SMALL DAYS AND NIGHTS

SMALL DAYS
AND NIGHTS

Tishani Doshi

BLOOMSBURY CIRCUS
LONDON • OXFORD • NEW YORK • NEW DELHI • SYDNEY

BLOOMSBURY CIRCUS
Bloomsbury Publishing Plc
50 Bedford Square, London, WC1B 3DP, UK

BLOOMSBURY, BLOOMSBURY CIRCUS and the Bloomsbury Circus logo
are trademarks of Bloomsbury Publishing Plc

First published in Great Britain 2019

ISBN: HB: 978-1-5266-0375-3; TPB: 978-1-5266-0374-6; EBOOK: 978-1-5266-0377-7

2 4 6 8 10 9 7 5 3 1

Typeset by Integra Software Services Pvt. Ltd
Printed and bound in Great Britain by CPI Group (UK) Ltd, Croydon CR0 4YY

MIX
Paper from
responsible sources
FSC® C020471

To find out more about our authors and books visit www.bloomsbury.com and sign
up for our newsletters

For Ajay, Carlo and the Ar Lan y Môr legion

It's in the little towns that one discovers a country, in the kind of knowledge that comes from small days and nights.

James Salter, *A Sport and a Pastime*

PROLOGUE

My sister Lucia.

How strange it is to say the word.

For three years we have lived together in a house without men. It is a large pink house with blue shutters and verandas, and a garden set on ten acres of beachfront land.

That we live here, in the deep south of India on this spit of isolated beach, is a matter of concern for the neighbouring villagers. The headman, Valluvan, who has named his daughters after Hindu goddesses – Bhubaneswari, Karpagavalli, Manjubharghavi, and inexplicably given his sole son the name Lenin – invites me to discuss issues of safety once a month. He insists I bring Lucia even though she has no interest in tea or politics.

It was Valluvan who suggested we bring a woman from the village to stay with us.

'You put one small house in your compound,' he instructed, 'and you take this lady. She has nothing. Husband has disappeared. Parents are dead. No children. Her name is Mallika. She can help with the cooking and cleaning. And she can keep watch.'

Mallika is short and dark like most of the women in Paramankeni. She is beautiful even though her front teeth are big and crossed over, her fingers shooting up to cover her mouth every time she laughs. Her eyes are her best feature – brimming with calculation and astonishingly free of the wide range of sadness she has certainly suffered. Sometimes I spy on her from the terrace when she's watering the lawn or hanging clothes out to dry. She is always draped in a bright polyester sari and a fresh flower in the bun of her hair. Every bit of gold she owns, she wears – earrings, nose-ring, a bangle on each twig-like wrist.

The three of us have managed to create a togetherness here with the dogs. In the beginning Mallika could not understand what was wrong with Lucia but she soon learned her habits. She was quick to pick up a few English words as well. 'Ya, ya,' she says impatiently when I struggle through my Tamil explanations. I think she watches American sitcoms on the television in her room, because when new friends visit, she shakes hands with them and says, 'Hi. I'm Mallika.'

The night before the puppies arrive we hear sounds in the garden. Loud, gut-wrenching moans from the undergrowth that wake us from sleep. Lucia shuffles across the corridor from her bedroom to mine. 'Grace,' she says, 'the new babies are coming.'

We go out on the terrace and lean over the balcony handrail. Everything is dark except for a rim of moonlight on the ocean, where we can see the outline of a few fishing trawlers. It is October. The heat of summer is behind us but the days still feel bedraggled and worn. In a few weeks the rains will arrive, transforming everything. For now, only the hibiscus and bougainvillea valiantly put out flowers. We go back and lie on my bed together, fans whirring madly above our heads.

In the morning she is eager to begin. We go in pyjamas and rubber slippers to check on the dogs. Hunter has hunkered in the neem bush close to the beach gate, Thompson has claimed the land behind the garage, and Flopsy is furthest away, in the casuarina groves behind the house. Between them we have thirteen new puppies. They are minuscule: eyes shut, blindly sucking at their mothers' teats. They lie in a heap, one on top of the other, noses and paws, making tentative squeaky sounds. They move constantly, searching for warmth, these black-and-white finger-long creatures of fur and heart. It is an effort not to pick them up and squeeze their tiny bodies.

As they grow stronger, they will begin to explore and find their way to the house, towards the new source of food. When we return from our evening beach walks with the big dogs they'll spring out at us from the bushes along the path — a harlequin splodge attacking our toes. 'What will we do, Lucy?' I say. 'There's too many of them.'

But it is marvellous — all this life.

Lucia and I drive to the AVM nursery to buy a row of flame trees to block our neighbour's ugly orange house. The toothless gardener who works there reminds me to put red soil and earthworm fertiliser in the garden beds regularly. He keeps a stack of sweets by the cash register and gives Lucia a packet of Cadbury's Gems, which she demands I open immediately. On the drive home she pops the Gems into her mouth one by one, according to colour.

It is a still day. Nothing moves. Even the sea is lifeless — a sheet of metal suspended out of the sky's head like an exhausted grey tongue. It's the kind of day that allows for openings – makes me wonder how it happened that in another life I lived in America. I had a husband, a job, people I socialised with. Not friends exactly. There had been only one friend after a decade of living in America, and she moved away before I did. But there was the structure of a certain kind of life, one I'd imagined for myself before occupying it. And I had learned how to navigate that life even though I frequently felt removed from it.

That was me, wasn't it? Being neighbourly and taking Rosemary Callahan's kid to the school bus every morning because she and her husband left early for work. That was me feeling queasy about the sight of so many children piled in together, but smiling and patting the brat on his head anyhow, wishing him a good day because it was the dutiful thing to do. And still me – putting on something smart for work, driving half an hour to sit in my cubicle at the customer service department of Duke Energy, eating my grilled cheese sandwich for lunch, saying, *How y'all doin?* as if that's the way words were meant to come out of my mouth.

Blake sent me a photograph recently, of us taken at the dance where we met. I'm showing off my skinny legs in a blousy geometric dress, my waist is encased with a thick studded belt, and every accessory on my person, including my pumps, are variations on the shade of Pepto-Bismol. Blake is smiling widely with his too-white teeth, a pansy wilting in the buttonhole of his shoulder-padded blazer. We are both sporting hairdos that resemble filo pastry – feathery tufts cascading around our emaciated faces.

On the back of the photograph Blake had inscribed: *B&G, 'Summertime', Kodaikanal, 1994. Love at first blossom?*

Back home, in our driveway, there's a man leaning against a motorbike. As soon as he sees the car he hurries to open the gate and gives us a cheerful salute as we drive through. I pull the handbrake and step out.

'Yes? Can I help you?'

'Ah, hello, madam. I'm interested in buying land in this area. Can you help me?'

'I'm not interested in selling.'

'But you're a foreigner, no?' He squints. 'How can you own land in India?'

'I own this land and I'm not interested in selling. Please look somewhere else.'

Before I can climb back into the car, he thrusts a business card into my hand.

'Sorry, okay, please don't be offending? In case you change your mind, my name is Jiva. I'm a real-estate broker. Just you call me in case anything is changing.'

Opening the front door I let loose at Mallika. 'Why aren't you locking the fucking gate? Don't you know any bloody fellow can just come in here whenever he feels like? What's the point of keeping you, I don't know. What are you people good for anyway?'

Sometimes I sound so much like my father it disgusts me.

PART ONE

I

Return is never the experience you hope for. After all those lost years in America I wanted to walk into the streets and know them, but there is a new tightness to the city, an exuberance that is difficult to understand.

Madras. August 2010. A swell of bodies. At arrivals there's a crush of families and hotel chauffeurs, bouquets wrapped in plastic and welcome boards. It's past one in the morning. What kind of parents are these who bring their bawling children out so late into the night?

The air attacks you at the threshold. Heavy, sweaty air, which smells of something that was once sweet, now rotting. Damp in the armpits and crotch. Jeans sticking to thighs.

Taxi drivers and porters are jostling about trying to cadge a passenger. *Taxi, madam, taxi?* Prepaid customers roll their luggage primly towards Fast Track and Akbar Cars without making eye contact. Madrasis returning home are on their mobile phones, instructing people to hurry and meet them at the pickup point.

Murali is waiting for me in the usual place. He is old and as dark as the night, hairy-eared and half blind. The way he drives, it will take us five hours instead of three, but Ma always valued loyalty over ability, even though she herself could rarely be relied upon to be steadfast.

'Still smoking, Murali?'

'What to do, madam? Now I'm an old man, no? Difficult to change.'

I'd ask him for a cigarette, but that would mean upsetting the order of things.

He's trying to take my luggage off me now. 'Please let me do it, Murali. Look at these arms. I go to the gym, you know!'

He gives me a lopsided grin and lollops along to open the boot of the car.

There's a scar on Murali's back that runs from top to bottom like a lazy river, thick and muddy pink. I know because I've seen him shirtless in a lungi doing odd jobs for Ma around the apartment – his back bare, except for the scar and the savannah of tightly coiled black hairs along his shoulder blades. I had asked him about the scar one summer, emboldened from my first year of studying in America. It was the war, he explained. He told me how the Tamil suburb he'd lived in on the outskirts of Colombo had been set upon by their Sinhalese neighbours, who came with hatchets, tyres, kerosene. He escaped with a butcher's knife in his back, but his family perished. Now his life was in India.

I wonder who will say it first? Him or me?

I feel sure that Murali is a man who knows how to hold his own in the face of any silence.

We heave the bags into the boot. My mother must be the only person in India who still insists on travelling around in an Ambassador. But there's something reassuring about this car. It makes me feel as though I were riding in the belly of a whale on the crazy seas of the Tamil Nadu highways.

'Traffic is terrible, madam.'

'Yes it is.'

The new airport has been a decade in the making but it has the feel of a never-ending family summer project, with bits and pieces being added on to the main building as and when funds and the inclination to do something come through. Car horns are sounding out warnings, each more virile than the next. People move purposefully in this barrage of noise, glaring backwards at the offending vehicles, always with the same resigned look on their faces. Back to this shit again.

I've been travelling over twenty hours, but my body is suddenly alert. It's the thing that surprises me every time I land in India. Despite all the blatant deterioration, all the decomposition, things survive. In fact, they thrive. Things are ready to bludgeon you with their aliveness.

I began my life in this city, four kilometres from the sea, in the clammy hallways of St Isabel's. This was 16 April 1977, and if my birth certificate is to be believed, the exact moment when I was pulled from between my mother's thighs was 4.12 a.m. 'Your father wasn't there, of course,' Ma said, when I asked what it was like to give birth. 'Showed up hours after you were born, making all kinds of demands.'

Blood debilitated Papi. As did certain sounds. Sartorial inelegance wasn't something he went in for either. If my father had a say in the workings of the world, he would have made maternity wards off-limits to men.

I'd like to think my parents were held aloft with awe for at least a few days after my birth, but hindsight would indicate otherwise.

'Childbirth is painful,' Ma said. 'But obviously you know that. Nothing as painful as what your father made that doctor do. Put my legs back into those stirrups and scrape the walls of my uterus looking for that damn placenta. Then your father made me eat a blessed piece of it because he said it would help me lactate better. Some Italian house-wife's tale. That was the moment I knew we were doomed. Any man who forces cannibalism on his wife after child-birth is a monster. Nothing was going to change that, not even you.'

We were happy in our small house on Gilchrist Avenue in Madras, even though my parents fought frequently. Our neighbours were meek people, content to stroll to the end of the lane that joined Harrington Road with their shopping bags, waiting at the appointed time for vendors with their carts to buy vegetables. Fruit-sellers didn't come down our street calling out their wares, neither did knife-sharpeners or paper-collectors. My father was known as the crazy white man because he sometimes ran down the street waving a bamboo stick, threatening to beat people.

Papi was an acousticophobe. I don't know if it's some-thing he developed in his youth or if it ripened into existence over the years he spent in India, but he always believed science would save him. He worked for the Italian firm Eni. Items banned from our house included pressure cookers, mixi-grinders, vacuum cleaners, hairdryers, radios, and any kind of toy that emitted a noise. His only concession was music. After dinner, we'd clear a space and I'd watch as my father and mother danced to Paolo Conte on the patio of our dead-end-street house, thinking they'd do this forever.

My father wore earplugs while driving. At work
sat in a cork-lined office fitted out with double insul
tion windows. His staff had been instructed to whisper
when they addressed him, but no amount of precaution
could prevent the city of Madras from filtering through
his tympani. After a particularly bad bout of encounters,
Ma took him to her alternative-therapy doctors to try
hypnosis, an Ayurvedic diet, exposure therapy, behav-
ioural therapy, urine therapy – all to little effect. When he
suffered one of his attacks, my father would shake, sweat,
curl into a ball, beat the walls and scream. For this reason
we avoided restaurants and cinemas – the city's paltry
entertainments – because it would inevitably end with
Papi smacking a man across the head.

He almost killed our neighbour, a sweet Syrian
Christian widower called Moses Paulraj. Moses drove
a silver-coloured Fiat that made the sound of 'The Star-
Spangled Banner' when it reversed. These days most
cars have reversing alarms, but back then Moses was the
only person we knew whose car could sing. Moses was
not an adept parker, and it happened one day while we
were eating breakfast that we had been exposed to the
American national anthem for a very long time. For the
first few minutes my father just clutched at the tablecloth
and turned very pale. Ma cautioned from across the table.
'Calma, calma,' she said in a completely non-calm way.

Then it seemed that 'The Star-Spangled Banner' had
been upped a notch, as if a microphone had been attached
to the source of the noise and was magnifying it for the
sole purpose of annoying my father. He tapped his feet
restlessly, beating the table softly – hammering, hammering – moving his lips up and down, saying something in

Italian, softly first, then loudly, uncontrollably, spewing out invective, of which all I could understand was *i selvaggi*.

Papi had a rich vocabulary of names for Indians – *negretto*, *scimmione*, *watussi* – but *selvaggi* was his most favoured.

I'd never seen him like he was that morning with Moses – crying, breathing irregularly, fingers drumming manically. My mother was patting him on the shoulders, agitatedly repeating her entreaty for him to stay calm. He shoved her aside and brought his head down on the table so hard I thought he must have cracked his skull. Then, as if the table had been made of rubber, he lifted his face and screamed, '*BASTA!*'

For a moment it seemed that the scream had worked. But a second later the squeaky anthem could be heard valiantly playing on.

Papi wiped the tears off his cheeks, pushed his chair away from the table and marched down the garden path out of our front gate. He turned left into Moses Paulraj's driveway and made straight for the tendons of our poor neighbour's neck.

My mother, who was just a tiny stick insect of a thing then, ran after him and jumped on his back, screaming, 'Giacinto, stop it! I said stop it now, you crazy man.'

But it was only after my father saw Moses Paulraj's face twitching like a small dying bird – the closest he ever came to a religious experience, he later said – did he relax his fingers and step away from the vehicle.

I have been travelling these roads ever since Ma moved to Pondicherry. It's always a revelation, the shedding of the city and the opening-up of space as soon as you hit the coastal road. It's 3 a.m. now and the Bay of Bengal lies like an inkblot to the left, spreading and hissing as we drive through barely lit villages on either side of the road. We snail along, catching the glare of high beams in our pupils, often skidding off the tarmac because of an oncoming lorry barrelling drunkenly over the divider.

Coconut trees. Canopies of teak and tamarind. Flying foxes. Vacant bus stops. Temples and step-wells. Ugly new constructions, which I can just about decipher the outlines of in the dark. Police checkpoints and metal road barriers. Sometimes our headlights catch a spray of winged insects in their beams, the outline of a goat or dog, racing across into blackness.

From the rear-view mirror dangle two black-and-white photographs: Sri Aurobindo and the Mother – the mystics who lured my mother away from my father. Aurobindo is a bearded beauty, everything a sage should be. Eyes like bottomless wells gazing into the infinite. Over the years I succumbed to my mother's instigations to read his teachings about Integral Yoga. But her? The Mother, Mirra Alfassa, Aurobindo's spiritual associate? She I never got. People who met her said she could make you follow her anywhere. But in the pictures she looks like an alien, always with a banal saying typed along the bottom: *It is only in quietness and peace that one can know what is the best thing to do.*

For the past few minutes Murali has been trying to send someone a text; the car snakes wildly, bumping across the median.

'Please don't do that, Murali,' I snap. Immediately I feel like shit. That was Papi's voice, Papi's disgust. 'It's just dangerous, you know?'

'Yes, madam.'

We drive for another twenty minutes in silence, burrowing through the dark.

'How is Blake Sir?'

'All fine.'

I wish he would shut up. If we cannot speak properly, I would rather make this entry in silence without pleasantries.

I wonder whether I should have allowed Blake to come with me. It would have been our last trip together, and he might have helped ease things. But then I think about the way he always crouched in the back seat, pressing his khaki-clad knees together like a gangly bird, blinking at the oncoming lights, all the fear leaking out of his stringy body. And the questions. He would have had so many bloody questions.

It's after five in the morning when we arrive outside my mother's apartment building on Marine Street, a kilometre away from the Aurobindo Ashram.

Murali pockets his tip morosely and moves towards his luggage.

'No, no,' I say. 'I can take the bags. Really! You go home. I'll phone when I need you, Murali.'

I push open the gates. The same watchman, a Nepali guy, leans forward to peer at me through half-closed eyes, and after registering who I am, slopes back to snooze in his chair again. I step into the lift and pull the squeaky metal gate towards me. There is an automatic electrical voice that repeats again and again: 'Please shut the door. Please shut the door.'

I go up to the third floor. My mother's flat is marked with an avenue of potted ferns. Splotchy, lurid green things. The door is ajar. Inside, the paper lanterns in the drawing room are casting an orange glow over everything. There are photographs of the protecting talismans again – Aurobindo and the Mother – on the wall. From the veranda, pink fingers of dawn poke through the grilles like warnings.

Ma's best friend, Auntie Kavitha, sits on the day bed in a kaftan. She used to have such long beautiful hair but it's shorn now, cut close to the scalp like a soldier's, and it opens her face, pushes out the ridges of her cheekbones. Opposite her is Mrs Dalal, my mother's neighbour and fellow devotee. They're like two crows, these women, emaciated and agile, their voices rasping. They've been smoking and there are cups of tea on a tray beside them.

I nod at them and leave my luggage at the door.

My mother is in her bedroom in a freezer box on the floor. A grotesque stainless-steel contraption with an airtight glass lid. She is huge – arms and legs chunky as hams. That pretty mouth of hers slack, as though there were no longer teeth to support the pendulous lips. The skin on her face sags in abundance. And there's grey in her hair, so much grey, mottled and streaked, spreading out of the crown of her head like the skin of a forest animal.

Auntie Kavitha walks in behind me. She has that dull look people get when they've been crying too much. Face pinched with sleeplessness, eyeliner smudged. 'Grace, are you okay?'

'Yes. I'm okay. How are you?'

To be intimate with people you've known for a long time but don't really know is a difficult thing. I go over to her, lean in to hug, but it's clumsy and we immediately step away from each other.

'Does Papi know?'

'I thought perhaps *you* better…'

'Yes. Yes, of course. But what do we do now? Did Ma say what she wanted? We never talked about any of this.'

'She wanted to be cremated.'

'Okay, yes, if it's what she wanted.'

I don't know the first thing about how one goes about burning a body. Some years ago in Kathmandu, Blake and I had stood on the banks of the Bagmati River and watched as a series of corpses were hauled on to the river bank, waiting to be set alight on the pyres. I remember only the smell, the smoke from so many fires, drums and chants, bands of monkeys that charged up and down the hillside, the sadhus in saffron robes and dreadlocks who posed picturesquely in the doorways of temples, summoning people over for photographs. 'Don't go,' a tourist had said. 'They'll steal your soul.'

I remember as well the sight of those toes poking sadly out of the swaddling cloths. Those desolate dead human toes that in a few hours would be turned to ash.

'We have a slot at the crematorium for ten, so you should sleep a few hours.'

I wheel my luggage into Ma's room. Undress. Shower. Put on a cotton singlet and boxer shorts, and climb into my mother's bed. Her smell is still in the pillows and sheets, something between milk and rose with a hint of sourness. The heat of her. I lie spread-eagled on my stomach, breathing her in. I sleep deeply while my mother keeps watch from a freezer box a few feet away from me.

Do I dream? If I do, I remember only the feeling of it. I am in a place between places, childhood mostly, that transient land at the top of the Magic Faraway Tree, whirling, whirling.

Auntie Kavitha is leaning over me. 'Grace, get up. You should get dressed. People will start to come soon. We need to take your mother into the front room.'

'What should I wear?' I ask, looking at Auntie Kavitha, who has changed into a white cotton sari.

'I have a salwar kameez if you want. I'll get it for you.'

In half an hour the front room is full of people. Most of them are ashramites and from the nearby community of Auroville, but there are also random people my mother befriended – beach friends, whom she chatted to every evening from her outpost on the promenade by the Gandhi statue, restaurateurs, shop owners, the fridge-repair man. Three of my mother's siblings have come from Tharangambadi. Other than Auntie Kavitha and Murali, most of the people at my mother's funeral are strangers to me.

There's a run-down black Maruti van downstairs that will transport the body. A group of men lift up the box and carry her out of the door, and it is at this moment that someone starts to cry. I don't know who's sounding that cry for my mother leaving her home for the last time, but it draws something out of me as well. I begin to cry and Auntie Kavitha thumps me gently on the back, saying, 'It's okay, it's okay.' But my tears are short-lived because soon there's the practical question of how to get the freezer box down three flights of stairs without mishap. People shout. Slippers that have been left outside the door are kicked around. Murali takes charge of the situation, guiding people softly to move this way or that, and miraculously, the box reaches the ground floor and is manoeuvred into the back of the van.

We follow the hearse to the ashram crematorium. It is nothing like the banks of the Bagmati River. Mother is removed from the freezer box and people begin to prepare her body for fire. First a layer of ghee, then big clods of cow dung over her face, body, arms. They wall her body in with a kiln of bricks. And all this is done wordlessly, with no songs or crying. A beautiful old man with a heart-shaped face and bright-white hair puts a flaming torch to the pyre. Auntie Kavitha brandishes a pouch of rose petals from the folds of her sari and begins to fling them on the body. We stand around the fire in silence, and I'm trying to photograph this moment of my mother's final disappearance, but even as I watch, the whole scene is vanishing.

Afterwards, my relatives corner me in the street outside the crematorium and say how I must visit them in Tharangambadi. Have I forgotten all my cousins there? They tell me to be strong. That my mother was too young to die. Then they make the sign of the cross and head for their cars.

Auntie Kavitha is herding a woman over to meet me. This woman is skinny as a post, with deep creases around her black, teary eyes. 'Grace, I want you to meet Mrs Gayatri. She's an old friend of your mother's.'

Mrs Gayatri catapults her body into mine. 'This is the daughter from America!' she exclaims. '*Om Namah Shivayah!*'

People trickle back to my mother's flat. They sing *bhajans*. Auntie Kavitha organises tea and samosas. I want them gone. Unreasonably, I want Blake here. I want my father as well. But Papi is probably just waking up in his studio in Venice, putting the Bialetti on for coffee, checking to see if there's still a heel of bread left over from the day before.

'I think I should call my father,' I say to Auntie Kavitha. 'It's six a.m. there. He should be up.'

'Okay, but let me get rid of all these loiterers first. Everybody wants to hang around like bloody vultures.'

Within twenty minutes the apartment is empty. Auntie Kavitha moves assuredly around the kitchen. She removes a bottle of Talisker's from my mother's booze cabinet and reaches for two crystal glasses. She pours a heavy slug into each glass and then drops a gash of whisky on the floor. 'That's for your mother. The best woman I ever loved.'

I stare at the puddle of whisky on the floor and wonder who's going to clean that up.

'It's a gypsy tradition,' Auntie Kavitha says, 'to honour the dead. Technically, we should be out in the forest somewhere, and the whisky should be swallowed by the earth, and there should be brethren playing the guitar and singing sorrowful but celebratory songs. But seeing that your family are such a bunch of pricks, let's just imagine it, shall we? Drink up.'

I've never liked whisky. Never enjoyed the scorch of it at the back of my throat or the burning of it deep in my belly. But I lift the glass to my lips and drink all of it.

'Good girl.'

She pours another round. And another. Then, from the roll-top desk, she unveils a Kashmiri papier-mâché box. Inside are cigarette papers, coils of perfumed hash, tobacco filler. She rolls expertly and with concentration. Puts the joint in her mouth and sucks long, hungry drags.

'You want?'

I take the joint between my teeth and it reminds me of standing around the Kodaikanal Lake with Queenie and Blake, our lives teetering on the rim of change.

We go like this, smoking and drinking until my arms and legs feel like water.

'Now the first thing you must do is to stop calling me Auntie. How old are you now? Thirty-two? Thirty-three? Christ! I think we can speak to each other as adults. There's so much to talk about. How's your marriage going? Tell me that first.'

I tell her the truth. That my marriage has gone to shit. That Blake wants kids and I don't. That there's a loneliness that's been swallowing me up in America and the thought of returning to my life there pounds like a great engine inside me.

'Forget about America,' she says.

We sit on sofas facing each other. I feel like slumping down and closing my eyes.

'Grace, didn't you ever wonder where your mother disappeared to when you were a child? Didn't you ever think to ask?'

'I wasn't inquisitive enough, I guess. I had my own theories.'

'You should have asked.'

Slowly, we unwrap the past.

Kavitha Raman is unravelling every memory and replacing it with something else. It's the first time I hear the name Lucia. None of it makes sense. I am drunk. This is what I want to tell her. I am jet-lagged. I want to lie down. Tomorrow morning we must collect what's left of Mother's bones. But this woman persists in talking.

'There's time for sleep later,' she says. 'Now, you must listen.'

2

My mother disappeared every Thursday.

I knew no other mother who demanded a timeout, a rest from her maternal duties, except for mine. When I think of all the Thursdays she went missing and line them up, one against each other, there is nothing but sound: the great emptying sigh of the house, the soft swish-swish of her Mangalagiri sari rustling between her quick, powdered legs as she ran down the driveway away from us.

The patterns of Thursdays changed as I grew older, but for the time we lived in Madras, they held a steady course. On Thursdays we would eat breakfast half an hour earlier so that Ma could be dressed and ready to go by the time Kavitha Raman honked at the gate. 'Bye, *kanna*,' my mother would say, kissing the top of my head. '*Ciao*, Giacinto.' Or if it happened to be a day of reconciliation, '*Ciao, amore*.' And then she'd be gone, with her tatty brown handbag in one hand and a basket of fresh bread for her bridge group in the other.

It was always the same. Her leaving through the front door in a shroud of light, never turning to look back at us. And the savage return.

Long after Papi and I had finished eating dinner and were playing Briscola in the drawing room, she'd come back to us ruined and speechless, staring, as though she hoped we might not be there, dropping the empty wicker basket on the floor and striding into the bedroom to unwind the layers of sweaty cotton from the contours of her body. Then we'd hear the shower – half an hour of steam pounding on her head, drenching her long dark hair until the geyser ran out of hot water, and she was forced to step back into our lives.

'Why is she behaving like this?' I used to ask Papi, who I imagined must have had greater insight to the sorrow of my mother's Thursday escapades.

'You think I know?' he'd say. 'Other women dream of this arrangement – one day of the week, no cooking or cleaning, no questions, leave all the responsibilities to your *schiavetto* of a husband. *Sì*? But your mother, Grazia, she is not like other women. This much you should know.'

Papi called me Grazia, the Italian version of Grace. For this, and for the hazelnut milk chocolates he smuggled into my lunchbox and cigarette breath of him when he kissed me goodnight, I loved him. Yes, he could be grumpy, and there were days, especially after one of his attacks, when there was no reaching him. Yes, we could not have clocks in our house like normal people because of my father's fear that they would explode like bombs in the middle of the night and tear delicate, excruciating holes in his eardrums. But on Thursdays, when my mother disappeared, he made an effort to be the good parent, and as time went by, I came to treasure those days.

On Thursdays, Papi would have a glass of Maltova and four slices of bread-butter-jam waiting for me on the kitchen counter by the time the school van dropped me home. He would even help with my homework. Always impatient with my sluggish and roundabout methods, he'd do most of it, and then we'd hurry with towels in hand and rubber slippers on our feet, drive an hour south along the coast to one of the many deserted beaches, strip down to bathing suits and rush into the salty arms of the Bay of Bengal.

Those were happy evenings. The two of us getting thrashed about in the sea while the city held her noise at bay. My father would take care to wash the sand out from my curls when we returned, wring my bathing suit dry and stand our washed slippers up against the granite stone in the kitchen garden. We never intended to keep our beach expeditions secret, but as my mother never asked about our day and never told us about hers, it seemed fair to maintain a silence. I knew it was wrong to favour one parent over the other, but if I'd had to choose then, I would have chosen Papi.

My father, contrary to all expectations of his name, was a sullen man. He was baptised Giacinto Luciano Marisola — an exuberant potpourri of Italian optimism. Hyacinth, light, sea, island — all these were part of his name, but nothing of his personality. By nature, he was untrusting and unforgiving, and his years in India had only served to intensify those attributes. He was not stingy with his affections, but when he chose to deprive you of them, the devastation was brutal. There was violence in the silence he created, a terrible asphyxiation, and because we had no clues to the mysterious mechanisms within him, there was no way for us to set about making amends.

My mother frequently fell into dark moods as a result of his temperamental nature, and I remember her telling me in those moments, 'Never believe a name, Grace. Names deceive more than people do.'

My own name had been cause for a great argument between my parents. Papi had wanted to call me Filomena or Clementina after one of his grandmothers, and Ma had wanted Magdalena or Lumina after hers. Grace was finally agreed upon as a name that could travel widely and be easily pronounced. Also, as Ma pointed out, it did not remind one of an ageing matriarch. 'Grace is simple, Grace is good.'

Needless to say, I would have preferred any of the other names. But the middle path, as with so many other compromises in life, is the one that everyone can agree on precisely because it lacks nuance and daring.

My father arrived in India in 1971 to look for oil off the coast of Tamil Nadu. Coming to India had not been his dream, but it had been a way of escaping the claustrophobia of his childhood. He was born in the northern Italian town of Vicenza, the eldest son of a pharmacist, and had been expected to follow in his father's profession. As a child, he spent most of his summer holiday cooped up in the pharmacy on Corso Palladio, helping his father put prescriptions in paper bags and unearthing strips of medicines from the shelves in the stockroom. Aside from the rewards of an endless supply of coloured sugary sweets that his grandfather slipped him and the pocket money he earned, he could think of no worse fate for a man to endure than being the keeper of a shop.

Papi went on to study geotechnical and building engineering at the polytechnic in Turin. He promised my Nonno Danilo and Nonna Rosa that he would return to run the pharmacy, but had secretly relinquished his rights to his brother Fulvio, who, being unimaginative and overly attached to the town of his birth, was only too happy to take over a thriving business. Papi's ambitions were taken as a sign of courage, and when he set off to work for Eni, first in Rome, then Egypt, and finally India, he was treated with even greater respect, a modern poster child for the kind of fearless Vicentini who had gone before him – writers and explorers like Trissino and Pigafetta, who gave their names to Vicenza's statues and streets.

I think Papi must have been terribly lonely when he arrived in India. He was stationed in Tharangambadi, or Tranquebar, as it was known then – one of the first places where Christianity and the printing press entered India. A small coastal town in Tamil Nadu with a warren of streets and a biscuit-coloured Danish fort, it was overrun by flocks of crows and white-socked goats. After a long day at his offshore site, he would walk from the fort along the seafront, picking his way across the rocks, past the fishermen fixing their nets and the coy young schoolgirls with ribbons in their hair. Outside the crumbling wreck of what used to be the Governor's Bungalow there was an ancient Shiva temple on the beach, where he'd loiter, smoking cigarettes, wondering how long it would be before he could leave this wretched place.

The story of how my father met my mother is an unreliable one. To hear my mother talk about it, she was the one who made the first move. My father claimed the opposite. When I was a teenager, rifling through the drawers of my father's cupboard, I discovered his diary, written in unintelligible Italian, and found a few terse notes written by my mother.

20 Dec, 1971
Hello Mister,

My friends and I would appreciate it if you could teach us how to smoke. Meet us at the abandoned temple at six?

Meera Andrews

22 December, 1971
Hello again,

I think perhaps you have the wrong impression. Probably in Italy there is a different way to go about such things, but here in India, we don't go making loud announcements of wanting to make love to people. Kindly abide by the rules.

Meera Andrews

26 December, 1971
Dear Mr Giacinto,

I really don't know what you were thinking, showing up at my house on Christmas Day. You cannot imagine the embarrassment it caused me and my family. My teachers at college sometimes scold us by saying, 'Were you mad, dead or drunk when you came to class today?' and I feel I must say that you must have been mad, dead and drunk when you decided to knock on our door with your cock-and-bull story. In any case, my father is on to you. And my mother, despite having fed you to the gills (which is in any case her great mission in life), said that if I ever tried to see you alone she would skin me like a chicken. These are not empty threats. Seriously, are you deranged? You should know I'm least interested in you.

Meera
PS: I want to be a veterinarian (hence the vegetarianism, since you asked).

30 March, 1972
Dear G

Don't leave. I couldn't bear it.

My mother was nineteen when she met my father. I can almost see her: reed-thin, double plaits and half sari, twinkling nose-ring. Her family were a hybrid of Tamil Christians who had intermarried with Hindus, and as such, they were a syncretic household, befitting the town of Tranquebar, where every evening you would hear the *adhan* intermingling with the sounds of temple and church bells. Jesus was the main point of focus in my mother's house, of course, but there was a dedicated puja room where concessions were made for major Hindu deities.

Grandpa Samuel was treasurer at the Holy Rosary Catholic Church, which is where my parents first met. Later, Auntie Kavitha would tell me that it was my mother who pursued my father. That ever since she had known her, my mother had had an irrational longing to escape. 'Always, there was something calling her away.' And here was this strange, brooding foreign man. Surely, he would help her leave behind this congested brick house and her doltish siblings, her father who would have her be a nun, her mother who, boringly, favoured her sons?

Their wedding photo shows a small, unremarkable gathering outside the church. My parents look like people I don't know and never will. They aren't smiling exactly, but there's a sense that whatever they have around them is something of their own making. No one from my father's side of the family is present, although the family ring had been sent with a shipman from Vicenza – a simple cluster of emeralds and diamonds in the shape of a cross, courtesy of Nonna Rosa. My mother wore that ring every day of her life, the gold getting worn and dark, until she passed it on to me on the eve of my own unsuccessful marriage.

3

In the weeks after Ma's death I plummet into childhood. None of it seems credible.

Auntie Kavitha tells me I will learn nothing by confronting my father, but she understands my determination.

I called him the afternoon after Ma's funeral. It was as if he'd been expecting the news. 'I was in Guidecca, after dinner with a friend, walking by the water, and I saw a flash in the sky. I don't know why, but I thought of your mother. It was something so real, so powerful. I marked the time. It was five after midnight.'

I told him we hadn't established the exact time of Ma's death. She had had an unremarkable day. All morning and afternoon in the house. At five Murali had driven her to Nilgiris to do her weekly groceries. She'd complained of the heat. The maid who came to cook three times a week had been the last to see her alive. She left at 8 p.m. Dinner was paratha and vegetable stew. Ma got into bed and never got up.

'She always hoped for this,' Papi said. 'She was so scared of death, of pain, of any kind of physical hardship. "Wouldn't it be lovely if we could all decide when we've had enough, climb into bed and that could be the end of it?" She told me that once. She was always a lucky woman.'

I wanted to say, 'And was Lucia a lucky thing that happened too?' but I hadn't met Lucia yet, and she was as unreal to me as Ma's death.

'How do you feel, Papi?' I asked.

'I feel alone,' he said, 'as ever.'

We are in Ma's apartment in Pondicherry. Every evening we walk along the beach, and for a few hours in the morning, we sort her belongings into boxes. Auntie Kavitha's grief is different from mine. She looks like a person demolished. She has no appetite for anything but whisky.

'It doesn't make sense to distrust the past,' she tells me. 'Everything that happened, happened.'

'But you mean when she was taking all those overnight buses to Madras, she wasn't going to bridge tournaments?'

'Your mother was an average bridge player at best. Far too impatient.'

My grief is filled with anger because she has overwritten every memory with a kind of deception. There – young, beautiful mother, how could you keep the lie up for so long?

I don't know what it means that I am dreaming of houses, but it must be a sign of insecurity. In the nights after Ma's death I am always in the rooms of a house, the walls crumbling, doors and windows flung open. I am frantic, searching for something or someone. The dream often begins in the house on Gilchrist Avenue in Madras, but inevitably it turns into Mahalakshmi, our house in Kodaikanal, where we moved when I was eleven. Sometimes the house is a ruin. Sometimes it's exactly as it was when Ma, Papi and I used to live there.

I see the manic play of a white dachshund and his ball on the grass. I stand at the edge of the garden looking all the way down to the plains, a shimmering rust patchwork of land 7,000 feet below, like a mirage in the heat. Some nights I wake in a sweat because it's as though one of them is standing behind me, ready to push. Papi. Ma. I can make no sense of it. This house with ivy, with brambles of raspberry and Queen Anne's lace growing in wild bushes all along the compound wall. This house that my father found and which I fell in love with as soon as I saw it. Mahalakshmi.

We moved there soon after Papi's incident with Moses Paulraj. It was decided we needed to live in a quieter place. Papi found it – a grey stone cottage with a portico and columns, nestled in the corner of the Kurinji Temple Road. The watchman used to tell stories of previous owners who had either hung themselves or lost children at birth. He'd look at me slyly to see if I was scared. 'But we live here now,' I'd say adamantly.

I'd spoken of my longing to return there with Auntie Kavitha the day we cremated Ma. 'I can go with you,' she offered.

It's as though everything was set forward in motion because of that house.

Papi left Madras first. He was a superstitious man when it came to travel. A large part of his family had drowned in the sinking of the SS *Bolivian* in 1919, a tragedy his grandmother never tired of despairing about, so we usually travelled separately, to ensure that if disaster struck, it would not eliminate our family in entirety.

Ma followed a week later. And I was brought soon after by Kavitha Raman. I had never been separated from my parents before, but I remember completely trusting Auntie Kavitha. I was quite unafraid of the journey and the new life waiting for me.

When we arrived at the Kodai Road Station we climbed into a taxi that Papi had organised, which took us up winding roads and through deep *shola* forests where bands of monkeys appeared and disappeared, and a great waterfall called the Silver Cascades washed down the cliffs. Auntie Kavitha frequently said, 'Oh, Grace, isn't it beautiful! Don't you think it's so beautiful?' And even though I felt slightly ill in my stomach from all the winding curves and bends, I nodded in assent.

I remember being in the taxi a very long time, and it was only after we stopped at the five-fingered lake at the entrance of town – Auntie Kavitha pointing to the boats in the mist and the horses whinnying and stomping in a cluster by the bicycle-rental stand – that I actually began to think it really was very beautiful. Ten minutes later we arrived at Mahalakshmi, where my parents stood on the front steps holding hands and smiling widely. Something about the sight of their togetherness, or the relief of being reunited with them, cracked a dent in my bravado, and I stumbled out of the car onto the front lawn to vomit and cry simultaneously.

Our first months in Kodai were difficult. Ma, who had grown up by the sea, found the mountains cruel and isolating. Papi, who had spent his youth skiing in the Dolomites and camping on the Monte Cornetto, tried convincing her that it was not all harshness. He knew, after all, what it meant to be separated from everything you knew. He had given up his life in Italy to be here with us. After a while, he said, the hills would offer a kind of peace the sea could never bring.

For my part, everything would have been fine if I hadn't been forced to go to the convent, which shall remain nameless, at the end of the long road that led from our house to the Naidupuram market. My friends and I called it the Prison for Poor Catholic Girls (PPCG), even though more than half the girls were from Hindu families. The indoctrination, in any case, was Catholic to the extreme.

I was one of the few day scholars at PPCG. Most of the girls were boarders from wealthy families in Madras, Madurai and Coimbatore. They weren't allowed out of the compound unless it was for authorised walks, or if a family member came to visit. Newspapers, films and magazines were banned, and if you were caught with cigarettes or alcohol, you faced certain expulsion. For birthdays, girls were allowed to have a supervised outing, providing their parents sent enough money. And in the eleventh and twelfth standard, you were allowed to attend the much-anticipated annual dance with the international school, which was exciting primarily because it involved boys.

As we lived just five minutes down the road, the sisters allowed me the privilege of going back home at the end of each day, but it was always cited as the main reason for my many perceived shortcomings. 'Grace Marisola,' they'd admonish, 'just because no one disciplines you at home, don't think you can come here and corrupt the other girls.'

Papi was the only truly happy one among us. He was a different person from the father in Madras. Jovial, relaxed. The climate in Kodai suited him, the trees and flowers were familiar to him, and there was finally some quiet and calm. Every weekend he went off on a trek with the local hiking club, and in this way made Indian acquaintances without my mother's intervention. He continued to work as a consultant for Eni on a part-time basis, forced to make site visits every few months, but otherwise allowed to work from home. The company would send him large dossiers, which he'd go through in his studio – a shed at the end of the garden. Here he'd work from ten to six every day, spreading sheets of paper on the table in front of him, fountain pen in hand, equations and formulas scribbled on notepaper and stuck on the walls around him. For lunch he would come into the kitchen and make himself a sand- wich and an espresso, smoke a cigarette on the front lawn in the sun and then return to his desk. At four he'd take a break to pick me up from school. My father's hands were soft and stubby. Walking home, I would put my hand in his until our palms became sweaty, after which I'd draw away.

Once a week I'd be dispatched to the post office in the bazaar to make sure that a dossier was couriered to Madras or Rome. And in this way, a kind of communication existed between him and the outside world. Our wealth must have been greatly diminished, but as with many things at that age, I had no understanding of relativity. I never felt anything but richness in those early years. We lived in a beautiful house, we had our health, my parents battled frequently but always made their peace, and I had only the nuns to mar my contentment.

When I think of my parents now, I try to think of them in happier times. In those days before I entered their lives – the languid year they spent in Tranquebar after their marriage, the excitement of those first years in the house on Gilchrist Avenue in Madras.

I was witness to scenes of love from time to time, occasional moments of togetherness in Mahalakshmi, the drawing room lit with a fire, the books glowing on the shelves. It was enough, then, to hear my mother in the kitchen preparing a meagre supper of soup and bread. Papi emerging from his studio after a day's work, entering the house with a volume of Ungaretti or Zanzotto. I think poetry was the only luxury my father allowed himself, the only love my parents shared. How many times he tried to get me to learn Italian by reading poetry – '*A ogni nuovo clima che incontro mi trovo languente … Godere un solo minuto di vita iniziale cerco un paese innocente.*'

But I had no ear for languages, no love for them either. I was more interested in the music Papi played after dinner. While Ma and I cleared the table, he would pick something from his record collection, depending on his mood – Louis Armstrong or Paolo Conte or Sarah Vaughan. Whatever he chose, whatever their most recent argument, Ma would dance with him.

It was their way of salvaging the day, of forgiving. And it was marvellous to watch. My father in his perfectly tailored Italian shirts and trousers, always so formal for every occasion. My mother in a sari or a floor-length dress and cardigan. The two of them sliding across the wooden floors of Mahalakshmi like two serpents in their battle dance. It was the most civilised thing about my childhood, and though I remember exactly when they stopped dancing, it was only much later that I figured out why.

4

A city such as this shouldn't have the right to exist. It is a dream on water. A seaweed-stinking dream.

I've been here three weeks, staying in an apartment off the Campo San Giacomo dell'Orio. A light-filled place with large windows that look out onto small canals where singing *gondolieri* steer their sleek black vessels through labyrinths of water. At first I used to stand by the windows, listening to strains of 'O sole mio', 'Volare', 'Santa Lucia' – music I didn't know I knew, but which must have folded into the grey of my cerebral cortex as a child. After days of listening to the same songs over and over, I close the windows because they are ruining the dream.

The apartment is mostly white except for two purple velvet armchairs, a Turkish rug that covers the entire floor, and a wall of books. Every evening, after my long day of walking, I slide a title off the shelf, purely on whimsy, hoping the pages will bring some kind of revelation.

The woman, Ilaria, who owns this apartment, is a photographer. Her black-and-white photographs of semi-nude men and women are framed in discreet corners. I found Ilaria on the internet. She had been looking for someone to sublet the place while away on sabbatical in Marrakesh.

India is a mother country!! Ilaria had written in her email. *Every time I go there I remember one of my past lives. It's the only place where I feel I'm coming home. Sorry not to be able to meet you, but my friend Roberto will bring you the keys and explain everything to you. It's easy!*

Along with Ilaria's welcome note, which included a list of instructions of things not to tamper with – crystals in the bathroom, runes on the bedroom floor, seashell sculpture above the bed – she had enclosed a pamphlet that someone had passed to her in a street in Calcutta. It was one of those New Age self-help things, on which she had scrawled – *I hope you find everything you're looking for in Venice.*

Play cosmic with your mind and body!
Protect nature and remove poverty!

Being is simple, being somebody is complicated.
Silence is simple, speech is complicated.

Last century was 'use and throw',
Now 'be mother to each to grow!'

The pamphlet, though ridiculous, makes me wistful for everything I've just left behind. I carry it around in the side pocket of my handbag as a kind of talisman.

I am alone here in Venice, and this is not a city that is built for loneliness. Too many honeymooning couples and groups of families and students, wandering around hypnotised by their tour guides' coloured flags.

The Venetians I encounter are a dolorous species, drawn inwards towards their bodies. They slope through the streets at a pace, with certainty. Perhaps it's the effect of being surrounded by so much beauty. Perhaps it's a form of containment – a result of being hemmed in by buildings, sky, horizon, the ever-present water and its multitude of reflections. But they are nothing like the throngs who have come in June, like me. Tourists. Dizzy as dragonflies in the narrow alleyways, confused and bedazzled, peering from one glass shop window to the next.

I sleep with the blinds raised, poised for the morning sun to hit me in the face. Breakfast is at the Café Orientale, a tea room along the Rio Marin canal. Then I walk. Fortified by sugar, I walk for hours, getting lost, finding myself again. I eat lunch at the cheapest trattorias I can find. I could afford to do better, but I'm used to skimping. The food is mostly terrible, regardless.

Every day brings new tourists, rattling the wheels of their suitcases over the cobblestones, peering behind each corner of the maze, hoping to find their *pensiones*. Midway they pause to gape at the perfection of a small bridge, the serendipity of a gondoliere passing beneath it, singing.

Those dashing gondolieri in their striped T-shirts and straw hats – aren't they tired of playing supporting roles in other people's dreams?

I am waiting for something to happen, but it must happen without any conniving. I must keep walking until the moment comes upon me.

In the evenings, I stop at one of the bars behind the Rialto, for Spritz and *cicheti*. I don't talk to anyone. I'm not interested in conversation. I stay away from museums and Vivaldi concerts and the Piazza San Marco. Nothing I want to happen will happen in any of these places.

Sometimes I take the number 1 *vaporetto* all the way to the Lido, marvelling at how the light skates off the tops of buildings. What colour is that? Burnt sienna? Rust? They don't look real, those Venetian houses standing in water, with their cornices and frescoes. It is all mirage – floating and shifting – and only when the Grand Canal sweeps into the lagoon after the Santa Maria della Salute does the vision open, whiplashed by light. Space. And more space. Giudecca gleams like a beacon on the other side. And beyond – the islands of Murano, Burano, Torcello – a kaleidoscope of bridges, buildings, colour upon colour.

One day a man's golden retriever leaps on to the vaporetto but the man gets left behind because of a stampede of Chinese tourists. The conductor says it's okay. He knows this dog. His owner will find him at the next stop. And sure enough, there he is, at the Accademia, flushed and out of breath. 'Amilcare,' the owner says. 'There you are, Amilcare.' The dog bounds off loyally behind his owner. I long for a golden dog of my own.

I return every night with blistered toes. I come home from walking and sit in the tub with bath salts for half an hour. The bath is made of boat wood and there's a skylight in the roof, which makes you feel like you're sailing away in the waters surrounding you.

I keep few supplies in the apartment. Fruit, bread, pasta, *peperoncino*, a ruined knob of garlic, Parmesan, olive oil, several bottles of red wine. After a bath I prepare a goblet of wine with a plate of fruit and cheese and read till I'm slightly drunk. I've found the thing I'm looking for. Joseph Brodsky. Not the poems, but his book on Venice. He talks of the city in winter, how it is like Greta Garbo swimming, about the streets – how they are like library shelves, about feeling like a cat and saying *meow!*

After reading *Watermark* I go to visit Mr Brodsky. His grave is overrun with rose bushes. Not far from him lie two compatriots – Diaghilev and Stravinsky. I feel the beginning of something changing in the San Michele cemetery under those long archways of cypress, amongst the cool brick walls and tombs.

How different a burial is from a burning.

I go looking for the members of my missing family who drowned in the sinking of the SS *Bolivian* on 9 April 1919. But I do not know their names. Tapetto, Bruno, Camilla, Felicita, Emilio, Pio. Could any of these people be related to me?

There are seagulls everywhere. They are loud and huge like big flying cats. One of them swoops over me, lets loose a spray of shit and then springs away, squawking madly.

I stop at the grave of a young ballerina. Her family entombed her pink satin slippers along with her. *Expectantes Resurrectionem.*

The roses are in full bloom. Red and white. And there's a cacophony of birdsong. Palm trees seem incongruous, but here they are, their roots entangled in the dust of bones.

Before I'd left to come here, Kavitha Raman had told me about a temple in Kerala where people went to find out about their lives. All you needed to supply them with was your name and date of birth. And then a priest would disappear into the archives and return with a papyrus bearing all the details of your meagre life. Imagine the folly of living in the face of an idea like this! All the destinies of all the people in the world predetermined and inked.

A stranger could read the book of your life and tell you things you didn't even know.

'Would you go?' she had asked. 'After everything you now know, would you still go?'

'No,' I said. 'It would be too terrifying.'

In the St Michele cemetery I search for a grave bearing my own name. It was common, wasn't it? Italians, naming their children after dead grandfathers and grandmothers, never thinking how morbid it might be for a child to stumble upon a marker with their name etched in moss. I don't find a grave with my name on it, but I do find a Giacinto Marisola. Even though I know it's not my father, seeing his name on stone fills me with dread, a feeling of being orphaned.

Later that afternoon I agree to meet with Ilaria's friend Roberto, who brought me the keys to the apartment. An idea settles that I might allow things to happen between us, should they proceed in that direction.

Roberto is a mathematician who works at the University of Ca' Foscari. He is a small man made big with ideas. He's wearing a waistcoast, a leather jacket and slim, mud-coloured jeans. He has delicate hands and disorderly hair.

We get a table on the sunny side of the Campo Santa Margherita, close to his office. It is a busy place, overrun with students. Roberto doesn't drink alcohol or coffee. 'It overexcites me,' he says, somewhat ashamedly. He compensates with pear juice and crisps.

I order Proseccos and listen for an hour about the theories he's working on. One is about how atoms reflect the movement of tourists on bridges in Venice. Another is about the dynamics of lists. Still another is about genes and homosexuality in men, and how this is in fact not a Darwinian paradox.

'The research shows that homosexuality is linked to the X chromosomes,' Roberto says. 'It finds that women related to a gay man's mother are more fecund; they have more children. And so it's a kind of by-product evolved in women, a tax for this super-fecund woman. The gay male son balances the process. The genes don't get washed out, but they spread around. We refer to it as the cock-loving gene. Passed on by the mother.

'We were barking up the wrong tree forever. Of course, homosexuals are more obvious and noticeable than fecund women, so it was much subtler. But the penetrating gaze of science tells us we were looking at things wrong.'

'What about lesbians?'

'Oh, different story. It's not clear yet. Do you have children?'

'No.'

'Do you want them?'

'Not particularly.'

We sit like this for a while longer, watching as children and dogs race around. There is a fearlessness about them. They have no need to worry about cars, to look left or right before crossing.

Roberto's phone rings. '*Arrivo, arrivo!*' he yells into it. 'I'm sorry, but I must go. Let's meet again.' He places €20 on the table, pecks both my cheeks and heads off with a strut.

I walk back to the apartment and what I think is this: that my life seems to have passed without any great tumult of feeling. Only music has had the capacity to upturn me. I have longed for more, for all the grand emotion that stems from sex, friendship, nature, art, God – but I have always found myself lacking. What has mattered after all? Not family. Not love. Not politics. Not literature. Only music, with its dark mutability.

At home I speak to Blake on Skype with the video turned off. I tell him the internet connection isn't strong enough. The truth is I can't bear to see his face. We are still in the process of talking things through, but I wish he would just let me go. Everything in my life has changed. Surely he must understand that. But we persist with the talks, because to disengage from one another after a decade of togetherness without an adequate amount of tug and pull would suggest that there was little there to begin with.

He tells me he doesn't need to have children.

I tell him he does, that he is exactly the kind of person who needs to have children. Just not with me.

'Did you meet your sister before you left?'

I tell him no. I am waiting to settle things first. Another lie.

That night I fall asleep listening to the *bmph-bmph* whale-like noises of the *vaporetti*, wondering about the shapes of chromosomes – how one extra chromosome can alter the alchemy of things. It is a dreamless, seamless sleep.

I see Papi on my twenty-second day in Venice. He's sitting in the shade of the Santa Maria della Visitazione in Zattere, eating an ice cream – chocolate and hazelnut, his staple. He's wearing a trilby and sunglasses so I cannot see his eyes, but it's him. The lines around his mouth have grown deeper, and his skin is papery, darker than it ever was in

India. He's watching people pass by as if all of this were pleasant. An afternoon in the sun with a gelato. As if the horns of those big ocean liners weren't tearing into his nerves. As if it were a damn pleasure to have those feathered rats hover so close to him.

I watch him for a few minutes, wondering, will he turn towards me? Will some mysterious force make him aware of my presence?

Watching him, I understand that it is perfectly possible to exist in the world without being aware that someone close to you, someone of your flesh and blood, is moving about in the same air as you, occupying the same streets. That it takes all kinds of coincidences for trajectories to collide. But mostly we move about the world without collisions.

It reminds me of when I used to make those long trips between America and India. Getting off at the other end and looking for a face. Blake in America. Ma in India. Would I see them first, or would they see me? It was our game. Who was more in tune with the other? There was magic in walking into a place you didn't quite belong to, in the knowing that at least one person from that entire mass of people belonged to you.

I walk up to stand right in front of Papi, blocking the light.

He looks up, confused, blinking. Removes his hat. 'Grazia? *Cara?*' My father has never been one for surprises.

These past few weeks in Venice I've been trying to recollect all the meaningful conversations I've had with Papi. Moments when he might have imparted something close to wisdom, or at least given me clues as to how I, his daughter, should live.

He was certainly the more active of my parents. Besides teaching me to swim and conquer algebra, besides music and constellations and poetry and whatever passing interest I may have in trees and the habits of birds, Papi was the parent who confided in me, who allowed me into his moods. My mother was always at a remove in that sense. Whenever I had questions she neatly deflected them to my father. He could be strict, forbidding even, sending me alone on errands to the bazaar saying, 'Nothing will happen to you.' And always I wanted to ask, 'How do you know? Is it worth the risk?' Nothing ever happened. The world mostly ignored me. He was the parent I understood as a child, the one I grew estranged from when I left home, but still, I cannot think of a single real thing that was ever said between us.

'What are you doing here, Grazia? When did you arrive?'

'I don't know what to say to you.' I leave him under a church awning with a melting ice-cream cone.

Later that evening I ring the bell of his apartment in the Calle del Fumo near the Fondamente Nove. I take my time walking up the four floors. Papi holds me for a long time at the door. His place is exactly as it had been since he moved here – crowded with books, a bust of Leonardo da Vinci that he'd bought at a flea market, boxes of records, the same heavy, dark furniture. Not a single object to signify that he'd spent twenty-five years in India.

He prepares spaghetti alle vongole for dinner, taking great care with the mussels, coating them in garlic and wine. Shirtsleeves rolled up to the elbows.

'Who's that singing?' I ask.

'Mariza. She's a *fado* singer. Wonderful, isn't she?'

We listen to this voice booming over us – sad and sweet. She's singing about love, undoubtedly, but if she'd been singing about plastic carrier bags, she would still have had the same effect – of installing orchestras in our diaphragms, complete with an audience of cheering people, as if we were somehow responsible for the enchantment she alone was creating.

We listen and drink and eat, and after there is no more music, in the long silence of an October night, my father begins.

'The baby was born a Mongoloid,' he says. 'It was 1973 in India, and no one knew what to do. You should have seen the hospital, Grazia. People on the floors. Dirty. Clueless people. Your mother and I were not equipped. The doctors gave us our options. They said there was a good chance she wouldn't survive. We decided together. I want you to know that. Whatever your mother has made you believe, this was something we decided together.'

5

I find my sister at the Sneha Centre for Girls in Injambakkam. It is November in Madras. Roads laid waste by rain. Mosquitoes vying for every inch of exposed skin.

Nothing about it is scary. Not the narrow funnel of Periyar Street or the lone, crooked laburnum leaning over the gate. Not even the towers of plastic clogging the exposed drains.

I think of my mother; my newly dead mother who has bequeathed me land, a house, a sister.

The place is more terrible inside than out.

All the walls are a uniform concrete grey, and the cork-boards – the only splash of colour in the rooms – are filled with pictorial charts of vegetables and types of professions. Sad, uninventive socialist charts, left over from when India used to be friends with Russia. The windows are barred with intricate grilles, and the bedraggled children stare off into nothing, holding themselves, rocking. Some of them have gimpy legs and they drag themselves across the floor with their hands.

Mrs Gayatri, who I first met at Ma's funeral, shows me the dark room with the wooden bench where the epileptics are hauled off to be strapped down, the kitchen, the terrace, the activity room, where the more advanced children make bags out of newspapers.

There are thirty girls in all. Girls, I say, though most of them, including my sister, are women.

One of them is an albino. Sugandhi. She sits in a dark corner. A giant, ghostlike creature with a disproportionately huge head, pink eyes, ash-white hair. When I enter the room she lifts a long arm to point at me. She is relentless with her questions. *Who are you? What's your name? What are you doing here? Are you married?*

Mrs Gayatri shoves me towards her. 'She wants to shake your hand.'

I take that ghost hand in mine. Those long, musical fingers. Somebody's child. Maybe even somebody's sister.

I tell her my name. 'I'm Lucy's sister,' I say.

No one at the Sneha Centre has ever called my sister Lucia. Lucy is easier on the Tamil tongue.

Mrs Gayatri guides me through her office, up the stairway to the large hall where the girls sleep. There are twenty-eight jute mats rolled and standing up against the wall, twenty-eight pillows and twenty-eight sets of folded sheets. A single shelf built into the wall runs all the way across the room, where the girls store their clothes, toys, towels, toothbrushes.

Only two girls have private rooms. One has cerebral palsy, the other is my sister. Rich girls.

'Lucy's waiting,' Mrs Gayatri says. 'Quite excited, naturally, but also nervous.'

Mrs Gayatri is a remarkable woman, almost two-dimensional if you look at her sideways. The paragon of a woman who works in social services. Completely flattened out by life. Trying to look optimistic and cheery but, having seen too much to be angry about, just looks perpetually worried.

'What should I call you?' I ask, after we had been acquainted a few weeks.

'Everyone calls me Teacher,' she laughed. 'Even my husband.'

The first sight of my sister.

She looks like a jumbo peach. Round glasses perched on a snub nose. Perfect almond upturned eyes. Tiny little ears that grow away from her face like flowers in search of light. Peach *kurti*, blue wide-legged jeans, peach plastic hoop earrings, peach slippers. Hair – limp and brown and long.

She is heavier than me. Plump everywhere – shoulders, breasts, hips, thighs, bum.

'Hi Grace.'

She smiles. Two rows of tiny, jagged, widely spaced teeth.

'Hi.'

'Come and meet my babies.' She slides off the bed and takes my hand. Laces her fingers through mine. Gives them a squeeze.

There are rows of stuffed animals of varying size, colour and condition, perched on the shelves of my sister's room. A frame sits on the bedside table with a photograph of my mother and Lucia. Ma is skinny, unrecognisable. She's looking down at Lucia at her hip, who's fat and bright-eyed, clutching on to a yellow teddy bear in a red-and-black vest. The same bear lies in a heap on the bed, looking somewhat diminished by the years.

'That's Baloo, the first of the birthday toys. Your mother used to bring one every year. Sorry, they're a bit dirty. Lucy gets agitated if we even talk of washing them.'

Lucia is introducing me to each of her babies. Many named from *The Jungle Book*, her favourite story. The newer ones have nonsense names like Pootchie and Booboo.

'You know your mother used to come every week? She always took Lucy to see a film, whatever was playing. Hardly any English films in those days, but it didn't matter. Birthdays were extra-special. She'd stay overnight and organise a party for all the children. Cake, balloons, mutton biryani, colouring books and crayons for everyone. We all looked forward to your mother's visits. She always brought her lovely homemade bread.'

Now Lucia is dragging out all her clothes and laying them on the bed. Smocks. A dozen of them – floral, baggy, shapeless things. We'll have to get rid of those. Nighties, salwar kameezes, jeans, T-shirts. One ridiculous frothy pink frock. A couple of bejewelled *ghagras* for the annual Diwali and Christmas dance shows. Underwear – granny-style vests and knickers, pointy cotton bras. Petticoats. A pink terry-towelling bathrobe that I remember my mother wearing for many years. Sensible, sturdy Teva sandals for her flat, splayed feet. Rubber chappals and a pair of pink-and-silver Nikes.

'It's all a little old-fashioned,' Teacher says, glancing at me apologetically.

'Doesn't matter, we'll pack it all.'

'Where's Mummy?' Lucia asks, suddenly, blinking.

'Lucy, we already talked about this. This is your sister Grace. You're going to go live with her. Mummy's not here any more. Mummy's gone to God.'

'But I love Mummy.'

'But Grace is here for you now. She's going to take care of you like Mummy did.'

'No,' Lucia says, shouting louder and louder. 'No, no, no, go away. I want Mummy.'

A week after I visit Lucia at the Sneha Centre, she agrees to come and visit me at home. It is one of those lost days in the middle of the monsoon. No rain for a week but the air still heavy with it. The sky drips into the sea like an endless watercolour of grey, smudged only with a spume of white waves and a few scattered trawlers bobbing in the distance. The garden is spiky with green, shiny and luminous. Egrets sail and land languidly like Cessnas in the brush, while painted ladies skitter madly between bushes of bright yellow oleander.

The dog, Raja, who has only recently adopted me, sits in the long grasses, surveying the newcomers.

Lucia arrives with her friend, Priya Darshini, also a Down's girl, and Teacher. They climb out of the taxi in flowery get-ups with sunhats and sunglasses, which they keep calling 'coolers'.

'Like my coolers, Grace-akka?'

'What about *my* coolers, Grace-akka?'

'You look like film stars!' I say, carrying their bags into the house.

I try to see the house the way they might see it, the way it appeared to me when my mother's lawyer Mr Sriram brought me to see it. A pink blob on a mound of grass with blue shutters and a red-tiled roof set in a garden, and several acres of brush a few hundred metres from the sea.

'Such a big place,' Teacher exclaims. 'Don't you feel scared staying here all by yourself?'

Teacher is searching the house for clues, but there are no photographs, no personal touches to infer anything of my previous life. Some of the furniture I'd salvaged from my mother's flat – two wicker sofas, a couple of planter's chairs, the dining table and an old rosewood bench from my grandparents' Queen Street house in Tranquebar.

The two upstairs bedrooms are sparse and functional. 'I'm still getting settled in,' I explain. 'There's a lot to unpack, and a whole load in storage, but I really don't want to clutter this place up. I like it empty.'

'What about safety? Any problems with the locals? Have you met any of your neighbours?'

'Nobody's bothered with me much. I've seen the *thalai-var* of course, a nice man called Valluvan, given him some money to keep him happy. It just takes getting used to. And besides, I have my Raja. He protects me.'

Priya and Lucy are eager to get to the beach. They've changed into bathing suits – demure one-pieces with attached frilly skirts.

'Don't you both look cute,' I say. 'Let's go.'

A Tamil Nadu beach at midday is something to marvel at. All that sweep of vast, uninterrupted sand. All those vanished people sitting in the safety of shade protecting their complexions.

Not to say there aren't chunks of coastline clotted with the odd row of tourists roasting themselves on sarongs. But there are few resorts, and fewer travellers who have tired of Goa and Kerala, who have swapped coasts to see what kind of ocean the Bay of Bengal is. Nothing like the sweet-lipped Arabian, is what. This sea is a rough, unpredictable, bash-you-about kind of sea, and at the peak of the day's heat the beach is a desert. This is the time I love it best. The catamarans are parked quietly on the sand, and the pal-myras and casuarinas stand, braced for any calamity. Only when the sun begins to dip to the west does life slowly resurge. In the cities people stream out to the sea like ants towards sugar – a carnival at dusk with mini Ferris-wheels, candyfloss stalls, peanut vendors. Here in Paramankeni it's the time when goat herders lead their animals home, fishermen sit by their boats smoking and mending their nets, and village boys rush out in their underwear, diving in and out of the waves. On weekends, there will sometimes be a group of city slickers playing volleyball in the ramshackle resort down the road, but it is still mostly isolated.

I lead the way up the stone path. Raja follows eagerly, past the thatch shack and the water pump, up to the brick wall and wooden gate. Midway, Raja lifts his hind leg to scratch himself, but after a few feverish cycles, he gives up and forges ahead. After the last bout of rain the beach plums have grown, gushing out of their beds like a rash, so I must bend back their large, rubbery leaves in order to push open the gate. We step out onto the burning sand, which is stippled with bits of Styrofoam and flotsam – dried husk of coconut, a carpet of purple-flowered weed.

I set up the beach umbrella for Teacher and roll my trousers over my knees before walking over to the girls.

We stand in the waves, the three of us – Lucia and Priya shriek every time a big wave slaps at their feet. An hour later, they become braver, dig holes in the shore and give Teacher their coolers and sunhats for safekeeping. They sit in these bunkers, burrowing their bums deep in the sand, and every time a wave knocks them over they flail their arms about and say, 'Save us, save us.'

Raja runs worriedly up and down the coast, refusing to get his paws wet. A beach dog that is terrified of water.

We take a break from the waves for a picnic lunch. Biryani and Coca-Cola, but as soon as they've shovelled a plateful of food down their gullets they're back in their bunkers, screeching.

At four, Teacher begins to complain, saying the girls are getting too black.

'You better get going,' I say. 'I don't want you driving on that road in the dark.'

'No no,' they shout. 'We don't want to go.'

Teacher gets up and starts waggling her finger at them. 'You want to come again, don't you? We can come next week, but you can't behave like this. What will Grace-akka think?'

When the girls finally stand up, their swimsuits are full of sand. They're wobbly from all the extra weight, and they're giggling because every time they take a step forward, mud slides down their thighs.

'Look! Like kaka in the pants!'

They point at each other and laugh till they're choking.

'Come on. We'll hose you down inside. And you too,' I say to Raja. 'Let's get you some food.'

Lucia is intrigued by Raja. He has decided that she must love him, so he's exerting all his charm, following her, letting her pat his head, gazing up at her with his wet brown eyes.

'What a scam! He's putting on a show for you, Lucy. See this big flea circling his head? That's where his heart really lies. That's his beloved wife, Rani. They're always together. Raja and Rani.'

When they pile into the taxi, Raja follows them all the way up the long driveway to the front gate. He squeezes under the gate and chases after them through the village, past the traditional thatch and newer concrete houses, past wells and bicycles, roosters, cows, children – his legs hurtling over ditches and heaps of stone rubble. And only when the car bumps over the little bridge, crossing the lagoon and fixing on to the main road, does he turn around and make his way home to me.

The next morning Teacher calls to say, 'Lucy wants to try. If it's okay with you, we'll come next weekend to spend the night.'

6

How often I dream of going back to sit on one of those cold, hard benches at PPCG just to listen to the heavens crashing down, even if it means being in the presence of those cretinous nuns for a few hours.

There is nothing in the world like hill rain – epic, torrential – all drum rolls and whiplash. The smell of the earth, potent and warm like mud in your nostrils. It is the smell of sex, of a lover returning. And the nuns, knowing it, fearing it, herded us into the chapel for safekeeping, lit candles and incense, prayed and prayed for the storms to pass.

My parents would come for me in the Ambassador. Ma at the wheel, tiny and bug-eyed; Papi with a raincoat and an umbrella, running to fetch me from the chapel. There was always hot chocolate and Miles Davis in Mahalakshmi when it rained. Papi would light a fire, and Ma and I would bring out blankets so we could huddle around the drawing-room table and play rummy. Outside, eucalyptus trees shook nervously in the gale, and stray dogs took shelter in the portico. Those were probably our closest moments as a family, and still, I would have given anything to be with Queenie and the other girls in the dorm.

I wonder where it comes from? That strange foreboding of childhood? That the universe is conspiring to keep secrets from you. Did it begin in Kodai? Or earlier?

I remember little of my early life in Madras. It was always a place of exits and entries – a dreamy, transitional city, where time was either expanding or closing in. In Madras I had not felt lonely. Ma told me I had two friends at Rosary Metric, the school I attended from standard one through to five, although I have no recollection of them or the things we might have played. Savitri and Ayesha: two pigtailed, smiling girls. There are photographs of the three of us at successive annual days at school, dressed as peacocks and flower sellers and the Three Kings. There's one taken of us at sports day in chaste, knee-length shorts. We are holding hands and smirking as if we'd just shared a joke. All the photographs of our years in Madras are as drained of colour and out of focus as my memories.

I know for sure, though, that when I lived in Madras I had not felt the acute need for a witness in my life. When we moved to Kodai I began to have a real yearning for someone who shared my memories. Someone other than my parents.

My friend Queenie always used to say, 'You're so lucky, Grace. You never have to fight for attention or have two brats constantly slobbering all over your things.' She was the eldest of three girls, the star of the family. Pressure was always on her. But I watched when Queenie's mother and sisters came to pick her up for holidays. The history she shared with her sisters bound them together from birth. How could she ever be truly alone? Sure, you could grow up in the same house and experience everything differently, but there would always be certain episodes that either brought laughter in the remembrance of them, or clots of purple bruising. Long after Queenie and I drifted apart, she would still have her sisters. They would call each other on the phone, their families would meet. And perhaps they would complain in secret, as all families do. But blood prevails. Sisters outlast friends. For me, this was something.

The summer I turned sixteen we went to Italy, and I remember dragging my parents around all the museums of Venice and Padua, from one Visitation of the Angel Gabriel to the next, looking for beauty among all those Resurrections and Ascensions and Last Suppers. It was the summer I kissed the Bernardi brothers, who lived next door to Nonno and Nonna in their canary-yellow apartment building on Corso Fogazzaro, and I had returned feeling emboldened and changed. It only took a week to deflate everything. We'd been invited to Ma's bridge partner Sundar Rajagopalan's house for dinner. It was threatening rain, and Ma was the only one who really wanted to go. My parents were in their bedroom, arguing. I sat in the bay window reading, waiting for them to be finished.

'You're going to complain about this after I've spent a month cooped up with your family?' Ma was saying. 'He's our friend, Giacinto. One of the few we have. But if you don't want to come, that's fine. Just don't try to make me feel guilty about going.'

'Oh, friend. Yes. We know whose friend he is. Let's be clear.'

'Yes, yes, let's be clear. We wouldn't want there to be any fucking unclarity on anything.'

'This is not a word. Unclarity.'

'Grace, let's go,' Ma screamed, slamming the bedroom door. 'Your father isn't coming.'

Ma drove wildly, emitting a series of sharp, incomprehensible grunts as we sped along the treacherous hill roads. It was a misty night and I had to wipe the windows with the car cloth and shine the torch out through the windscreen so we could see. She was wearing a sparkly dress she'd bought in one of those fancy boutiques in Vicenza, and a maroon woollen shawl draped across her shoulders.

The party was small but raucous, like most of the parties I got dragged to in those years. The Rolling Stones or the Bee Gees would inevitably be banging away in the background, and there was always a lot of hard drink involved. Most of my parents' friends were functioning alcoholics. Not that I'd even get a taste of beer. I'd be stuck with a Gold Spot and a bowl of tapioca chips in a room playing Risk with the Swaminathan twins and Amin Bilimoria.

Sundar Rajagopalan lived in one of those old Kodai stone houses, which seem to have been designed specifically to promote pneumonia. The floors and walls emitted a cold, uniform dampness. Overstuffed taxidermied birds lined the entrance, while mounted deer heads looked on morosely from above. Any space that wasn't utilised by a dead animal was seized by one of Uncle Sundar's paintings – ugly, abstract abominations of what looked to me like giant red-feathered phalluses. Add to that the awful smell of piss and deterioration that no amount of long-stemmed lilies could smother. That was my mother's idea of a good time.

During dinner parties at Uncle Sundar's, the grown-ups usually sat in the bar room while the children were herded into the shrine room – a grotto-like enclosure with candy-floss-coloured wallpaper and alcoves filled with icons and statues of every god ever invented. Uncle Sundar's mother, who lived with him, and probably had something to do with the pervasive piss smell, was a devout woman who believed in appeasing the gods equally.

That night we found dogs in the shrine room. Uncle Sundar's dachshund, Boogie, was now consigned to a bed of blankets with three puppies sucking at her teats – two black and one white. Boogie growled when we came close, but she allowed Uncle Sundar to pick up the little white pup and plop it in my lap. He had pale eyes and a huge, wrinkled forehead and when his little body shivered in my hands, my heart corresponded metronomically.

'Do you want him, Champ?'

Ma gave me one of her glares when I said yes. 'We have to ask your father,' she started. 'And what happens when we go visit Grandma and Grandpa?'

I didn't care. I wasn't about to let go of that pup.

'You know what?' Uncle Sundar said. 'Keep him for a couple of weeks. If it doesn't work out, you can always bring him back, and if you need me to look after him when you're away, I'm happy to do that too.'

In that instant I loved Uncle Sundar. All the irritation I felt towards him because he dyed his hair black from a bottle and wore too-tight pants and most probably put his teapot into the backsides of other men flatlined.

It was past midnight by the time we got home. Not a single light had been left on to welcome us. The puppy quaked in my lap – a pale, white, whimpering sausage.

'Salsicciotto,' I said. 'That's what I'm going to call you.'

'He's your responsibility, Grace,' my mother said, dragging her feet wearily. 'You have to clean up his crap and feed him and walk him. Understand? And no letting him sleep on the bed.'

I don't know what time it was when the lights in my parents' room were turned on. My father would have waited for my mother to fall asleep. I can see him patiently flexing his toes in his striped pyjamas. The anger inside him churning. He would have waited till her face softened, till that little ridge between her eyebrows eased and the corners of her mouth relaxed. He would have let her flip onto her stomach, as she always did before falling into the deep. And then he would have flicked on the lamp.

'Sleeping? You can sleep through everything, can't you?'

'Put the light out, Giacinto, we can talk in the morning. You're going to wake everyone up.'

'But everyone is already awake.'

There was that usual tightness that entered my body when they began. A slow pummelling in my stomach. If I tried to cover my ears, the menace would be there too, saying, *Listen, this is important* – all the disappointment they seemed to carry for each other rolled like waves out of them, one accusation after the other.

'What the hell is wrong with you? Why do you behave like this?'

'Maybe because I like when my wife goes around town without me. Maybe because I like being like a little castrated thing, crying that my wife is carrying on with mister so and so ...'

'You wake up and shit comes streaming out of your mouth, Giacinto. I swear, if you think I can't have my own opinions and desires ...'

'Desires? *Cara*. Don't disillusion yourself. There must be a fridge between your legs ...'

That's when Ma raised the lamp and threw it at him.

I heard the crash of glass, footsteps, the front door slamming.

'Where are you going, Meera?'

By the time he opened the door she was gone. The car had growled out of the gate and into the night.

I could hear Papi stand outside my door. Please don't let him come in, I thought. Just leave me alone, the two of you. I don't care if you kill each other. He stood there for a while, panting, and then padded softly away.

That night it rained so hard I felt I was being thrashed around on a ship in the middle of a storm. Salsicciotto curled up close to me with his soft ears and paws. He peed continuously through the sheets, and I held him in that pungent pool of wet. I thought about how it felt to hold a small creature of blood, tongue and heart, and how it might feel to let go of everything and walk into the future.

*

Our lives began to move in different directions after that night. I was growing up despite my grievances against adulthood, and the changes within me were a kind of smothering, like driving down the *ghats* every summer to visit family I desperately wanted to love but didn't.

I still feel it whenever I come down those hills. That suffocation in my throat, the air, thick and red. A 7,000-foot descent. Always the same song in my head. *She'll be coming 'round the mountain when she comes ... She'll be riding six white horses when she comes ... She'll be wearing pink pyjamas when she comes ... Singing ay ay yippee yippee ay.*

I am by the window, peeling off the layers of clothes to make space for humidity, for summer. The change is like a sloughing off. Out come my toes from socks and shoes. Off comes my jumper and scarf. Underneath, the skin behind my neck is already soft with sweat. Two hours of curves and hairpin bends. Sometimes the taxi driver takes the corners too fast and there's a stirring in my belly that claws up my throat. *Slow down, mister*, I say, and the driver turns around and grins slavishly. But five minutes later he's off like the Road Runner again.

The rise of nausea and the subsiding. Again and again and again. And just when I think I can't bear it any more, we're hitting the base of the Palani Hills, riding the flat of the plains, bumping along ragtag villages where chickens and children are constantly racing across the road lined with corpulent teak trees with black-and-white painted bands around their trunks. Paddy fields glimmer like swimming pools at the base of brown hills. Lorries and buses barrel down the highway with muscular headlights and horns. A warm, soupy breeze begins to blow softly through the window.

We are cheating death, all the time, passing one overcrowded town, then another, and another. The litany of village names buzzing in my ears like flies with a hundred lives – Kanakkanpatti, Oddanchatram, Batlagundu, Palakkanuthu. Neon boards flash with the faces of film stars, advertising beauty salons and eateries. The cows that congregate around rubbish bins are skinny, with coats of dust. Shops line the narrow streets. Tiny cubbyholes where you can buy birthday cake frocks and plastic cricket bats, brass pots and toilet scrubbers. Shit and spit. Everywhere, shit and spit and jasmine and mari-gold. And somewhere in the distance, the sea.

7

In those early days of discovering my sister, I kept looking back to scenes of my life, hoping for clues, openings where she could walk through. But we will never sit in a room with our parents as a complete family. We will never know what those rhythms might have been. Our childhoods are consigned to a kind of captivity, forced to exist in two compartments separate from one another.

The irreversibility of having a child. This is what I think about as I watch Lucia, trying to learn her ways.

Teacher had already told me that Lucia loves cornflakes. That she loves Coca-Cola, chicken fried rice, finger chips, mutton fry, vanilla ice cream, car rides, train rides, horse rides, bike rides, Tom and Jerry, Shivaji Ganesan, the colour pink, afternoon naps, going to the doctor, swimming pools, merry-go-rounds, stuffed animals, parties, cinemas, dancing.

I was learning that Lucia also loved to lie like a crab on her back, moving her arms and legs up and down rhythmically, her blouse sometimes rising to show the soft mound of her belly. That she was double-jointed and could hook both ankles around her neck and swing from side to side like a pendulum. That when she got into her singing mood she could rock and sing operatic gibberish for hours.

Her hands were like two pats of butter. They were my father's hands – soft and stubby, the right forefinger shorter than the left because she jammed it in a door when she was ten. Sometimes she would slip the tips of her fingers into her panties and graze herself against the mattress.

I cried every day when Lucia came to live with me. Shameful crying, done in bouts on the floor of my bedroom. I had expected to feel less estranged from the world, but Lucia brought heaviness. She was a big girl and she occupied the house in a way that was neither timid nor hushed. At nights I had imaginary conversations with my dead mother. Mostly, me ranting at her: 'Don't think I don't know why you hurried off to die. Don't think baking bread for a group of imbeciles once a week condones anything. You abandon your child and have the guts to tell me that I'm a selfish person?' Once, I even whispered my exit plan, which began to seem more and more like an inevitability with the sea beating at the shore and the wind gusting through the house. 'Barbiturates, Mother. What do you think about that? Barbiturates for the both of us.'

Some days I feel the sadness build. Other days it blindsides me. It is different from what I felt in America – that large, one-size-fits-all American loneliness.

When my new friends ask about my life there, I tell them about those first months. The fall of 1996. Those North Carolina skies. Walking up Selwyn Avenue to the A&P to buy microwavable Uncle Ben's Rice. Heaps of yellow and orange leaves clustered along the streets as if it were a movie set. The lines all clean and straight. The houses, gigantic and gateless.

America fills you out, exerts her homogeneous hunger upon you, making it so that no matter how much you have, you always want more. I grew stout in America on a diet of French fries, Budweisers, brownies and ranch dressing. Within a year I went from being a raw-boned teenager to a chunky amoeba of an adult with a muffin top and endangered clavicles.

I tell them about my job at the cafeteria, and about Ms Betty, the cafeteria supervisor − a pint-sized black lady with the heart of a Cadillac. It was Ms Betty who saved me on those never-ending North Carolina evenings when the skies grew ragged with pink, and everything that was young and flourishing seemed to be outside, just out of reach − under the shade of dogwood and sugarberries, in the quad where sorority sisters exchanged whispers and lacrosse players stretched out like cheetahs on waterproof blankets spread upon grass of such perfect height and prickle, it made me untenably sad.

'You ain't gonna find what you is looking for out there,' Ms Betty used to say, every time she caught me gaping through the glass doors of the Students' Centre.

'You ain't gonna find it in your friends nor your fine boyfriend neither. You blind, is what.'

She was right. After all, what kind of crazy person moves from one country's deep south to another country's deeper south?

North Carolina. North Dakota. None of it had conjured up any particular picture as I sat in my bay window in Mahalakshmi with college forms and SAT tutorials, dreaming my getaway. It was where Blake Henderson was going and where I would follow. Perhaps I'd been inducted long before meeting Blake. Back in Madras, with Moses Paulraj and his American-anthem-singing car penetrating every early-morning dream. Perhaps it was the reason why I went with Blake in the first place, because I knew that America would be big enough and lonely enough to accommodate me.

When I finally arrived in America I had not been prepared to feel so poor. I had not understood how it would make me cling to Blake, who visited me in Charlotte every weekend from Chapel Hill, taking me out to Burger King for big Whoppers – the two of us chewing on that cheap food, bristling in the glee of our independence. And later, gliding through the shiny corridors of South Park Mall, dragging our greasy fingers through all those racks of beautiful clothes. I hadn't realised there had been so much want in me.

I remember once, at the top of Tanglewood Lane in Myers Park, Blake had just picked me up from a babysitting job. We were putting our seatbelts on, getting ready to drive to Freedom Park, when there was a knock against the glass. An old woman with huge rheumy eyes and a straggly grey bob leaned in to peer at us. I lowered the glass.

'Hello?'

'Are you running out of people?' she said. She was looking at us in a hard, mean way. Not like a confused little old lady. 'Have you never lost anyone, then? You never missed someone by mistake?'

We just blinked at her.

'Well?' the old lady asked. 'Have you?'

'Are *you* missing someone, ma'am?' Blake finally asked.

And suddenly, her face softened. 'Yes. My husband. He's going to be angry at me, that's for sure.'

I wanted to ask the lady, who are you? Are you lost? Should we call someone? But I just stared at her, dumb, speechless. Finally we left her there, saying, 'Okay now, you have a good day,' and she looked at us, angry again, disgusted. 'Yes, I'll try.'

After freshman year I moved out of the dorm to share an apartment with an Ethiopian girl, Misrak, who, when she grew homesick, sat in bed and gnawed on doughy rings of *injera*. We were reading *Brave New World* together and listening to Nusrat Fateh Ali Khan. Every Wednesday we hit the nightclubs with our fake IDs. We'd stand on wooden boxes in cheap black dresses and shake and move, thinking, Yes sir, here we are in America.

There were things I hadn't been prepared for in America, like counting dimes to buy rancid bean burritos from Taco Bell, the melancholy of a Wal-Mart store at 2 a.m., reverse-wearing underwear. All the sprawl and waste and marvel of American life.

And when I say American life, I mean the lives of the rich bankers in the neighbourhood around the college where Misrak and I folded laundry and pulled boogers out of their kids' noses for five bucks an hour.

Street after street of mansion and lawn, each competing in bigness, each with its own overfed Labrador unencumbered by a single blood-sucking tick, stunned into dumb submission by an invisible electric fence.

And this abundance of gleaming created something sick in me – not a yearning for home exactly, but the imprint of a lost, forgotten thing, and I knew if I wanted to catch that lost thing I would have to leave America.

In hindsight, I could say it was Lucia. That I had always been carrying around this sense of loss in me. But in those days I went searching for other things – in the face of the old man fumbling around for treasures among the bric-a-brac of the Dollar Store, or the immigrant woman trawling through the aisles of Food Lion, fondling all the fruits and vegetables in search of the fattest and the sweetest. I'd think of that poor, helpless woman in Myers Park looking for all the missing people in her life, and it seemed to me that in every corner of America there was someone growing sick with loneliness. And all that started up a mad swirling inside me of what I can only describe as grief. I don't know whether it had anything to do with being poor, or lonely, or America itself, but it had nothing to do with missing my parents.

It was as if my entire life before hadn't been real. Those had just been days of waiting and filling time before the real thing could begin.

But sitting with Misrak on the mattresses of our one-bedroom apartment, smoking late into the night, talking about everything from Kantian ethics to the glories of a deplumed cunt – that was life.

Listening to Nusrat, who was the soundtrack of all our days. Something in his voice scoured every nameless emotion from inside our bodies and gave it a name. He was all curvatures of sound, a spray of fine-grained grit against the face, sex and god in the same room. And we never tired of him. Misrak would get up and dance, wriggling her shoulders up and down, all frenzied and primal, and I'd spare a thought for Papi, who would have called her a *watussi*, for sure. I'd spear the walls with a broom, whirling and screaming, 'Alive? Are you feeling alive, motherfuckers?' to the neighbours, who always wanted us to keep things down.

The walls were so thin and we were so young. And I know that every one of those nights we spent in number

161 Woodland Apartments, we were shining beings. Those were moments of pure living. We were *sonias* – long-haired, full-bodied believers in whatever it is that was starting.

I feel so far away from that now, from the beauty and closeness of those days. Who can I speak to in this wilderness? Not Lucia, with our single-sentence conversations. Not Mallika, with my rickety, broken-down Tamil. Not the dogs.

I miss the clarity of American roads. I think of them when I'm faced with acres of landfill emitting poisonous smoke, kilometres of road without a single rubbish bin, plastic clogging up the canals and lakes, all the disfiguring of what could be pristine. I think of the many road trips we made in Misrak's Cherry Red, and I feel nostalgic for a country that allows everybody to have everything if they want it.

Those journeys have layered themselves one on top of each other. New York, Washington DC, Charleston. The car's air conditioner was always in a state of disrepair, so we travelled with the windows down and hot air rushing in. 'Turn it up, turn it up,' Misrak would say, if the radio played Tina Turner's 'Private Dancer' or Prince's 'Purple Rain'. Those were our anthems. She would take off her top and fling it in the back seat, look straight ahead in a lacy bra, with one hand on the steering wheel and a cigarette in her mouth. Passing truck drivers would toot their horns. 'What are you doing?' I said, the first time she did it. But soon I was doing it too. Whipping off my shirt like a stripper, laughing as those men tooted their horns. Third-world Thelma and Louise. This is what being with Misrak made me feel.

Only once we travelled with our boyfriends. Spring break 1995.

We decided in Athens, the diner we went to on the corner of Independence Boulevard and East 4th. It used to be open 24/7, and it's where you'd find Misrak and me at the end of a long night, in our corner booth, leaning our imminent hangovers into red Rexine seat backs.

It was Misrak who wanted to go to Myrtle Beach. Four years in America, with graduation looming, and she still hadn't taken a proper break. Always sleeping on Ethiopian couches on cheap road trips or tagging along as a nanny with a white family to go on holiday with other white families. 'I want to stay in a proper hotel and have fun!' she said. 'Come on. Don't you think Chichi is ready for it?'

Chichi had burst onto the scene a few months earlier at a party, where he had impressed Misrak with his agile shoulders and silver Maserati. He was studying pre-med at Chapel Hill and had so far proven that few things had the potential to animate him: the sight of Misrak's chest was one; a series of cocktails, preferably Long Island Iced Teas, was another.

I remember him sitting in the back of Blake's car, staring glumly out of the window at the parade of flowering trees down I-74. Everywhere – bullets of colour. An upheaval of brown, like skin turned inside out to expose festering wounds of purple and pink. All those flowering trees, the names of which could compete only with the names of the seemingly make-believe towns we were passing through. Darlington, McBee, Monroe, crape myrtle, magnolia, redbud. Perfect little explosions.

In Myrtle Beach I found out more about Chichi. That he was an Eritrean; that he'd been taking care of his mother and sisters ever since his father deposited them in the United States in 1986. That he had drive – not immigrant drive, which was shabby and somewhat sycophantic, but entitlement drive, the same kind of drive Blake had.

Misrak and Chichi fought constantly in Myrtle Beach. They may have spoken the same language, but they came from different sides of a disputed border. When we came home to Woodland Apartments she said, 'It's never going to work with us. I just don't see it.' And just like that, Chichi of the agile shoulders and silver Maserati was out.

I too should have seen clearly the incompatibility of our spirits. Blake and I, holding hands, walking along the scummy seashore. Him thinking that we were moving atop some giant swell of togetherness in a cheesy Richard Bach kind of way, calling me Ducky, saying things like, 'You and I aren't going to be one of those couples who fight or have secrets,' and me hating it, hating him for not realising that I hated him. Hating my dearest friend because she knew exactly what she was and what she couldn't abide, whereas I, whose life had been constructed from all manner of flimsy things – I was malleable.

I would have a moment of clarity in Myrtle Beach, of understanding why I didn't belong in America. All those orange umbrellas dotting the beach, and the grease of so many baking bodies slathered in tanning oil. The combined exhalation of all that burning fat.

It reminded me of Jesolo, the seaside of my father's childhood – a bleak port town on the Adriatic.

He took us once. I must have been twelve or thirteen. My mother spent most of her time cowering in the shade with an outsized hat and socks on her hands, complaining,

'I'm already brown, Giacinto! Brown people don't want to get browner.'

Around us the heave of summer. Barrel-chested men in Speedos and mamas with flaccid biceps beckoning to their beloved Giorgios and Ludovicos to come and eat their *panini alla porchetta*.

Day after day, the same routine. To the beach by nine – flip and roast, flip and roast – *riposino*, swim, walk, dinner, sleep, repeat.

I remember gawking at all the flesh – the women in bikinis, so filled out and unabashed. My mother, by contrast, swaddled in towels like a bloody Bedouin. I longed to own my body like those women did, even if their pasta paunches pushed over their waists, and their cylindrical thighs shook with cellulite.

How old was I when I had the courage to buy my first bikini? I know I didn't have one in Myrtle Beach, because I remember watching Misrak emerge from the cabana and taking in the wonder of her quietly along with Blake and Chichi. That she could transform two bits of red nylon – some cheap thing she'd bought on sale without even trying on – two bits of triangle and string, and *still* look like one of those characters from *Baywatch*, bounding gloriously down the beach. That she had made no particular effort to look that way, unlike all the other girls with their patiently honed midriffs and manufactured thigh gaps.

It would take years before I had the courage to step out in a two-piece, always making sure to lift my thighs in photographs so they wouldn't look like bags of cement. By then, Misrak had found Jake, a boy from the Midwest, to marry. He contained her fire, softened it, gave her three kids and a white picket fence.

'She done found her place,' Ms Betty would have said.

I think about that now. Misrak's busy American life. Some of the Amharic still clinging to the throat, but the rest of the accent hammered out into something steady and recognisable. I think of the trips she must make with her family to beachside towns, and wonder if anything about the large migration of humans on holiday depresses her.

I think of my father, out in the Adriatic Sea, away from the din of the world – a small, unrecognisable blip. And I know it's really me I'm seeing. Standing behind glass.

PART TWO

8

Mornings at the beach can arrive like a whore in a jangly, too-tight dress at the end of a long and sleepless night. Lucia and I lie with our toes pointing east under mosquito nets in second-floor bedrooms with the doors flung open and the fans whizzing over our heads like helicopters. By six, when the sun is crawling its way out of the sea's belly and forcing its way through the blinds, I have already been up for hours, distracted by music from the temple in the village, which judders to life at 4 a.m. – *Brahma Muhurta* – God's hour, although there is nothing devotional that I can ascertain about this music. Tinny, Tamil film songs that pulsate across the air with no high-rise buildings to block their trajectory.

It isn't always that way, of course. Sometimes I sleep like a person lost to the world, buried and dead, my eyes caked shut with goop, deep ridges in my face from the sheets. There is no freshness in those mornings, no cool tingle of dawn. I wake in a bucket of heat. Lucia standing by the bed, poking at me, 'I'm hungry, Grace. Gimme cornflakes.'

Breakfast is a grand affair served in multiple courses. Freshly squeezed orange juice, diced papaya, multiple helpings of cornflakes drenched with sugar, a soft-boiled egg with a piece of soft, white, buttered bread cut up into soldiers.

Teacher says I've spoiled her. Tells me that when Lucia was at the Sneha Centre, she used to eat *idlis* for breakfast like the rest of the kids without complaint. 'You've given her new tastes,' she said. 'Once these children change their routines, it's very hard to change back.'

Teacher can sometimes be a sanctimonious bitch, but I try to keep things cordial.

It's strange to be unemployed. To have no project in life other than this. I spend time in the garden, trying to coax vegetables out of the ground, learning the names of shrubs and trees. There's so much beauty here, but always, the reminder of decay. Salt eating into the parliament hinges, washers in taps disintegrating, coats of rust thickening the lips of every mechanical appliance. It could drive you mad. This rushing about to preserve the doorjambs.

We measure the seasons by insects. Mosquitoes, black ants, mayflies, bees, wasps, moths, dragonflies, red beetles, and mosquitoes again.

We are in the middle of January now and the sea is settling into a hushed simmer. Fishermen go out in their catamarans early in the morning – their engines rattling like machine guns, low and wide across the water. The beach is a war zone, littered with carcases of olive ridley turtles caught in nets and discarded on the shore. They look like prehistoric sculptures in the sand. Dürer etchings. Crows pick at the flesh of their small, wise turtle heads. Our legion of dogs push their noses deep into the eroding carapaces, coming back home with the stink of death on them.

When Lucia first moved in I couldn't sleep at all. Teacher stayed a few nights to guide me through her routines, but after she left, when it was just the two of us, I used to lie awake, my mind popping and buzzing with fears. It was madness in a way. To live so far from everything.

Auntie Kavitha had assured me that whatever I chose to do, she could be relied upon to help. 'You don't have to do this, Grace. Your mother never expected it. All she wanted was for you to be able to see Lucy from time to time, to know her in a way. But you don't need to give up your life.'

I had wanted to give up my life, though. I was desperate for it.

With Lucia the patterns of cohabitation were different. Nothing like it had been with Blake. No snagged conversations. No pull and tug about the future. No talk of babies. Only puppy babies.

In the beginning we overcame our shyness for each other by fussing over Raja. He surprised me – the way he stuck to Lucia on the beach, the manner in which he curled himself by her feet when we sat outside for meals, shifting his attentions in order to welcome her.

A month later he disappeared. I tried reassuring Lucia that he would be okay, that he had other friends to visit along this stretch of ocean. But she wouldn't be placated.

Every few minutes she'd ask, 'Where's Raja?' Her right hand flung out, jabbing at the air, her left hand softly beating her thigh. 'Where's Raja? Where's Raja?' And when this produced no results, she screamed in frustration, rocking backwards and forwards on her feet, hands still jabbing, finally flinging herself on the floor in desperation. 'Where's Raja? Where's Raja?' Until she wasn't listening to anything I was saying, just repeating his name over my voice like an incantation. Raja. Raja. Raja.

Only after she had tired herself and gone off into a corner, subdued and hoarse, did the shouting stop. But all through the day she kept her eye hawked to the horizon for a sign of gold. After four nights even I began to worry. There were packs of dogs along this beach who could demolish and drown him in minutes. There were people who could be just as cruel for the sport of it. He had never stayed away so long.

On the fifth day, when he finally appeared, strutting up the garden path from the beach, Lucia ran towards him shouting, 'Raja, Raja.' Shadowing behind him was a black bitch – sleek and gorgeous, with a tikka of white in the fur of her forehead. This was Bagheera, Raja's great love. And between the two of them they spun kingdoms.

9

Vik comes over when it's dark and we fuck in the bedroom with the lights out and the door locked. We smoke a joint afterwards, our bodies slick and beautiful, and because he is young, we often go again.

The nights he's here, Lucia is restless, pacing the corridor, switching the lights on and off. The dogs are restless too – setting off with their orchestra of howling every time some poor creature gets too close to the walls. Vik and I laugh at the madness of it, but he doesn't stay long enough to really see it.

In the morning we rush to the sea in our bathing suits. The dogs chase after us. We ignore the shitters squatting further along the beach where the new constructions are rising up. All along the coast they are committed to cloning claustrophobic, ugly holiday homes, which will sit empty most of the year. Men have been hauled in from different parts of the country to work in this wasteland. Some have never seen the ocean. Some may even be terrified of it, although they don't show it. There's something dangerous about these men, the way they don't avert their eyes.

'What will you do?' Vik often says, usually when he's pulling up his shorts and reaching for his car keys.

'We'll have to see how things turn out,' I say. But I'm as scared of the future as anyone.

The longing I have for Vik is unlike any I've ever had. I first saw him at a Christmas party in someone's ancestral house. Ochre walls, marble floors. There were chairs in the garden and women in bandage dresses complaining that their heels were getting stuck in the mud. Everyone coked out of their heads – all swagger and crazy-eyed. I sat, trying not to look alarmed by the scene, which didn't correspond to any idea of Madras I had in my head. Vik slipped into the chair beside me in cargo shorts and T-shirt. Short, lean, bearded. A mouth full of teeth. 'This is all such bullshit, right?' he said. 'But it's part of what we live.'

He comes and goes. Every time he's gone too long I tell myself I won't let him back in. Lies. He knows he only has to send a sign and I will set about preparing myself, preparing the house.

The first time we do it is in my car. I pick him up at his parents' apartment building with a flask of red wine at my feet. It's late in Madras, and I have been driving around the streets, staring at people, trying to make eye contact. But people are resilient. They stare away from me at some point ahead in the darkness.

'There you are,' Vik says, sliding into the passenger seat.

We drive around and drink. I park outside the first house I ever lived in. The dead-end house on Gilchrist Avenue with its patio and ring of ashoka trees. It looks smaller now, ramshackle. Eventually, it will be torn down to make way for an apartment building, like Moses Paulraj's house next door.

'I had a bedroom with mustard paisley wallpaper,' I say. 'And I used to play with Fisher-Price toys. I made whole townships with those toys. But you probably don't even know what a fucking Fisher-Price toy is, right?'

'I fucking know,' he says, smiling. There is nothing to trust about this man. Still, I want to crawl inside him.

'I was a fat kid,' he says, as if to offer something of his own childhood.

'And did that traumatise you?'

'I used to beat the shit out of anyone in my class if they called me fatso.'

'A bully, then.'

'And you, convent girl? What were you like?'

I'm trying to imagine the kind of girl he normally goes with. One of those bandage-dress women at the party. Newfangled modern Indian woman. Smoker, drinker, drug-user, moneyed, gym fiend.

'I used to clean the shit in other people's toilet bowls when I was in America. I babysat, I worked in the cafeteria and the graveyard shift in the library. And you don't ever want to play pool with me because I will skin your ass.'

'We'll see about that.'

After the deadness of Blake this is an awakening. I clamber on top of him and we are in a hurry to put our hands on one another. I feel like a teenager hiding out in the forest. There are dogs at the end of the street barking. The sex is brief and exhilarating. I sit there, legs crushed, breathing in the smell of him.

There is a rap on the roof of the car. A cop at the window. He presses his face against the glass. He looks at us, mean and leering. I slide off, rearrange my skirt.

'Hang on,' Vik says. He zips up, gets out, guides the cop back to his patrol car up the road. Fifteen minutes later, he's back. 'I love this country,' he says. 'Everyone has a price.'

*

It's easy to fall into brutishness here. For days I wander about in a tatty sarong, legs unshaven, hair anarchic. The wind eats into your face. No amount of coconut oil will salvage it. Everything corrodes. The rusted hooks, the locks crumbling on the latches of the gate, the sea beyond – breathing. Pointless to fight it. No swaddle of air-conditioned city life here. No sparkly dresses or expensive moisturisers to delude you into thinking you can stall the clocks. How I long for it.

'Don't you have a full-length mirror?' Auntie Kavitha asks when she comes to visit. 'You'll forget what you look like.'

Like mother like daughter, she's probably thinking.

We sit on the veranda smoking while Lucia naps.

'How are you doing?' she asks. 'Really. Do you get out much?'

'Once or twice a month,' I say. 'I stay with my friends Samir and Rohini in Madras. I leave Lucia behind with Mallika, who always looks at me as if to say, What's so important that you must leave your sister behind? Teacher would be happy to have her stay, but Lucy will not go. She won't return to the room of her old life. But I leave her anyway, because I know if I can't be with people it will erode me. Who can I speak to, after all?'

'You didn't have to do this, you know.'

'You keep saying that.'

When I was a teenager I used to think that my mother and Auntie Kavitha were lovers. I'd imagine them on their Thursday jaunts – laughing, doing girly things like lunching and shopping, then retreating to one of the rooms in Auntie Kavitha's palatial house. Disrobing each other on a mirrored double bed. Being soft in the way women are.

Knowing doesn't change the way you remember things. Auntie Kavitha and I have talked about this before. The way memory is always dancing around our imaginary truths.

Lucia walks down the staircase with fistfuls of socks and handkerchiefs.

'Hi Lucy,' Auntie Kavitha says.

Lucia pauses at the bottom of the stairs. 'Gimme biscuits,' she says.

'Say hello to Auntie first!'

'Hello Auntie.'

I settle Lucia at the table inside with a glass of milk and a plate of bourbons split in half so all the chocolate is on one side of the biscuit. She will take half an hour to eat them, swinging her socks as she slowly chews.

'It isn't difficult,' I say. 'It's just the repetitiveness of it.'

After Auntie Kavitha leaves, Lucia and I go out on the beach with the dogs. We have five of them now. Raja, our golden one. Bagheera, our Nubian queen, and their three black-and-white daughters – Hunter, Thompson and Flopsy. They rush out of the gate and put their snouts in the air, sniffing to see if enemy packs are nearby. We charge after them, Lucia and I, flinging our rubber slippers in the sand, feeling the scrub between our toes. The dogs run in and out of the waves, wetting their paws, except for Raja, who is afraid of water. We walk past the newly constructed ashram, where white-robed foreigners some-times drift out to do yoga by the reclining stone Buddha. Past the derelict beach resort with its dead date palms and sagging volleyball net, where on weekends groups of city men gather to drink beer.

We pass the scattering of half-built houses constructed too close to the sea. Muslim fishermen from the neighbouring village are out with their lines. They look like office clerks with long-sleeved shirts and trousers. They must have jobs they can hurry away from, because at four they are standing in the sand with their skullcaps and their small cloth bags of tackle – casting and reeling, casting and reeling. When they see us approach, they lift their lines high so we can crouch under, or they press them close to the sand for us to jump over. They do not like the dogs, and sometimes raise their hands to shoo them away. But they always smile at Lucia. 'Sister?' they ask as I pass. I do what I always do when any of the locals try to speak with me. I pretend I am not from this place. I smile benignly with no sense that I have understood their question. I wave at them instead, and Lucia, because she is happy, waves too.

We keep walking till there is nothing but beach and casuarina, shell and flotsam. The dogs are manic. They bite and play, and I imagine because joy is tearing out of them, they turn to us and howl. Lucia and I do it too: raise our heads to the sky and howl as if the sea was a window and we were climbing out of it.

A death in the village. All night there are drums. I close the shutters and windows along the west-facing wall, but the pounding-thumping sounds roll through. Mallika tells me that the man who died was an important man – a school headmaster, which means there will be drums all week.

In the morning I find Lucia awake in bed, legs stretched out, her collection of new friends – a ragtag group of napkins, handkerchiefs and socks – lined up meticulously on either side of her. She has given up on her stuffed animals and jigsaw puzzles. All the old toys sit mildewing in the corner. These new friends go everywhere with her. She spends hours picking each one up, gently flipping it forwards and backwards, flick flick flick with her wrists, proceeding to go down the entire marching order, only to start again. Sometimes she sings as she does this, rocking her body forwards and backwards. If one of these friends goes missing, or if I try to put them in the washing machine, she hollers at me, 'Gimme back blue, Grace ... gimme blue.'

'You look tired, Lucy. Didn't you sleep?'

She shakes her head.

'Too much noise, right? I know. Shall we have a bath, then? Get going for the day?'

I run the water in the bucket and nudge the plastic stool over with my feet. Lucia's bathroom is open to the sky, so when I look up I can see part of a new construction next door, black-shouldered kites swooping and darting, clouds in the shape of a dancing bear.

'C'mon,' I rally. 'C'mon, c'mon.'

She stands in front of me, waiting for me to strip her down to panties and brassiere. She has lost a little weight thanks to our daily walks, although she's still a hearty girl — arms and legs, bum and breasts and face.

She lowers herself carefully onto the stool and I pour mugs of warm water over her. I squeeze a glob of body wash into the bath sponge and hand it to her so she can scrub under her arms and between her toes. There are faint strings of hair along her arms and legs. I refill the bucket three times.

'More,' she says, when she sees me about to fetch the towel.

'Just one more, then.'

I fill the bucket and I do what my grandmother used to do to me. It's the one fond memory I have of Grandma Loretta. When we used to visit them in Tranquebar, she would make us girl cousins line up in the bathroom, and for each of us, she'd pour a bucket of water over our heads like a waterfall, saying, '*Karuvi*, karuvi, karuvi,' slowly first, and then whoosh, the final splash, which took your breath away.

I do this to Lucia — 'Karuvi, karuvi, karuvi' — and when the water's finished, she stands, and I wrap the towel around her while I help to remove her wet underwear. Such care to modesty. This is the way Teacher taught me to bathe her. And when she's dry, on goes the talcum powder, a storm of it. She does this cheerfully, dousing her armpits with talc, then putting out her palm and patting splodges of powder on her face and in the ridges of her neck.

We are having golden days at the beach. The sea is flat, the horizon white. Boats shimmer in the distance, the noise of their motors faint and far. Everything is held in a sun-bleached March lull.

Bagheera was on the lawn with a dead chicken this morning. She had her puppies a few weeks ago, but she still won't allow us to follow her to them. Mallika thinks she must have had a big litter because of the way she's skulking around the house, perpetually hungry, her teats swollen and pink. Her three daughters are pregnant too. Lucia is delirious at the idea of so many puppies. 'After this, we're bringing the Blue Cross in to fix them,' I warn her. 'That's the end of the puppies. How are we going to look after so many dogs?'

I've stayed away from Madras and Vik for a month. I see on Facebook that he's busy with boozy Sunday brunches at five-star hotels. There was a photograph of him with a group of people, none of whom I know. And there was a girl – in white, looking at him and laughing. I cannot explain, but I know there's something there. She is copper-skinned with thick eyebrows. One of those women who does not dwell on her beauty but knows how to use it.

I carry this picture of her around in me for days, making myself sick. I'd known from the start that the world he was so dismissive of was one he needed. He might read Schopenhauer, take Vipassana courses, befriend older women and generally do things no other men of his group might, but eventually, the indoctrination was strong. There was a string that pulled him back to the centre of family, to the allegiance of school friends, to the making of money. At some point he would have to give me up.

Lucia and I are watching David Attenborough's *Planet Earth* series every evening. It seems an apt prelude to what lies ahead. The circle of life, et cetera. The more I watch, the more I believe Hinduism has captured the essence of life as a philosophy. Everything hinges on the circumstances of your birth, after all – the kind of life you have, the kind of death. Will you be a measly krill? Or will you be a turtle who makes the journey back and forth from its birthplace for eighty years. Or will you be truly amazing? A wondrous octopus, a dugong, a rhizome?

'That man has come,' Mallika says, standing at the door.

When I lean over the banister I see that it's Vik, with a bottle of wine and Chinese takeaway.

'You're here.'

'Isn't it about time?' he calls back.

He comes upstairs, hovers uneasily at Lucia's bedroom door.

'Hey,' he says, looking at her. 'Hey,' he says again. 'She's not big on saying hello, huh?'

'She doesn't really know you. Besides, when you come over, I basically dump her, so what do you expect?'

We eat dinner together. This is a first. *Bringing It All Back Home* on the stereo, fancy bone-china plates on the table. Vik heats the takeaway on the stove with a kitchen towel flung over his left shoulder, sticking his finger in the Szechuan chicken to test if it's hot enough. Lucia is in her usual chair, picking her nose determinedly. She's flapping a tatty blue sock back and forth.

'Stop it, Lucy,' I say. But she ignores me, continues to flap and pick.

Dinner is stilted. There's no mention of the girl with copper skin and bushy eyebrows. No explanation for why there's been such a long silence.

'How long are you going to live out here for anyway?' Vik asks. 'Do you even have the number of the local cop?'

'What for?'

'Villagers can be dangerous pricks.'

'We haven't had any trouble.'

'You could sell this place, you know? The land prices are insane. Find a place in the city. You could get a job, find a vocational centre for your sister.'

'But we like it here.'

'Okay. Sure. I'm just saying. It's no place for a woman alone. Sorry, this is India. This is just how it is. You want to go all *Little House on the Prairie* or whatever, but that doesn't work here. You want a garden, put it on the terrace of your city flat. You want a dog, get a Lhasa Apso.'

The sex that night is different. Something has been dismantled. Afterwards, he holds me in the usual way, arms enfolding, stomach to back. 'What's wrong?' he whispers. I pretend to be asleep.

This morning, incessant cries from the brush. I shrug on a housecoat and go downstairs. The French doors are open. Lucia and Mallika are standing all the way down by the brick compound wall.

I find my slippers and a straw hat and walk over to them. They are examining Bagheera, who is lying on her side in the shade of a neem bush with six puppies suckling at her. Six splotches of black and white. Mallika and Lucia crouch beside her, grinning.

'What's going on?'

'See how many, Grace,' Lucia points.

Mallika yanks the pups one by one off Bagheera's teats to check their sex. 'Boy!' she announces proudly when she sees a sliver of penis. The girls, of which there are three, she tosses aside, and they blindly grope their way back to their mother.

'Good girl,' I say to Bagheera, who looks as though she can't wait to sequester herself from all these demanding tongues.

'Do you hear?' I say, pointing backwards. 'There's a sound coming from there?'

The three of us walk towards the house, trying not to get our legs caught in the bramble and thorn.

'Why haven't you worn your slippers?' I scold Mallika, who's bending over to disengage her leg from a creeper.

'It's time to do the weeding,' she says, cutting across the brush, following the noise. She stoops, lifts up a stack of palmyra leaves, and underneath there's a puppy sitting in the sand, crying violently. It's mostly white, with two black patches around its eyes like a panda and a twirly black line above its mouth. There's a piece of twine caught around its neck. Pink paws, bluish eyes, a mouth full of mud.

'Pick it up!' Lucia shrieks.

Mallika unties the twine from around the puppy's neck, revealing a raw pink gash in the fur. It's a fat thing, looks almost like a kitten.

'How'd you get all the way out here? Let's get you back to Mama.'

We trudge back to Bagheera and put the puppy down in the sand. She tries to lift herself but her hind legs give way, collapse under her weight. She sits there spread out like a miniature exotic rug, crying.

'What's wrong, girl? Too fat to stand up? There there,' I say, picking her up and placing her directly on one of Bagheera's teats.

The sight of all those puppies jostling and feeding is startling.

Bagheera suddenly stands and shakes the pups off her, scratches violently at a halo of fleas and walks in the direction of the house.

'She doesn't want her,' Mallika says.

'What do you mean?'

'You saw the puppy's back legs? She can't stand up. I think the mother left her there to die.'

'Take the puppy back to the house with Lucia. Try giving it some water. I'm going to the beach.'

*

There's a scattering of geckos when I lift the latch of the gate. Ten a.m. The beach is a desert. I sit in the sand burning my backside, feeling the hot wind lash at my ankles. Everything gleams and blurs in this harsh light. The dogs have found their way through the holes in the brick wall. It isn't beach time, but they're happy to be out. Raja, Hunter, Thompson, Flopsy – skidding their bums across the sand.

To my right is the village of Paramankeni. From this distance you cannot see the rivers of plastic clogging up the sewers. Only coconut trees that arch gracefully towards the sea, a clutter of brightly coloured fishing boats, a jumble of nets. There's something in all this stillness that expands time, pulls it up and around you. It's terrifying to be alone in it.

I've been thinking of Blake. Wondering whether it has all been a mistake. If life isn't about what's raw or necessary, but merely what you can endure. Perhaps it was not so difficult, the things I found monotonous, the facile conversations, the dead-dead sex. Perhaps I should have seen it as a comfort rather than a danger.

I roll up my pyjama bottoms and walk into the sea. The water is cooler than I expected, refreshing. I wish I could take everything off and swim out to where the waves are breaking. But I just stand there, holding my hitched-up pants, peering at the horizon through my glasses.

Two figures are walking towards me from the village. Boys. Men. Seventeen, eighteen, hard to say. They're in short-sleeved shirts and lungis. Spry, wiry, walnut-coloured. They park themselves on a ridge of sand a little away from where my slippers are. They smoke and stare. The dogs have emerged from the shade of bushes and are making soft snarly noises, just to say, 'We're here.' I feel afraid and I'm not even sure why. But there's something about these boys. The way they're leering at me. I've seen it in some of the migrant men, who always seem to be playing in the movie version of their lives – but this is not that. This is real and unsettling. It's desire and hate, and I feel stripped away.

I walk towards them and slide my feet into my slippers. They are still staring at me. 'What?' I bark. 'What are you looking at? What do you want? Not enough beach for you, you have to come and sit right here?'

I know they don't understand what I'm saying, but I can only say it in English because the few Tamil words I know have disappeared. It's a fear that's jerking around inside me. I'm telling myself it's only the stories I've been reading in the news lately – all those girls and women raped and dumped and hanging from trees. It's Mallika's penis-worshipping the puppies that's bothering me, the bloody propagation of patriarchy by women in this country. I'm telling myself that I'm strong. I'm standing outside my own house, the dogs are here, it's fucking daylight! Nothing is going to happen. But I'm a quivering mess by the time I get to the gate. The dogs whisk through, shaking the sand off their coats, all gambol and play. I latch the gate, and I run up the stone path to the house, and by the time I get to my room and lock the door, I'm weeping.

The headman Valluvan's house is not the largest in the village, but the land around it sprawls with coconut and mango trees, and his wife, Nila, who's constantly hunched over a broom, keeps it as clean as a shrine.

When I get there, he's sitting in his usual place – on the *thinnai*, reading a newspaper. He's wearing a white short-sleeved shirt and blue checked lungi, and his gold watch glints in the sun when he waves.

'Didn't bring your sister?'

'She's too busy taking care of a new puppy,' I say, standing in his yard and looking around.

The clothes line sags with children's clothes and a row of plastic pots filled with water sit in the baking sand. 'Something's different? You put on a new roof?'

'Yes,' Valluvan says. 'We got rid of the thatch and put tiles.'

'Looks nice and pukkah.'

'Hot today, isn't it?' he says.

We always exchange pleasantries about the weather, even though it's only ever too hot, too rainy or too dry. There is never not enough heat.

I leave my slippers beside a cluster of others lined up outside the house and follow Valluvan inside. He flicks on three glaring tube lights and motions to one of the squat jute stools in the room.

Most times I visit we talk about village politics and the state of Valluvan's crops. Today he wants to talk about safety. 'There was a death in Mugaiyur,' he says. 'Near here. A fellow called Perumal. He was a lorry driver but had some kind of land-brokering business on the side. Yesterday afternoon a group of thugs dragged him out of his house and beat him to death with sticks.'

I stare at the teal-painted wall ahead. There's a calendar, which is still stuck on the month of July, and a photograph of a smiling woman saint they call Amma, who gives benediction to her devotees by hugging them.

'Some of us think that these brokers will be coming for our land next. There is a coal-plant project they want to build near here and all these government goons are involved. There's little we can do. You should join us. Find a city lawyer to help us.'

Valluvan narrows his eyes and pinches his forehead. He has the brightest cuticles I've ever seen. There are strands of grey creeping into his moustache and the sides of his hair.

'We have to be quick. There are so many of these fellows hanging around, asking questions. It would be better to be prepared.'

Nila appears at the doorway all of a sudden in a strange kind of get-up – a gaudy, shapeless kaftan with a thin cotton towel thrown across the frilly front of it.

'Tea?' she asks.

'No, no. I'm going now. I just came to check in.'

'Why don't you ask one of your man friends?' Valluvan says, as I stand. 'Maybe they can help.'

Was that a sneer? I can't tell. But when I look back at them from the road, I see that it's not judgement in their eyes but fear.

I walk back through the village – the houses all a mix of exposed brick, thatch, cow dung and mud. There's obviously some kind of caste hierarchy here, but I don't know exactly how it works. Some have motorbikes, some have cows and chickens and goats. All of them are poorer than they'd like to be.

There's an empty plot of land at the corner of the village, and the road that leads to my house. It's protected by a massive concrete wall, but when I pass the gate and look inside, I see there's a man squatting in the scrub, shitting. Alongside this road runs what remains of the Buckingham Canal. Not so long ago the city of Madras was navigable only through its water canals. Now this canal is a murky green strip where women sometimes stand knee-deep in water, bent over looking for clams, while battalions of lorries on the highway charge by with their horns.

The whole day feels threadbare and alone. I'm thinking of the video Lucia and I saw last night of a young scientist who has figured out a way to dredge the ocean of its 5 trillion tonnes of plastic. In a few years 99 per cent of seabirds will have bits of plastic inside them. I dreamed of those five gigantic garbage patches in the ocean, big twirling gyres of crap. Ours might be the last generation to see big animals in the wild. Imagine. A world without the rhinoceros, elephant, tiger. And still we go, in this country, lurching wildly into the future with our incomparable biological imperatives. One point two billion people and *still* fucking. We should put that on a bumper sticker.

When I get home I call Vik. 'I need to see you,' I say. 'And I need the name of a really good lawyer.'

13

Lucia wakes later and later. The new puppy sleeps in a basket on the floor beside her. She is still having trouble with her hind legs. We have named her Golly, shortened for Good Golly Miss Molly.

At nights Lucia is up several times, in and out of the loo to splash water on her face, opening and slamming the bathroom door. In the morning I look into her room and she is sleeping like a turtle, awash in the middle of her bed, stomach to mattress, legs and arms tucked under her, chin to one side. The puppy has shat on the newspapers spread on the floor and is crying. I pick her up and take her downstairs to Bagheera, who is lying under a frangipani with the rest of the pups tugging at her. I shove one of the other pups aside and plonk Golly on a teat.

I go out on the beach with the rest of the dogs. Catamarans are being steered onto shore and fishermen are hauling in their nets. I think of walking and walking and never turning back.

I turn around and walk back. I shave my legs. I set up the mirror in the sunlight and tweeze the extra hairs from around my eyebrows and above my lip.

At breakfast I say to Lucy, 'I'm going to Madras for two nights. You're going to stay here with Mallika. Better be a good girl, okay? If you're good, I'll bring you some mutton biryani. Okay?'

Lucia looks away, flipping her blue sock back and forth.

After a while she says, 'Where's Mummy?'

'Mummy's gone to God, Lucy. Remember? Mummy used to look after you and now I do.'

Sometimes Lucia's eyes fill up with tears, but as far as I can tell this is not connected to any kind of sadness. She will be sitting at the table, or on the couch with one leg hitched up to her ear, tapping and swishing, and she'll be somewhere else, far away from anywhere. The tears never spill. They just stay there, and then vanish.

As I'm stacking the breakfast dishes in the sink, the dogs set to barking. 'Who is it, Lucy? Go see!'

When I come out of the pantry, Lucia hasn't moved.

At the door I see the Sneha Centre van parked at the shed and Teacher hobbling out.

'What's wrong?' I say, walking towards her. Normally Teacher doesn't come without calling first. 'Did you do something to your leg?'

'Oh, it's nothing,' Teacher says, hobbling with increased determination. 'I fell.'

There is another woman walking behind her — pyramid-shaped with thinning hair. She shuffles respectfully behind Teacher.

'Lucy, kanna,' Teacher shouts as she enters the house. She leaves her slippers at the door and steps over the wooden threshold with care.

There is a quality of exaggeration about Teacher that I have come to hate. Even when she speaks, it is as if she has been holding in all her thoughts, waiting for the moment you ask a question, and then she bombards you until you have to cut her off.

Lucia is smiling. After a brief glance at Teacher to establish her identity, she has now looked away, eyes twinkling, tossing the sock back and forth with renewed vigour.

'Ey,' Teacher says. 'Where are you looking off to? I'm here. Lucy, look at me.'

She parks herself next to Lucia on the cushion and wrests away the sock.

Lucia turns to her and starts pulling Teacher's hair out of her bun.

Teacher giggles. 'She doesn't like my hair tied up. Funny girl. I always had to keep my hair in a plait when Lucy stayed with us. I can't believe I forgot about that. Ey, Lucy, say, "Good morning, Teacher."'

Lucia repeats mechanically, 'Good morning, Teacher.'

The other woman has inched into the house. She sits beside Teacher and announces, 'She looks depressed.'

'Sorry, who are you?' I say.

'Mrs Subhalakshmi is a psychoanalyst. She works with special-needs children.'

'Sorry to ask,' Mrs Subhalakshmi says, 'but do you think this has been the right move for her? Do you have daily activities planned? Are you engaging enough? She seems much more withdrawn than when I saw her last.'

'I was actually on my way out,' I say, looking at Teacher. 'You might have called to let me know you were coming.'

'Do you leave her often?' the shrink asks.

'Once or twice a month, yes.'

Mallika has sauntered into the house and started washing dishes even though it's earlier than her usual time to do so. She wants to listen in on the action. Teacher must have called her last night to find out whether I'd be here and to make sure the gate would be unlocked.

'The problem is that if I don't leave her I might go mad,' I say, smiling insincerely.

'Of course, of course,' Teacher soothes. 'Nobody is saying you shouldn't go, but is it the best thing for her to be alone? Shouldn't you drop her off with me on your way, and pick her up on the way back? That way she can be with her peers. Otherwise, here she is all alone. What do you think?'

'Remember the last time we tried that? How much she kicked and screamed and I had to come and get her?'

'Yes, but that was so long ago. Now she must be missing us.'

The shrink wants to prescribe antidepressants for Lucia.

'Why?' I say. 'So she can be more of a zombie?'

The shrink looks at Teacher as if to say, So this is what you're up against.

'We can take a call a few months down the road,' she says. 'Next time, perhaps you can bring Lucy to my clinic. We were just passing by here, so thought we'd drop in.'

'Of course,' I say.

After they've gone I realise I didn't even offer them a glass of water.

Mallika loads the car with the rubbish bags, cooler box and shopping bags. 'Don't forget to bring liquid cleaner to wash the floors,' she says. 'And a new broom. A proper one this time.' I press 500 rupees in her hands and remind her to lock the gate when I'm gone.

The nights I'm away, Mallika sleeps on a jute mat in the corridor between my room and Lucia's room. When I call to ask whether Lucy is being good, Mallika says, 'What is there for her? Eat and bathroom and sleep. She is fine.'

I take the two kilometres from the house onto the highway slowly because it is always a little startling to re-enter the world. On my way out I see two bee-eaters perched on the electrical wires, a bespectacled goat herder sitting outside his house, smoking.

Once on the highway, I turn up the music. I briefly think of taking off my top and driving in my bra. Hoot hoot. Here is the world and it is chaotic and loud.

This new highway is like a serpent, widening and thickening, swallowing all the villages that lie in its path. There are posters of our portly chief minister and her glowing face plastered on both sides of the road – placards and cutouts, ribbons fluttering in the breeze. Every time I see a smudge in the road I imagine it's a dead dog and I swerve away. I pass all the familiar landmarks – the nuclear township of Kalpakkam, where I dump our rubbish and where I sometimes buy vegetables and fruit. The historic town of Mahabalipuram – degenerate and creepy, filled with crusty white tourists and rude locals. Past the Hotel Mammalla, Lucy's favourite rest stop. On and on. The desalination plant on the right, dizzying in its ugliness. The road shimmers through it all.

Apartment blocks rise up from the flats with names like Horizon Properties and Coastal Dreams. I think about the kinds of families that will move here. Where will they get their water from? What will they do with their rubbish? Closer to the city things get more hectic and jumbled. Bakeries and furniture shops and mini-malls. Traffic chokes and stutters. Everything is pressing down on me, but I feel freer than I have in days. This evening at Samir and Rohini's flat I will smoke many joints and drink a gallon of bad red wine. I will lay my head down in Vik's lap and allow him to take me to the top of the terrace and push me against the water tank. I will remember my birth-control pill and vitamins, and when I sleep, I will not be listening for the sound of dogs or for the sound of my sister moving around in the dark.

14

If there was an Indian bourgeois symbol for dog, it would be the Pomeranian. White, fluffy, yippety. It's the kind of animal that looks good in a woman's lap, the brightness of its fur radiating like a small white church.

Samir and Rohini have two such animals, Loulou and Leela. They are really Rohini's dogs. She bathes and brushes them, takes them for long walks around the colony, waits patiently while they squat on their haunches and piss outside other people's gates. Most of the neighbourhood dogs are walked by bored watchmen who sit with other bored watchmen at street corners, smoking and gossiping while their poor charges tug at their leashes. I think of the wildness of our dogs. The acres of beach that belong to them, and how in this, at least, they are lucky.

I meet a new person at Samir and Rohini's. He is called Praveen. At one point in his life he must have been gangly. Now he has the body of a middle-aged man trying to keep up. His jawline has thickened with alcohol, but his shoulders and legs are still powerful from years of playing a club sport – tennis or squash. He is talking about psychedelic music, something about which I know nothing.

'Who cares?' I say. 'Tell me about the rich wives in this city.' Living in isolation has made me a brusque person. 'I hear you're friendly with them.'

Praveen laughs. 'Let me tell you something about rich girls,' he says. 'God had different ways of getting back at them. Most of them are not that great to look at. They got to feel they can prove themselves, right? So they catch hold of some young, beefy, brainless stud and marry him. They're saying to the other ladies, Bitch, look what I got. The dynamics are changing, see? Earlier it was the good-looking girls that got married to the rich ugly guys. Now it's happening the other way around too.'

Rohini had already told me about her friend Praveen the bachelor, who sometimes serviced the bored housewives of the city. Praveen manufactures small parts for cars. He lives with his mother. He does all kinds of drugs. Now that we are sharing a joint, Praveen is making a joke about Pomeranians. He tells me how the bored housewives sometimes use them for *you know what*.

'What?' I shriek.

'Cunnilingus.'

'Get out,' I say. 'I thought that was your job.'

Samir and Rohini's neighbour Tanya is here with her child, a two-year-old girl who sits on the floor in a pretty smocked dress, playing with her stuffed pig. Tanya had a baby with a man who disappeared three months after the child was born. She is talking about how she can't have sex any more because it makes her physically sick to think about it. Praveen mutters, 'Yeah yeah, no one's dying to have sex with you either.'

I want to call Praveen out on this. Say something about how the burden of child-rearing always falls on the woman. That he is judging her because she is overweight and dishevelled. But I like him too much and am bored of everyone else.

In the corner someone is talking about her mother's insane jealousy. 'My mother's a Scorpio. Her whole life was jealousy. After thirty-five years of marriage she left my father because he danced with another woman at a wedding. Can you believe it?'

Across the room there is Gauri, forty-something, starting up about her failed marriage. Twenty years she and her husband have shared a bed. They have a son. 'Everybody thinks we're fine, but we haven't had sex in fifteen years. That's not a relationship, is it? He has his own thing going on, I have my own thing. I mean, I suppose it's fine. For the sake of our son.' And the next moment. 'No, it's not fine. It's sick. It's sick.'

'It's human,' Samir interjects. 'We all have things like that.'

'We do?' Rohini says, flashing him a look, before wrapping herself around the trunk of her husband, as if to prove to the rest of us that they are still strong, that while they can understand other people's idiosyncrasies, they are far too much in love to suffer such problems themselves.

'All this must be silly *Sex and the City* shit to you,' Praveen says.

'Something like that,' I say. 'Although, shit, this city has changed.'

'But seriously, are you sorted out there? It's brave and all, but are you going to be okay living out there by yourself?'

I know they discuss me in my absence. The eccentric dog woman and her sister with problems. I know they speak of me in tones admiring and disbelieving, like, What does she do all day, and doesn't she get lonely, and how long do you think she can keep it up, and who knows how safe it is because you hear about what goes on in villages, plus climate change, and I hear she doesn't even have security — just one woman who's half her size and is supposed to be the guard.

I skate around the wives. They are an unforgiving breed. I make sure to sit with them, to reassure and cajole. It is the only way for a woman alone to survive in this city.

Rohini keeps her hair short and wears low-cut jersey dresses with chunky necklaces. She laughs vigorously and has a way of tossing her head back, opening her tiny throat, exposing the small pearls of her mouth. She has never lived alone, and any travel she has done has been with Samir, but she is always talking about Paris, about the ideas of some philosopher — never quite able to get to the point, except to let you know that she can say Rousseau. There is something carnal about her, and it is this asset that she constantly brings to the surface. I can't get a sense of her beyond this, except to understand that she is ashamed of her provincialism, that she is ambitious with no discernible talent, and is trying on different personas as she goes along, in the hope of one day sliding into her self.

When Samir met her, he told me this is the reason why he came back to India. To find someone like her.

Samir and Blake went to the Kodai International School together. They weren't great friends, but when they reconnected in America, the memory of their friendship deepened. I remember sitting across the glass-topped dining table in our apartment in Charlotte one Thanksgiving, the smell of Blake's chicken curry still heavy in the air, Samir saying, 'Maybe I'll just go home.'

He'd been sleeping on our couch for a week, listening to Pink Floyd's *Dark Side of the Moon* repeatedly. He wore the same flannel shirt and jeans for days, didn't shave, didn't help to clean up, did nothing except talk about how he had stopped feeling. He went on and on about the dullness. Blake was patient with him. I, less so. We would drive to Blockbuster most evenings to rent a film. For half an hour we would parade up and down the aisles of that brightly lit store, trying to home in on something that would make us laugh. By the end of the week I wanted to shake him. 'Make him leave,' I said to Blake one night, after we had turned off the lights, and the strains of 'The Great Gig in the Sky' floated up the carpeted stairway into our bedroom.

When Samir finally left, Blake and I were uneasy with each other. Whatever balance we had created for ourselves had been pulled apart.

Now when I look at Samir it is as though he became that sloth who slept on our couch simply to prod me out my own inertness. Because here in Madras he is transformed – clean-shaven, ripply with muscles, forehead shiny with sweat. He serves mojitos and gets broody only when he is stoned and listening to Leonard Cohen. He is always saying how moving back to India was a premonition, that even in the darkest moments he knew that life was eventually going to go right. 'I didn't know, but I knew, you know? Coming home was the beginning of that. Rohini was the continuation.'

'So are you guys going to have kids or what?' Gauri asks Rohini.

Gauri, who because she has just vomited her story, expects some recompense.

'Why are people so obsessed with kids? My God!' Rohini says. 'I mean we just got married. What's the hurry?'

'Just asking, ya. No need to get uptight.'

'I know, but everyone *just* asks. It's like an epidemic. What if I don't want to have kids? What if I don't want to have to go through all that ...'

Tanya, the jilted neighbour, stiffens. 'For sure,' she says, wanting to sound equable. 'It's not for everyone. It's a huge thing to have a child. I mean, look at me.' She trails off somewhat sadly, not able to get past the plea for us to look at her.

Praveen comes back in from the balcony, where he's been smoking. 'Your man is here,' he says.

A few minutes later the doorbell rings, and it is Vik.

He is already drunk and smiling. An open bottle of red in his hands. I teeter over to collapse into him.

I'm surprised that Praveen and Vik know each other. They are friends, even though there must be twenty years between them. It's a curious thing about this city. Some men never retire from the party circuit. They may marry or remain bachelors like Praveen, but come Saturday night they strike out, stags about town. Their circle widens with new entrants – precocious high-school kids and college boys, mostly wealthy, with gelled hair and slim-fit shirts damp with cologne. They call each other *machan*. There is a looseness about them. I envy it.

I watch Praveen and Vik standing together, and I imagine they are saying something about me. The novelty of having met someone new, of having talked as a person to another with no bind – that has gone. He already knew about me. Of course he did. *Your man is here.*

'Grace, can you help?' Rohini says, dragging me into the kitchen.

It is one of those narrow apartment kitchens designed for a maid who comes for a few hours to do all the kitchen work and then disappears. Two women are standing next to the water filter and talking, blocking the path.

'Sorry, sorry,' Rohini says, shoving them out of the way. 'I'm going to put the food out.'

We put the biryani into big bowls – one vegetarian, one mutton. Raitha, pappads, pickles. 'That Gauri,' Rohini says. 'Such a bloody nosy person. Every time I see her she asks me when I'm going to have kids. Fuck. I mean, what the hell?'

'Well,' I say, 'having a kid has kind of been the centre-piece of her life, so I suppose for people like that it's hard to imagine what else there could be.'

'And you?'

'What?'

'Are you going to have kids?'

I laugh. 'You're doing a Gauri on me.'

'I've earned it, right?'

'I've inherited a kid. That's plenty.'

We haul the platters of food onto the table. I've already put some biryani aside in Tupperware boxes to take back for Mallika and Lucia. A stab of sadness. That feeling of being among people and feeling alone. Of understanding that this is not your life but it will have to do.

'Jaan,' Vik says, coming over to me. He has taken to calling me Jaan. My Life. My Love. 'Come with me.'

'No,' I say. 'I want to eat first. Let's eat.'

We take plates of food onto the balcony. There are no stars to be seen, but all around, in the surrounding apartment buildings, the blue lights of televisions are flickering in the windows. Vik sits beside me, spooning biryani into his mouth. He has a way of eating, his left hand turned over like a leaf under his chin to catch any spilled grains of rice.

'I don't think we can do this any more,' I say.

He puts his plate aside, puts that left leaf-like hand on my thigh. 'What are you talking about, Jaan? It's you and me. Forget about everything else.'

We both know it's hardly enough but for tonight I let it go. We walk back into the flat. Loulou and Leela are tussling on the carpet. They're growling and snarling, and Tanya's toddler, who sits just a foot away from them, is bawling, saying, 'Mummy, Mummy, they took Mr Pig.'

The Pomeranians cannot be broken up. Rohini is standing above them, shrieking, 'Stop it, stop it!' but the dogs don't hear. They are intent on destroying the thing – teeth bared, their tiny bodies jerking around. They tear at the toy until all the stuffing of Mr Pig's entrails has been gouged out and strewn over the carpet. After they finish, the fur on their backs that has been standing on end subsides a little, and they step away from each other. Rohini beats their noses with the flat of her fingers. 'Bad, bad dogs,' she shouts.

Tanya scoops up her child, who is so tired she is letting loose a long string of sounds from her mouth, refusing to sit still at her mother's hip, lurching up and down violently, her cheeks red, her eyes drawn shut like two black pins. The noise comes from the centre of her, and I feel it pulling something out of me – unreasonable and insistent. Tanya goes to her flat next door without saying anything to anyone. Praveen follows in her wake. 'I'll just make sure she's all right.'

15

Lucia is having nightmares. I found her twice this week, sitting on the floor of the corridor between our bedrooms, shouting. I run to her half asleep, saying, 'What is it, Lucy? What happened?' But she is unable to explain, frantically jabbing her hand in the air at the imagined terrors. The moon shines through the grilles of the windows, lighting the corridor as if it were a stage. I look at my sister and the puppy, Golly, who is unhelpfully licking her toes. 'Let's get you back to bed,' I say. I settle her in and stroke her fore-head, the way Ma used to when I needed consoling, but she is already shrugging away, reaching for her socks and hankies underneath the pillow, drawing them out one by one. 'Go away,' she says, turning her back to me.

The new puppies have arrived. Even though Mallika has given away all the male pups from Bahgeera's litter to work-ers at various construction sites, we still have twenty-two dogs. And while most of them are still suckling, it will soon become impossible to feed them. When it was just Raja and Bagheera I used to cook rice and meat and feed them in separate bowls. Now I buy ten-kilo bags of dry dog food and scatter the pellets on the patio. Only Raja still gets his food in a bowl, but he doesn't like this processed food; he crunches at it desultorily, and leaves the remains for the mothers to fight over.

He hates the puppies. They come at him like locusts, snapping at his penis, thinking there might be milk there. Lucy has named this batch after Bollywood stars – Preity, Kat, Bebo, Dimple … Their sister, Golly, is universally despised because she's the house bitch. Her hind legs are better now, but she is still fat, still slow.

Ma's lawyer, Mr Sriram, comes to the house to discuss the issue of the upcoming coal plant, on Vik's recommendation.

'How odd,' I'd said to Vik. 'I ask for the name of a lawyer, and you suggest the one I already know.'

Mr Sriram is a thin man with vitiligo. He lives in Madras, but I haven't seen him since he brought me to look at the house after Ma died.

'This must be strange for you,' he'd said, as he drove through the front gate and the long scrubby driveway.

It was strange. To think of my mother buying a plot of land, imagining she'd live out here like a pioneer, keeping secrets. I saw a grove of bright green trees. Mr Sriram said they were cashew. All along the ground were sunburnt weeds. There was a well – white and gleaming – an anachronism. Who builds wells like this any more? I had a vision of Ma leaning over the concrete rim, dropping the bucket into the cool moss of water, hauling it up with a frayed coir rope. It was like re-entering a scene from childhood. Women with their pots lined up at the well. Women at the street tap. Women waiting for the metro water tanker. You could trace a line from the present all the way back to Mohenjo-daro and there would be women with pots in the curve of their hips, waiting to collect water.

Mr Sriram knew when to be quiet and when to speak. He had allowed me to wander around the house by myself.

When I came downstairs, he was sitting in a chair, reading a newspaper he'd brought with him.

'I expect you'll want to sell?'

'No,' I had said. 'I want to keep it. I think I might even want to live here.'

Now, almost two and a half years later, I look at him directly in the face. The vitiligo has spread. His face is almost white, except for a few streaks of brown along his forehead and under his chin.

'The house looks more lived in,' he says. 'Much better. Your mother hardly came here. Mostly she stayed in Pondicherry, but she had an idea that this could be a retreat of sorts.'

Mr Sriram tells me that the ashram down the road has 100 acres and that they aren't interested in selling. 'It will be difficult for anyone to take that away. After the politicians, it's the God people who are the most powerful in this country.'

I tell him about the murder in Mugaiyur, how even though I lock all the doors before going to bed, I often wake up in the middle of the night to check the bolts and latches. 'Should I be worried for my safety?'

Mr Sriram agrees that hiring a security guard might not be the best option because there have been so many cases, particularly with women living alone, where the security guard is the perpetrator of the crime. 'Have you received any direct threats?' he asks.

I cannot explain the vague sense of foreboding that hums in my body. It is not paranoia exactly, but I am always alert, always on the watch to convert any stray look into something ominous.

When I see Valluvan later I will tell him that for the moment we are safe. The proposed coal plant ten kilometres down the coast has not been given the green light yet, but at some point, the monsters will come.

Before Mr Sriram leaves, I try to thrust a puppy on him. He had been idly stroking Dimple's head. 'Take her,' I say, 'really. We need to find homes for them.'

'Oh, no,' he says. 'My daughter only wants a pug like that one in the Vodafone advertisement.'

Sometimes I think it is all an elaborate hoax. That my sister is perfectly fine. Is able to wash her own bum, put the sanitary pad in the strip of her knickers, yank them up over her thighs and then hold forth on Sebastião Salgado.

I will walk down one morning and everything will be changed, as if in a fairy tale. Frog to prince. Tree to woman. Lucia will have breakfast ready. Perhaps she will be a genius omelette-maker. She will have an English accent for reasons unclear to everyone. But every word she utters will have the clipped weight of English authority. She will be funny, bossy, knowing – in the manner of an older sister. 'That's not how it happened,' she'll say, correcting some truant memory of mine. Or bolstering, 'Oh, yes, Papi could be a real pain about those kinds of things.'

Or maybe it will happen differently. She'll be released from catatonia by some miracle drug, like in that movie *Awakenings*.

The best would be if no transformation were involved. If she were just acting. If all this was part of a huge art project, something Marina Abramović might have thought up. Three months of silence? How about thirty-eight years?

I try to catch her out. Snoop on her while she's on the bed droning, watch from the balcony as she sits on the floor of the patio with her pile of hankies and socks beside her, the puppies crawling over the flesh of her legs.

I think of setting the house on fire just to see what she would do.

She is unremittingly dense. We repeat the same actions day after day. Beyond shoving a spoon in her mouth, there is little she can do for herself.

Everything becomes slowed down and elongated. The simplest of activities. Eating. Bathing. Dressing. 'Hurry, hurry,' I sometimes shout, losing my patience after two hours of watching her chew. I try adapting to her speed. I bring a book to the table to read in between prodding, but I can't really get into the story if I have to keep taking my eye away from the page. Finally I take the plate away and say, 'That's enough, your stomach is getting too big,' and she yells, 'No. Gimme more.'

She has started a new trick. Coming into my bedroom to play with the strings on the blinds. She barges in, walks up to the window that looks out on the sea, grabs hold of the string with the bobble on the end of it and swings it, tip tap tip tap. If the blinds are raised and she cannot reach the string, she just stands there, trying to lift her arms as high as she can. When she tires of stretching, she goes back to her room. Stupid little bitch, I want to say. There's a stool right there! Move it to the window. Stand on it!

The rains begin at the start of November. Everything smells musky and rich. Green things start shooting out of the ground. Then come the insects – millipedes, mayflies, midges, moths, mosquitoes. The evenings we can't go for walks Lucia and I sit in the drawing room with jigsaw puzzles, listening to the rain beat down for hours. At night the sea is at our throats even though I've bolted the balcony doors and fastened all the windows and shutters.

The dogs move from their hideouts in the garden to the shelter of the front veranda. After a few days of continuous rain we allow them inside. The rubber linings under the doors have been eaten away, so I lay rolled-up towels on the floor by the doors to keep the water out. The electricity goes for hours. The fridge leaks. The whole house stinks of wet dog. Golly is happiest of all, reunited with her clan, except they barely acknowledge her. She puffs herself up like a frigate bird and rolls into the other pups boisterously. Mostly they ignore her, but sometimes she gets pinned to the ground with a set of teeth at her jugular. Lucia comes to her rescue. 'She's just a baby, stop it!'

I think of the rains we used to have in Kodai, the warm binds of those forced familial afternoons in Mahalakshmi. I begin a letter to Papi, trying to tell him about this life, but it's difficult to know where to start. I send a photograph of Lucia and Golly instead. He writes back: *Is everything okay?*

When I think of my childhood it is always with a sense of emptiness. I cannot know whether it really was that way, or whether I look at my parents now as having failed in some basic task. I know men and women frequently abandon one family to begin another, that it is sometimes impossible to reconcile the two, so the old family is forgotten. That the same people who failed utterly on their first attempt at parenthood are champions the second time around. I know people believe they have the right to change their life whenever they want, but this is different.

Papi insists it was the right thing to do, that for the kind of person he is, he could live only with complete renunciation. 'This thing your mother did, of going once a week, it tortured her. Her whole life was guilt. It is a moral question, Grazia. Will you give up your one life to completely devote it to this child who will never be independent, or will you do the kind, responsible thing, which is to entrust this child to someone who can take care of her, who is paid to look after her in a community of other children who suffer like her?'

He could never answer my question about their duty to me, their other child, who grew up as an only child when she didn't need to. 'Children don't get to say how a family is run,' Papi said. 'We decided for you, and it was always agreed that we would tell you when you needed to know.'

I remember trying to find amongst one of my many cousins a sister, brother, friend, but it was useless. I was always the bastard at the wedding, the stranger at the feast. If I could have forged at least one connection, it might have proved to me that we were of the same tribe, but the more family reunions I went to, the more I realised it had been my parents' intention all along to create a life that had nothing to do with their own beginnings. All my aunts and uncles on both sides had chosen to live within a two-kilometre radius of their parents, while my parents had taken the first opportunity to flee. I struggled with the forced intimacy of our family gatherings as much as my parents did, and so it was always a relief to return home, the three of us – to fall into our usual patterns of subterfuge and bickering, to be away from the particular politics we had temporarily been thrust into.

Now that I have Lucia in my life, that sense of loss has lifted, but other heavy things have come to settle on my shoulders.

*

Lucia's nightmares have subsided, but one afternoon she screams so loudly all the dogs start howling. I run into her room, and she is standing on the bed hopping about. 'Mouse, mouse,' she shrieks. Golly is curled up uselessly in her basket, peering out with no intention of moving. I go to the bathroom and grab a mop with a wooden handle. 'Where is it?' I say, and she points under the linen cupboard. I start jumping about too, whacking the end of the mop on the concrete floor, shouting, 'Get out of there!' and when the mouse runs – Jesus, it's huge – I try to beat it but it's quick, and soon it's jumping up the blinds. Who knew mice could jump so high? I whack the blinds madly, and the mouse falls on the floor, scrabbling away until I get it. I hit it, a dull thud in the centre of its body. I keep beating it. It's as though I'm standing outside myself as I do this. Lucia is screaming, the dogs are barking. Mallika has run upstairs to see what the commotion is about. When she sees it's a mouse, she laughs and picks the dead thing up by its tail. 'Looks like it was pregnant,' she says. 'Good thing you caught it.'

I am shaking and sweating. 'I've never killed an animal before,' I say.

Mallika grunts. 'Maybe you should get rid of all these dogs and get some cats instead.'

She walks downstairs swinging the mouse by its tail. I watch her go over to the compound wall, lifting her legs high over the wet brambles. She stands at the brick, steadies one hand over the top of the wall and flings the carcase over. Within seconds a black-shouldered kite swoops down to take this unexpected prize in its mouth and disappears into the sky.

16

There is a ring of traffic around the mall so thick and tightly crammed I feel like giving up and turning around. Midweek, midday, but still we are among a pilgrimage of cars, motorbikes, mopeds, cycles, trucks, auto-rickshaws, buses, scooters – all spewing fumes into the air. The trees lining the street look weak and hung-over. We are here to find a dress for Lucia. She sits in the passenger seat wearing jeans and a striped T-shirt, one chubby leg hitched up under her. Two men on a motorbike at the traffic light beside us look at her transfixed and begin to make faces at her. Lucia carries on with her singing, oblivious to their stares.

Once inside the mall I grab hold of Lucia's hand. She shakes me away, follows at a distance from me. This is new. Her and me in a public place. I should have brought someone along – Rohini, Auntie Kavitha, my new friend Praveen – someone to bolster my confidence. People are looking, trying not to, but looking anyway. Something about the features of her face – the flattened-out nose, the slanting eyes, the tongue too big for her mouth. I feel, what? Defensive? I want to absorb these stares, divert their looks by talking loudly to Lucia as though she understands everything, as if there is nothing so different about her.

'Shall we go in here, Lucy? You love Benetton, don't you?'

We look through the racks of clothing. Everything I choose is somehow too dull, too tailored, not to Lucia's liking.

I find a long red dress made of jersey and spandex with a square-cut top, three-quarter sleeves and slits up the sides that end demurely at the knee.

'What about this? Come, let's go try it on.'

In the changing room we peel the jeans off. 'I told you, we should have put you in something else. This is such a pain to do, Lucy.'

I put the dress over her head and it is too tight. I call to the salesgirl, 'Can we get this in a size forty-four, please?'

A few minutes later I make Lucia walk out of the changing room to look at herself in the full-length mirror. The dress catches over all her fat bits, but the colour is strong and makes her look healthy. 'I like it,' I say.

Lucia tugs at the material around her waist and pulls at it, irritated. 'No,' she says.

'Okay. We'll keep looking.'

The mall is packed. Two weeks from Christmas, so there are carols on loop, a giant artificial tree in the centre of the ground floor, flecked with bits of cotton and tinsel. In one corner a scary-looking mechanical Santa with a sleigh filled with presents waves his hand up and down. Blue-eyed elves nod maniacally with him. Around this winter wonderland runs a toy train making high-pitched choo-choo noises. Families gather around this installation and take photographs. College kids in skinny jeans pout in groups. Clusters of men, always clusters of men – hands in their pockets, fingers chocked to balls.

It is nothing like the expeditions Ma and I used to make to Spencer's before it burned down. Such a dearth of stuff in those pre-liberalisation days. Christmas had still been about presents, but they used to be such meagre everyday things, like an orange or an apple in your stocking, a pair of plastic earrings. Rarely something extravagant like a new bicycle or a Walkman. This is new India – crazy, glitzy, spending India.

Lucia and I manoeuvre through the crowds. We stop for an ice cream at Baskin-Robbins. My toes are sore and my head hurts. I'm lugging around a bunch of things I've bought for the house already – wooden hangers, towels, ceramic knives. Still no dress.

We wander past a place called the Big Bazaar. Lucia drifts in. 'Not here, Lucy, come on. It's a mess.' But she is already flicking through the racks, pleased with what she sees. I spy the dress before she sees it. It is a sequinned pink thing, tiered, with a full skirt and an unflatteringly tight bodice. Sparkles everywhere. No point telling her it will make her look like a giant ball of candyfloss. We tussle in the changing room to squeeze her arms in, but once it's on, she flounces about on her toes and grins widely.

The drive home takes longer than usual. I have never made a trip to the city without spending at least one night there, so I feel the fatigue of the traffic, the crowds, the ting-tong mall music. Lucia sleeps, head knocking against the glass of the window, tongue poking out of her mouth. Does she dream of her new pink dress? I feel angry, powerless; I can't articulate it, but it has to do with the way people look at her. Families, children, grown people who can see there's something different about her but who are so unused to the sight they can only gape. I wanted to smash in some of their ugly faces. I had hoped for what? Empathy? A jaunty day out with my sister. Instead, I am drained, barely able to drive back home.

As soon as we are slipping through the long driveway, I feel the blood return to my legs. The dogs are around, making all kinds of noises, tails frantic, paws in the car, scratching at the seats.

Mallika unloads the packages from the boot. 'They were crying after you went,' she says. 'They thought you've gone, left them.'

I ask Mallika to make some instant noodles for dinner. Lucia is tired, but she looks pleased to see the dogs.

'Whose birthday is it going to be soon?' I say in a sing-song way. 'Whose happy birthday?'

She looks at me, smiles sideways and nods her head. 'Lucy's happy birthday.'

The next morning we see dolphins. Hundreds of dolphins swimming north, their silver-pink bodies undulating in and out of the waves. Lucia and I run into the ocean, and when the sand bar drops and she can no longer touch her feet to the ground, she clambers on top of my back, clasping her hands around my neck tightly, saying, 'Swim, Grace, swim fast.'

I swim far into the blue, further than I've ever been, but there's no sign of the dolphins. 'Maybe they looked closer than they really were? Maybe we were too late?'

We float there for a few minutes, turning around to look at the shore. The house looks like a pink speck in the distance, and the dogs, who followed us into the heat, are lined up like smudges of black along the beach.

And then the dolphins are upon us, around us, charging ahead. I can feel the weight of each body, the pulsating quick of this fish-mammal, larger than I expected – wild and cracking with power. Suddenly I am scared for the both of us, for being caught in the middle of this squad of nose and fin, but Lucia is shrieking, her fingers tight around my neck, 'Look, look!'

When we swim back to shore, the dogs storm out from under the shade of the casuarina groves. Raja and Bagheera bark and lick the salt off our toes as if to make sure we are who we were before we swam out in the sea.

The whole day is spent in the afterglow of the dolphins.

Mallika scolds me when she finds out. 'Where there are dolphins, there are sharks. What's wrong with you?'

Lucia and I watch the Attenborough episode about the deep ocean. All those strange sea creatures that lie at the bottom of the sea floor, blind and menacing. The fangtooth, the gulper eel, the hairy angler – grotesque things with out-of-proportion jaws, teeth, bodies. 'This world might be alien, but it's not without beauty,' David is saying, but Lucia is already asleep, cheeks grazed from the swim.

Mallika's long-dead family is being resurrected. Someone somewhere is dying of something, and suddenly she must be there.

'My half-sister's husband's cousin's son,' she says, when I ask why she must go to the hospital.

'He's only two,' she keeps saying. 'He has fits. I must go.'

The half-sister's husband's cousin is the head gardener at the ashram. They have organised an ambulance to take the child into the city, to the best hospital – Apollo. The ashram is bearing all costs. Mallika underlines this last fact as if to say, This is what good employers do: look after you at all costs.

'Go if you must, but I need you back for the party tomorrow.'

Of course, she does not come back the next day and when I call, her phone has been switched off.

The first guests arrive at twelve, and nine hours later Auntie Kavitha, Praveen and I sit on the balcony smoking while Lucia rocks madly on the floor, wired on Coca-Cola and cake, her tight pink dress in disarray.

'That went well, I thought,' Auntie Kavitha says.

'It was a freak show.'

'What do you mean, Miss G? It was cool,' Praveen interjects. 'Everyone had a banging time. Did you see your sister on the dance floor? What a cat!'

There had been non-stop Tamil pop songs. Teacher had all the girls in a circle clapping. Valluvan's kids monopolised the show with their film moves. Lenin, being the only boy, was particularly good with his pelvic thrusts. Before the cake-cutting, Teacher played the hokey-cokey. 'Your mother was the one who taught us how to do this. No matter whose birthday,' she panted, 'we always play the hokey-cokey.'

Lucy insisted that everyone join in. By the end of it I am dizzy and sad. I look at Lucia to see whether she feels it too, but she is busy flashing her teeth.

Vik hadn't come. I say nothing about his absence to anyone, but it feels definitive and I am ready to let it go.

The three of us look into the dark: only the dim lights of trawlers in the distance and a few milky stars.

'It's awesome here,' Praveen says, a magazine in his lap, fingers expertly rolling.

'I didn't think it would make me feel so strange to see all those kids in one room. It made me feel somehow exposed. Does that make sense?'

'It gets easier,' Auntie Kavitha says. 'Or maybe that's not the right word. It gets normal.'

'Teacher asked me for more money. She needs five lakhs to complete this new construction they're doing at the centre. I don't like the way she asked.'

'Your mother used to donate a lot. She basically floated that place, but can you imagine if Gayatri didn't do what she did? I mean, all those kids, she's the one person they can depend on.'

'So you're saying I should give it to her, even though I'm looking after Lucy now and I'm not my mother and don't need to siphon guilt money into that operation?'

'If you have it, you should give it.'

'I agree,' Praveen says. 'You never know how things will go.'

After they've gone I survey the mess. There are balloons and streamers everywhere. Millions of sparkly bits of paper from the crackers, and sand underfoot. I get Lucy to hold a big rubbish bag and stuff in the stacks of paper plates smeared with cake and bhelpuri, and anything else that might attract any mice. The caterer's boxes I stack in the fridge, the rest I leave for morning.

'Did you have a good birthday?' I ask Lucy, after I've helped her wash up.

'Super,' she says, fussing with Golly, making sure she's in her basket. 'Goodnight kanna, goodnight kanna,' she says to the sleeping dog.

Before going to bed I see the bulb outside Mallika's house light up. I call her, but the recorded message still says that this phone is switched off. I call her name through the windows but she does not holler back. I put on my slippers and walk over with a torch. The dogs rush after me, their quick feet making whispery noises in the brush.

She's squatting on the cement stoop of her house. The wicker chest I gave her has a set of vessels on top of it. The remains of a fire black in the sand. Plastic buckets, sagging clothes line, plastic bags and little silver packets of *gutka*, which she never admits to eating, glinting in the mud. It's like a bloody favela.

'So, what happened?' I say. 'You said you'd come back. We had the party. Thirty people came. I had to do all the cleaning up. No joke.'

She doesn't answer.

I ask, gentler, 'What happened, Mallika?'

'The child died,' she says, her lips spread in a mean scowl. 'I need to sleep.'

17

I wonder what stops them from rising up. From bringing hatchets and sickles and knives. If they stormed in, how would I stop them?

Villages surround us. Disorderly and overcrowded. To the right, further down the coast, are the areas under Valluvan's jurisdiction. With him I believe we are safe. But spreading beyond and behind us, all along the canal that runs parallel to the sea and further inland, behind the Odiyur Lake, jammed between fields of paddy, are rows and rows of flimsy huts that get demolished every time there are heavy rains. I don't know anything about those people and their lives.

Our closest neighbours are a rich industrial family who have built a solid orange-coloured five-bedroom house with a swimming pool. They visit a few times a year, but to ensure things are as they should be in their absence, they employ a convoy of servants. The house is a fortress. High cement walls, alarm systems, a Dobermann to keep guard. The wife visited me soon after the construction was completed. I took her around our rooms and she seemed charmed by the spartan nature of them. 'We should have made our house like yours,' she said. 'So open and nice. You're not planning to put in any AC? And you manage everything with only one woman?'

I was happy for her friendship. Whenever her staff dumped rubbish on the beach I'd text to alert her. *I'll inform my husband*, she would write back. And with this promise I felt sure things would change. I'd never met her husband, but when they started building the house I looked through binoculars to see what kind of people they were. I thought he might be a politician because of the speed with which the house had sprung out of the sand, and because there were always men in safari suits attached to him like barnacles, ready to do his bidding. It turns out he owns a factory where they make bicycles.

'Any time you want to use the pool, you should,' my friend had said. And I did, just once, with Lucia. The staff circled around, offering us soft beach towels and lime juice. Lucia jumped tirelessly in and out of the water, and in the end, I had to bribe her to leave with the promise of lunch in Pondicherry. I hadn't been able to relax. The dogs kept trying to get in and the watchman kept throwing stones at them even though I'd told him they weren't strays, that they belonged to us. Something I'm sure he already knew, as we walked past him every day.

I felt I'd transgressed some neighbourly line. The correct way to exist when you lived so far from the hordes was to observe each other across walls, not lie in full view in your bathing suit. By entering their territory I had made Lucia and myself susceptible. Instead of assuring me of human contact, it had made me feel defenceless. I left wondering whether the staff ever used the pool. If they slept in their master's beds. And if not, why not?

Before I left home for America, I went camping with Blake and his parents. I had lied, saying I was going on an overnight excursion with my science club. If my parents knew I was lying, they didn't reveal it. The Hendersons picked me up at the end of the Kurinji Temple Road. It was early in the morning, still dark, and I remember sliding into the seat next to Blake, resting a knee against his, understanding that between us there was some kind of longing. I can't remember the name of the place we went to, but we drove almost halfway down the ghats to get there. The vegetation was lush, a tract of land surrounded by terraced fields. Things that wouldn't have survived a few thousand feet higher in Kodai thrived there. Coffee, avocados, shiny tree tomatoes. There was a small wooden room on stilts that we might have used, but we were determined to experience the elements in their entirety.

Blake's father, Thomas, was a patient, deep-voiced man, a dentist by profession. If pushed he could tell the most beautiful stories of a childhood growing up on a farm in North Carolina. His wife, Molly, was the more exuberant of the pair. She was blonde and everything about her was healthy-looking. She had flawless teeth, as did Blake, but it was the strength of her arms and legs that I admired most. She started setting up the tents at once, all sinew and power. 'Y'all go forage for some fruit,' she said. 'And, Tom, go see if that stream water is good enough to drink.' When we returned, both tents were up, at a distance from one another. 'One for us and one for you guys, to give everyone a little privacy,' she said.

I can't remember what Blake and I whispered to each other at night. I know only that I didn't sleep well. The ground was stony and damp, making me cleave to Blake in his sleeping bag for warmth.

It was early when the noises started, because out of the tent I could see a slit of pink dawn. The noises were guttural, shouts and screams that seemed to come from behind us. Blake and I crawled out to see Tom and Molly crouching in the dirt. They wore matching flannel pyjamas, a show of domesticity that at the time excited me. It was difficult to understand what was happening because there were men running past us with weapons. They were running bare-foot in lungis and shirts with these instruments forged from metal in their hands. Some were sabre-like, others had heavy metal tops that could bludgeon a head, still others resembled tridents. All of it looked medieval and impossible. Molly suddenly ran towards the wooden room on stilts, jiggling with the lock, bashing in the door. 'Okay, kids, we're going to make a run for it!' Tom shouted, slowly and calmly. 'Follow me.' Blake grabbed hold of me and we ran. Once inside, Molly padlocked the door, and we watched as more and more men kept coming, holding their weapons firm, charging over the hill. It was as if they hadn't seen us. The object of their anger lay elsewhere, in the direction they were running.

When the last of them had run past us, we quickly dismantled the tents and drove home. Because Molly and Tom were religious people, and because they were Christian in the best possible way, they made only meas-ured statements about what we might have witnessed.

Papi would have called them savages. 'And we put up with it,' he would have said. 'We put up with it because this is the kind of backward country we live in.'

The Hendersons dropped me off at the end of my street. 'Are you going to be okay, honey?' Molly asked. She gave my shoulder a little squeeze. Blake mouthed 'I love you' from the back seat, and I turned away from him, annoyed by the inappropriateness of his utterance. We had just witnessed something frightening and this boy was talking of love.

The next morning I scanned the newspaper looking for an explanation. Buried in the local news was a small paragraph about caste violence in the Perumalmalai district. A high-caste girl had eloped with a Dalit boy. Members of the girl's village, led by her father, ransacked the other village, hacking the boy to death, burning several houses and injuring thirty people. The girl killed herself by drinking poison. It was a story so common, told so matter-of-factly, I might have missed it had I not been looking for it. I remember thinking then, as I still think, how strange that what they were most indignant about was that this boy dared to fuck one of their girls. How strange that they did not think to truncheon all the other forces that conspired to keep them down. That they could bear those indignities as though they were creatures made entirely of wounds.

A man is at the front door. I can see a sliver of him as I walk to the kitchen to prepare lunch. Who knows how long he's been standing there? The dogs had not barked. They must have disappeared further down the beach to make trouble.

I'm in shorts and a singlet, unshowered, slightly muddy from a morning swim.

'Yes?' I say.

He has a wide, uneven face. There's something scurrilous about the largeness of his mouth. A moustache creeps heavily over it, overshadowing his nose and eyes which are chiselled and keen. For a man he is wearing too much jewellery. Rings on five fingers and several gold chains that cut into the veins of his neck.

'Madam, I hope I'm not disturbing you? I wanted to enquire about land in this area.'

'Who are you? Haven't you come here before?'

'My name is Jiva,' he said. 'I'm a broker. I have clients who are interested in buying land here. Would you be interested in selling?'

He's still standing outside the door, and I am facing him from inside the house, looking past him to the motorbike he has parked in the garage.

'Who told you to come here?'

'As I said, my clients are interested in buying fifty acres for a project. They will be able to offer very good prices.'

'I'm not interested,' I say. 'I've already told you this. Please leave. And please don't come back here. This is private property.'

He's about to say something but I shout over him, 'Mallika, Mallika!' And he can obviously hear the fear in my voice because he says, 'Sorry, madam, please don't be misunderstanding.'

He turns to go, and I can see there are sweat stains on the back of his shirt. There is something graceful about the way his body moves. He slithers, and before Mallika can get to me, he is already halfway down the drive, the bike puttering and roaring.

'Wait here,' I shout at Mallika.

I go upstairs to check on Lucy. She's sleeping on the bed and Golly has snuck up to lie at her feet. I go into my bedroom. Put on a bra and tunic, change from shorts into long pants. I grab a straw hat and my sunglasses, put on sandals.

'Hundred fucking times I've said lock the bloody gate,' I shout at Mallika, dragging her by the hand. 'Why that's so difficult for you to do, I don't understand. Let's go now.'

At her house, Mallika puts on slippers. She hitches up her sari and follows as I storm down the driveway.

'Who was that man?' she asks, jogging to keep pace with me.

'Well, he wouldn't fucking be inside here if you were locking the gate.'

The grasses in the driveway are long and unruly at this time of year. They scratch through my trousers as I walk. The path seems to go on and on in this heat. Where had Ma got the money to buy so much land? Auntie Kavitha told me that the man who sold her the land was only selling in ten-acre plots. 'She asked my advice and I told her she was mad for thinking she could live out there by herself. But she got that land for a song.'

When we turn the corner it's as if we've stumbled into someone else's property. There is a group of people – men, women, children – rags of people, dark and bent over in the grass. A few of them straighten themselves to look at us. I turn to Mallika, bewildered. 'Now who the hell are these people? What are they doing and where have they come from?'

'They look like Adivasis,' she says, walking boisterously up to them. I stay behind. I can't hear what she's saying, but her body language is exercising authority.

'And?' I ask, when she returns. The people have resumed whatever they were doing, faces turned back towards the dirt.

'What I thought. They are Adivasis. They're looking for mice.'

'Mice?'

'To eat,' she says, simply.

As we walk past them, one of the men looks at me. His face is gutted and wrinkled, his ribs sharp as scalpels. He's wearing a dirty dhoti, out of which two of the skinniest, bandiest legs plant themselves on the earth. He rubs his stomach and brings his fingers to his mouth in the shape of a closed flower. It is a gesture of begging or thanks, I do not know, but I cannot react to it.

'Come,' I say to Mallika. 'I must speak with Valluvan.'

You know those sleeps when all your fears cram into the centre of your head and you're forced to contemplate the certainty that you will not only lose everyone you love but that you'll grow old alone and die in a troublesome way? Despair that begins inside the body – along the byways of arms and legs, the arteries and veins pumping blood vociferously, moving haplessly in the direction of disaster. Or perhaps nothing is intuition. Perhaps it is all retroactive premonition?

The day we lose the first of our dogs, I wake to that kind of morning.

First there is the smell of burning. A sharp, rancid smell of something giving way. It comes from the west, from the shuttered windows behind my bed. I wonder whether Mallika is setting another snake on fire, or if it's something more horrible – the house catching fire, a gas leak.

Outside it's dark and smoky. I reach for my spectacles and torch, and make my way downstairs to check the gas. Then I come back upstairs and go across the landing to Lucia's room. She's sleeping on her back, the bottoms of her feet meeting in a foot Namaste, hands thrown up over her head. Watching her like that, I want to climb into the bed and fan her thin brown hair against my chest and shoulders.

Out on my balcony, where the phone signal is strongest, I call Mallika.

'Where's all this smoke coming from?' I ask. 'Are you burning another snake? How many times have I told you they're not poisonous!'

'No, Ma. It's not a snake. Today is Bhogi. Everyone is burning their old things. You should close the windows.'

I'd forgotten about this tradition of people hauling all their useless things to burn in preparation for the New Year. I bolt the shutters and windows and climb back into bed to fall into a fearsome sleep, thinking only that I should remember to buy Mallika a new sari the next time I go to Madras. She'd expect it for the New Year.

A few hours later, Lucia's at the bed, tugging at the covers. 'Wake up, Grace, wake up.'

She doesn't let me change. 'Fast, fast,' she keeps shouting, so I pull on a robe and find slippers for my feet. Downstairs, Mallika looks sullen, wearing one of my old cardigans over her sari, arms wrapped tightly across her tummy.

We set off down the driveway – Mallika and Lucia ahead of me, marching. Lucy's thighs rub-squeaking against each other in pyjamas.

I take note of how many holes there are in the brick compound wall. That's where the goats come through – there and there. I marvel at how nicely the bougainvillea is coming along – huge, heaving hedges of magenta and orange sprawling over the brickwork. A speckled woodpecker sits in the middle of the path, making his noise, then disappears into a gulmohar.

The dogs are arranged like a question mark on the ground by the gate. Kat, Preity, the three mothers – Hunter,

Thompson and Flopsy — ungainly and heavy-titted. By the gate on the ground there's a package of newspaper with rice and meat. At first I cannot comprehend the scene, but then I see smears of vomit and blood around the mouths of the dogs and understand they've been poisoned.

'Get that out of here,' I say to Mallika. 'Anyone could pick that up and eat it.'

We come back with gloves and shovels. The poor, sad, dead dogs. Their black bodies are hardening in the sun and beginning to stink. Mallika asks if she should call for help. 'A man would be useful,' she says.

'No, I don't want anyone in here,' I say.

It takes hours to dig the holes. The sun is strong and a scratch of pain starts from my lower back and spreads into my shoulders. I plug on obstinately until the work is done. We wrap the dogs in plastic first, then sheets, and lay them in the ground. Lucia wants to say a prayer for each of them. 'Oh Father,' she starts, the rest of her words nonsensical, flowing out of her in some kind of litany.

'Tell Valluvan I want to see him,' I say to Mallika, and then I go back to the house to wash the death off me, leaving Lucia on a pile of mud in her pyjamas, rocking and singing.

Valluvan's wife, Nila, offers me hot, ghee-soaked *pongal* on a steel plate and a tumbler of tea. Valluvan himself looks luminous in a shiny white new lungi and *veshti*. He's fussing with the cows in the courtyard, whose horns have been painted red and black — the household's political colours — in preparation for New Year. The daughters dart about like parakeets in bright green pavadas with heavy gold borders, saying, 'Hi auntie,' while the boy, Lenin, just nods shyly.

'I'm sorry, I've brought nothing.'

'Never mind,' Valluvan says. 'Come, sit.'

The jute stools have been moved so I sit on the floor, crossing my legs awkwardly, the blood at the top of my thighs choked and dizzy.

'Someone has put poisoned food outside my house. Five of my dogs are dead.'

'That's not good.'

'That man who came to see me about selling the land recently, do you think it could have been him? I've phoned my friend at the Blue Cross, you know? He says I can file a police complaint.'

'There are so many bad elements in the village these days,' Valluvan says. 'They all want to become million-aires overnight. Not happy to be fishermen or farmers, no? They are only interested in this new gold, and we are sitting on it. I didn't think they'd try anything with you, though.'

'What can we do?'

'If I ask here, they will say that your dogs are eating their chickens at night, which is the truth. Here, if some-one kills your animals you kill theirs. But if it's that broker you're talking about, then it's hard to say.'

'But shouldn't they lock up their chickens? There are so many packs of hungry dogs around here. It could have been any dog! What kind of person puts poisoned food by the gate? What if someone's child picked it up?'

'You don't know these rowdies. They go around with axes and knives. They want to sell all this land and make resorts and coal factories. You are too educated, so they can't fool you. But so many others have already lost their land. Illiterate people who just put their thumbprint on any document. And the police – they are involved in all this. Don't think they're going to help you.'

'So, then?' I say. 'I should just do nothing, is it?'

'If you want your dogs to live, tie them up at night, simple.'

A mood settles over us all. Raja and Bagheera stretch out on the patio – morose and listless. The puppies are frantic for food. With the three mothers dead I don't know what to do. I take mashed-up dog food over to where they've been hiding in the neem bushes, and they rush out, a flurry of black and white, setting upon the bowls with blind hunger.

'Do you think they'll make it?' I ask Mallika.

'We'll have to see.'

Lucia doesn't want to go on our evening walk. It's the time of day we love best. To set out on the beach with the big dogs, to chase crabs and howl. All week we've been watching David Attenborough's *Planet Earth* series, and I've been putting on my Attenborough voice to entertain Lucia.

But there's going to be no walk today, or David Attenborough. At five in the evening, Lucia is still in her muddy pyjamas.

'Get up, Lucy. It's bath time, come on now, you can't sit like this forever.'

She doesn't look at me. She says nothing.

I go upstairs to run the water. 'Lucy,' I shout. 'Come for your bath.'

Ten minutes later I have to come downstairs again. 'Why aren't you talking to me? Lucia! Lucia! I said speak to me. Look at me.' I start pushing her shoulders, but she's staring away from me obstinately.

Finally, I have to call Mallika to help. 'Catch hold of her arms and I'll get her legs.'

'No, no,' Lucia shouts, lying down like a sack of stones.

'You have to, Lucia! You stink of dog, and you're dirty and you're not eating dinner in your pyjamas.'

But there's no reasoning with her. So I pinch her ankles and catch hold of them, while Mallika grabs her underneath the arms. She's kicking and screaming as we take her up the stairs, jerking her torso up and down to make it more difficult for us. We haul her onto the bed – the solid weight of her, and she's still shouting, no no no.

'Stop it, Lucy, stop it. Just get up,' I say, smacking her hard on the back. 'Why aren't you listening to me? Grab her, Mallika. You are going to have a bath whether you like it or not. It's not my fault the dogs are dead.'

We manage to get her into the bathroom, standing. I drag the shirt over her head while Mallika holds on to her waist. I'm about to pull the elasticated pyjama bottoms down her legs when she starts to urinate. A thick stream of piss. Standing there, just a few inches from the toilet. She doesn't cry, she doesn't shout. She just stands there and allows the piss to run between her legs, onto our arms and the bathroom floor. 'Lucia!' I shriek. 'Lucia!' And then I pin her shoulders to the bathroom wall, and beat her and beat her, while Mallika stands back to watch.

19

There are moments, even in the most intimate of relationships, when you're making love with someone and you feel nothing. It happened with Blake three years into our marriage. We were never an overly amorous couple, but in the early days we groped and had sex on stairways and believed in the unity of our bodies. Relationships tarnish, though, and for some, the erosions make them want to return to the body they've just hated, to claim it into being theirs again. I was never one for erosions. Once I began to see the dried skin around the elbows and the small hairs sprouting from earlobes, once I began to hold the body's smell – its own particular reek of dying – the day after day became untenable. With Vik, it had been golden. A giving over. I put my mouth to his and drank.

Now he's sitting across from me, I feel none of that. I see only a stranger. A boy – short and hairy. Full of ego with nothing to give.

We are in a hotel bar where a glass of wine costs an eighth of Mallika's monthly salary. It's a voluble gathering – Praveen, Rohini, Samir, Vik. Praveen is telling us how he's ready for monogamy. 'When you're single it becomes a case of carnality, you know? Like when's the next one?'

'You got to keep your shit quiet in this city, dude, otherwise you get fucked.' This is Vik talking. My young Vik. 'You need to have your hangouts, your underground places where you do your thing, you got to have your pad.'

'I don't want a wife or anything,' Praveen says. 'I'm just ready to be in a committed relationship. I'm forty-five, you know? I'm ready.'

'You're forty-five!' Rohini says. 'I'm impressed, Praveen. I'd have pegged you for younger.'

Rohini is obsessed with age. She tells me about all the women in the city who've had face fillers and boob jobs. Twice already, at the end of long nights, she's asked me what it was like to be with a man so much younger than myself. 'Divine,' I said. 'But really,' she asked, 'don't you worry?'

I sneer at her, but I know exactly what she's talking about because of course I fucking worry. I worry about Ms Bushy Brows and the bandage-dress women who are trying to make themselves so perfectly bland, how this has come to define what we call beautiful and this is what makes men raise their cocks up in the air, and so this is what women will do to themselves. 'It's only a thing of the moment,' I tell her.

'But get this,' Samir interjects. 'He's learned about commitment from his dog.'

Praveen blushes and Rohini is shrieking now, 'Bestiality, bestiality!'

'Seriously,' Praveen says. 'I've been learning loyalty from Sphinx. He's the only one who waits for me every day, you know? I never used to pay him much attention but now I'm like, Hey buddy, how's it going? It's an alien feeling for me. I'm trying to master it. I've been a bitch, a bastard.'

No one has asked how I'm coping with my recent dog tragedy because they're not furry house animals. Because they're a pack of wild things, the expectation is that wild things might happen to them, such as being poisoned en masse. Vik had said something to the effect of the numbers being under control now. Even Rohini, who proclaimed to be a canine freak, was only really interested in her two Poms. It feels silly to talk about grief, but I haven't been able to sleep, and when I drove down here I cried most of the way. I am angry too, because there is such easy acceptance of death. The cheapness of it. Those beautiful animals gone. And we chatter here about things I don't comprehend but am somehow part of.

'You've got such a pretty face,' Rohini says, turning to me all of a sudden. 'You should marry her, Vik. Why don't you just grow a pair of balls and marry her?'

I want to say that I'm already married and that it hadn't worked out so well the first time. That I didn't think monogamy was such a great idea. But I wanted to see how Vik would react.

'She won't have me,' Vik says, taking my hand. 'She keeps telling me it's over, so what can a man do? Just keep trying, right?'

The waiter circles around us with a bottle of wine, pours into our glasses.

'Boss,' Praveen says, looking at the waiter kindly, 'you need to take care of your body odour.'

'Jesus,' I say, laughing, 'that's rude.'

'Please, Miss G, it's not rude. I'm honest. I'm paying top dollar here. I'm not at the fucking Udipi Mathsya hotel.'

'Hygiene is super-important for Praveen,' Rohini says.

'Yeah, man, people in Madras don't have the concept of deodorant. It's a minefield out there. You got to be careful.'

'Want to get out of here?' Vik asks. A month ago I would have said hell yes. He would have taken me to one of his underground places. We would have leaned against enamel or wall, hands working quickly to unfasten buttons and flies, but now I want to keep his body at a distance from mine.

At one in the morning Rohini complains she's drunk and wants to go home. We signal for the bill. A man and woman saunter in. He's dressed all in black – shirt strained over stomach, legs like pencils, feet stuffed into old-fashioned leather moccasins. The girl is blobby in all the right bits. Teetering on heels, thrusting her chest out and pointing to the table she wants.

'Sheesh,' Praveen says. 'You have to wonder about these girls. Wearing runway clothes but going mewh mewh.'

'What's that? What's that fucking sound, mewh mewh?'

'Their personalities are so meek. They're servants, all of them.'

'They come from small towns,' Rohini says. 'That's what he means. Have you seen that Prashant's wife? She's like bus-conductor material.'

'I sure am glad you guys are my friends,' I say.

Praveen laughs. 'You're one demented bitch. That's why we love you.'

It becomes harder and harder to return to the beach. I set off Monday morning, hung-over, stop at the supermarket for supplies, mindlessly reach for bottles of pasta sauce, bags of rice, dog treats. There's always the feel of dirt after these weekends. I walk up and down the narrow aisles, pushing the trolley, dragging my slippers. The women at the cash register chatter like sewing machines and I wonder how they sustain such robust conversations. What do they find to speak about all day? The one who serves me has a face dented with acne. She coughs over my vegetables and then extends her hand for my credit card.

There are moments when I feel I have nothing to do with any of the life around me. I have no idea what most people find delectable, what pushes them to betray or lift up another person. Yesterday at brunch, someone asked what I thought about Aamir Khan's acting in *PK*. 'I don't watch Hindi movies,' I said. This woman was a former Ms Madras – a fetching thing with somewhat overexaggerated eyes and a stage-one zit marring her forehead. 'You don't watch Hindi movies,' she repeated. 'At all?' I told her I lived in a place far from cinemas, that mostly I watched cartoons and nature documentaries, but my interest in movies in any language had just died, and I hadn't bothered to question it. 'But don't you feel left out?' she asked. And it went like this, the former Ms Madras quizzing me about my village life, her hands getting increasingly hysterical as I told her about mouse killings and dog poisonings. I wanted to ask, Isn't it tiring to be a former? Doesn't that define the quality of your life to such an extent that you are always looking backwards? Former Ms Madras, former finance minister, former wife.

'You should hire a security team,' she said.

'So tell me,' I said, 'how did you meet your husband?'

The man she was married to sat across from her. He had flexible fingers that he bent backwards vigorously while listening, a delicate face, a carving knife for a mouth. 'She used to play tennikoit in school,' he answered. 'I met her at a party where I was flying my fucking balls off, went down on one knee and proposed. She said no, but I persisted. You married?'

'Yes. But I'm having an affair.'

Everyone but the former Ms Madras and her husband looked shocked. 'I like this girl,' the beauty queen said. 'Come and visit us when you're in town next. We'll force you to watch a movie. We have the most fabulous home-entertainment system. Now listen, be a sweetie and text me about putting pimple cream on my face when I get home, will you?'

Blake had written several emails proposing reconciliation. I had replied saying I'd met someone, that I was happy and was sorry he couldn't move on. Perhaps we should get divorced? He wrote back, a perturbed ramble about infidelity, which I thought quite unfair, because while we'd been together, I'd held steadfastly to him.

I'd always understood the nature of infidelity as something that stemmed from boredom or inadequacy. That the body sought out another body because we are primates, driven by primal intuitions. But with Blake my desires had shrivelled. Nothing in me wanted to be filled by another person. I had been told by my mother, when she still deigned to talk about bodily matters, that sex and love had nothing to do with one another, that a marriage could survive any kind of desert. Later, of course, Auntie Kavitha confirmed that Mother had been an unfaithful wife.

'There was that whole mess with Sundar,' she said. 'Although your mother was never really that keen on him.'

'Wait. I thought Uncle Sundar was gay?'

'No, no. And then there was that doctor in Madras who indulged your mother's tragic side. That was the more serious affair. It gave her a sense of controlling her life, because you know, your father was unrelenting about Lucy. He would not go see her. This broke your mother's heart.'

You never think your parents lead more deceitful lives than you, but of course they do. I remember the closed shutters of Mahalakshmi, the many weekend afternoons we spent in our private corners pretending to sleep or read, just to be away from each other for a few hours so that when we reconvened we'd be able to bear each other's presence again.

I've been thinking of taking Lucia up to Kodai for a few weeks even though the house is a ruin now. I heard the family fell out after the old man who owned the property died. Still, we could climb over the wall. I could show Lucia the view of the plains. We could stay at the club and take walks around the lake. We need a change, after all. The days are getting so warm, the sea so anxious.

20

The last days of March. All the puppies are dead. For three weeks I've lain in bed – fevered and sore as if fire ants had orgied in the bones of my tibia and humerus, the needles of my spine. In the rare moments of lucidity I had thought only of Lucia. What will happen to her if something happens to me?

This virus is spread by the female mosquito. It makes gulags of your joints. When it first hit me I woke disoriented, bladder full. I tried to lift myself from bed but it was as if my palms were made of sponge. I sank down immediately. I tried to shout but the noise coming from me was soft and rippled out into nothing. At ten, Lucia stormed in saying, 'Gimme breakfast.'

'Call Mallika,' I told her. 'Go get her.' Lucia started shoving me in the small of my back, as if to push me out of bed. 'Cornflakes, cornflakes,' she shouted, agitated that I wasn't moving. An hour later Mallika finally came upstairs. She stood at the doorway, hand at hip. 'What happened? You didn't come down to eat?'

'I need to go to the bathroom,' I said. 'Come here and help. I can't move.'

Mallika managed to sit me up in bed. 'You have a fever,' she said worriedly, pressing her palm against my forehead. 'What do you want me to do?'

'Help me to stand and walk me to the bathroom,' I said.

We shuffled over. Each step a mutilation. 'You'll have to take me all the way in.'

I lifted my nightie and sat on the pot. 'Stay here, Mallika, otherwise I might fall over.' I pissed with relief, feeling none of the humiliation I thought I would. 'Lift me up now,' I said. 'That's it. Wait, let me wash my face.'

Lucia followed, looking at us. 'Cornflakes, cornflakes,' she was saying, hand jabbing the air.

'Wait, idiot,' Mallika snapped. 'Can't you see your sister's not well? I'll feed you after.'

Hours later I looked up to see Auntie Kavitha in my reading chair. 'Do you want me to close the blinds?' she asked. 'Yes,' I said, staring out at the wrought-iron bars of the balcony grille, the sea framed between the curlicues. I was content with my sickness the way all guilty people feel when they are struck down. It felt deserving.

Auntie Kavitha was wearing a man's shirt and a long cotton skirt with mirrors sewn into the hem. Her short grey hair stood like bristle on her head. 'You've gone and got this vile chikungunya thing that's going around,' she said, allowing the blinds to hurtle down. 'Bloody mosquitoes.'

'Have you eaten?' I asked.

'Not hungry,' she said, standing with her feet apart as if to steady herself.

I could see the outline of her breasts in the half-light. Slight, elfin.

'I've stopped wearing underwear,' she'd told me the last time we were together. I can't think how the topic came up, but she'd said, 'What's the point? I don't need it any more.' I told her I felt the same, living out here, giving in to primitivism. Why not wear mismatched clothes, why bother with all the harnessing and holstering? 'I've never liked my breasts in any case,' I'd said. 'Ponderous fleshy things.' She laughed. 'Name me a woman who's satisfied with her breasts.'

Now she walked towards the bed and crept on to it with hands and knees. 'You're going to need help,' she said, lying beside me, hand on my forehead, fingertips soft and cool. 'I've brought my things.'

We live so close to death here. To lose all those puppies. And how? They hadn't even been named, they were still so small. Rolls of black-and-white fur, nails and tongue. After their mothers had been poisoned they moved from the bushes to the patio, ate mushed-up dog food softened with broth. They slept around the legs of the table, yelped in unison when I opened the doors in the morning. Mallika complained because there was always piss and shit on the patio floors. 'Can't you teach them to do their business in the garden?'

'Thirteen puppies,' I said. 'They'll have to learn themselves.'

One morning the runt of the lot vomited after feeding. Its body convulsed, pissing and quivering. It lasted a minute. When it was over it returned to the other dogs, legs slightly bowed. Lucia scooped it up and tenderly rubbed the goopy discharge from its eyes. 'Poor baby,' she cooed.

Throughout the day the pup had seizures. At night I brought it inside and stayed up with it in the sitting room. Lucia kept coming downstairs to turn the lights off, and Golly followed her, wagging her tail, sniffing the air. 'Go to bed,' I kept shouting. 'For fucksake go to sleep.' She ignored me and sat on the couch with her socks and handkerchiefs, rocking and singing. 'Golly needs to be away from the pup, Lucy,' I said. 'Understand? She needs to be away from her.' I dragged the dog upstairs and closed the bedroom door, and she howled a while before settling down. Bagheera, Raja and Dimple paced up and down the patio, pressing their noses to the window grilles.

Lucia stayed on the couch till she tired and fell asleep. I lay on the floor cushions with the pup in my lap. The pup kept running off to pee, shit, then circle around her mess, as if not understanding why her body was doing this. I got up and cleaned the crap with paper towels, then lured the pup back to me. She would sit in the folds of my dress for a short while, heart pounding madly, then off again. All night this macabre dance – silence and frenzy. That small black-and-white beast looking up in confusion as if to say, What is this, what is this coming for me?

At dawn the pup started foaming at the mouth. Her movements became more erratic, the circles she ran in wider and wider. Finally she ran upstairs and hid under my bed. I left her there, shaking and foaming, body damp with sweat. She no longer responded to me. It was as if she couldn't see or hear me. At six I went to get the crate from the garage. I made a cup of tea and woke Lucy. 'I'm taking the puppy to the doctor, okay? You'll have to be good and stay here with Mallika and look after the other dogs.'

On the phone with the vet he said to bring in all the puppies. 'They haven't finished their vaccination course but we'll see what we can do.'

Mallika helped gather the rest of the pups and put them in the crate. The infected pup I wrapped in a towel and laid on the seat beside me. I kept turning to see whether she was moving or not, but she lay rigid as a doll.

In a week they were all dead. We could not even put their bodies in the garden. They ended up in an animal hospital in Vepery. Because the symptoms of canine distemper and rabies were so similar, they'd have to be tested postmortem to make sure. The vet explained how the virus was in the nerves, not the blood, so they'd have to examine the brain tissue. I thought of a young student piercing a long needle into the fur of those soft puppy heads. The cadavers incinerated afterwards. What ritual could we perform for them? How to explain to Lucia that all this might be more terrible than what it already was? We needed to know for our own protection. I touched its piss, shit, saliva.

The rest of the dogs got booster shots, except for Raja, of course. He always knew when the vet was coming, running off through the holes in the brick wall, reappearing only when things were safe.

For weeks I dreamed terrible dreams. Of rabid dogs and lacerated tongues. Whatever sheath lay between us and the wild out-there had thinned to the point of vanishing. I could not sleep without clenching my fingers and hands, lacing the bones of my jaw.

The vet, who'd lost a colleague recently, had gone from being expansive about street dogs to suspicious. 'You can't be too careful,' he said, examining his gloved hands. 'I don't want to scare you unnecessarily, but my friend ...' He trailed off. 'He was treating these dogs and one of them barked and the spit flew in his eye. He just wiped it off, carried on. He was not a paranoid type. But he died such a horrible death.'

I thought there needed to be an aperture for rabies, that it necessarily involved teeth. But it can travel through spit and mucus and open wounds. I began washing my hands obsessively every time Raja licked me. I made Lucia do it too. 'You and your sister should take deworming tablets,' the vet said when he left. 'I hope you don't plan on getting any more dogs.'

We planted gardenia bushes, thirteen of them, all along the front lawn. A floral requiem.

I asked Mallika to hire some villagers to do the weeding. For a week, three women and two men ambled up the driveway with their shoddy equipment — a couple of shovels and a prehistoric pan-shaped thing that I'd seen women use on building sites to carry gravel on their heads. They started at nine and were gone by five. Between twelve-thirty and two, the hottest hours of the day, they rested for lunch in the shade of Mallika's small house. The remainder of the time they sat on their haunches in the dirt, yanking things from the ground with their bare hands.

'I want to pay the women the same rate,' I told Mallika. 'They're doing the same work, after all.'

'No, no,' Mallika said. 'The men do all the hard work, they clear all the thorny parts. If we don't give them more it will create tensions.'

At four I brewed a big vessel of tea. I made it milky and sweet. I called to Mallika, who had wrapped a towel around her head and squatted with the other women in the garden. 'Come and get the tea,' I shouted. She walked up the path, her skin polished with sweat.

Later, I called Praveen and told him I felt like a planta-
tion owner.

'Why's it like this here?' I asked. 'In America, every job
is a service. You do the job, you get paid, you fuck off. It's
transactional. But even when I was babysitting and cleaning people's houses, there was still some interaction. They
asked me to sit with them for dinner. They dropped me
home because I didn't have a car. I don't want to use the
word dignity, but it's what I'm reaching for. How am I
supposed to treat these people breaking their backs in
my garden for less than five hundred bucks a day? Why
is it making me so angry to look at them? Why don't
they fucking run into the house and smash the shit out of
everything?'

'It's the biggest mindfuck of this country. Only way to
keep sane is to get the hell out once in a while. And so,' he
pressed. 'It's really over with your man, is it? I saw him the
other day, Ms G. He's feeling it.'

This is a scene from a long time ago. How many evenings have I spent on this railway platform, sitting on an over-stuffed suitcase, slapping mosquitoes from my ankles?

Vendors are pacing the platforms with carts of *badam* milk and bananas, bottled water and magazines. It's as if they've been shouting forever, their voices billowing out from somewhere deep in their bodies. I keep craning my neck towards the direction of the train, but it does not come. The air is still and I am fatigued by the pointlessness of all the moving around. All the dirty, ravaged stray dogs.

I think of Papi. Of his betrayals. How he used to walk up and down this platform with me, pointing out the constellations. The Big Dipper and Orion's Belt, the Dog Star, Sirius. And me, pretending I could see those shapes in the sky, when really it was just night, vast and flamboyant, seeking to diminish us.

Ma used to closet herself in the upper-class waiting room on a bench, legs folded under her, book against her knees. 'It's smelly in here,' I'd complain, because the bathroom doors were always kept open, and the lavatories – little pits in the ground – emanated an odour that terrified me. It blanketed everything, that smell. Piss and chrome and blood – gamy and menstrual. The rotten, overripe smell of bodies in transit – bodies unwashed, all cloyingly masked by a bouquet of naphthalene balls and phenol. 'It smells outside too, darling,' Ma would say, her own scent something languid and animal. 'Go keep your father company. You know how anxious he gets.'

They've been ghosts this entire trip. Forcing themselves into frames, tripping us up, as if to remind us that the only reason we're here is because of them. I have been wondering where they found the courage to try again? To begin with a child they discarded and think maybe they could give it another go.

I had been prepared for ugliness because that's what grows in India, sprouts and flourishes like the hair on a dead person. But the space in which you go from adult to child, that leaf-thin whiplash, that I had not expected.

We drove through kilometres of *shola* forest, the taxi careening dangerously around corkscrew bends. Lucia was at the window, pushing her glasses up the snub of her nose. One knee flat on the seat, the other jammed into her armpit. Out of her mouth a song, or a kind of song.

'Look, Lucia,' I said, as we passed the Silver Cascades – that sad, depleted waterfall running crookedly down the rock face, overwhelmed by the many vanloads of people who had come to pose beside it over the years. And the monkeys manning the walls – they were still there, even though they looked more sore-assed and disgruntled than before. Above them skeletons of new constructions thrust out of the forest, and crowded around these were two-storeyed houses painted bright pink and purple, buildings made of such shoddy materials they seemed to sway slightly in the breeze.

Centuries before, Indian tribes had lived in these hills in megalithic dolmens, collecting honey. Later, botanists and enthusiastic American missionaries who dreamed of large congregations came and built churches and elegant bungalows. Couples took perambulations around Coaker's Walk and paused at the cliff's edge to give thanks to their own intelligence for having escaped the heat of down there. Now Kodai is a place that bursts in summer. Its inhabitants complain about the invaders from the plains with their pallid cheeks and fat hearts. They complain constantly, as I imagine descendants of a failed royal family do, aware that their ancestors lived in a time of greater beauty, that these reduced living conditions were a kind of poverty.

I had made plans to meet Uncle Sundar for dinner at the club. 'That old fox will pull out all the stops,' Auntie Kavitha had said. 'Are you sure you don't want me to come?'

Looking at him now, after all these years, I see how obvious it was. His eyebrows were radiant black arches, his hair a cathedral of black, even the way his jaws worked systematically through the club's stringy roast chicken, displaying slabs of strong ivory tooth now and again, showed a man of conscientiousness. I imagined him going through his weekly toilette. The bottle of hair dye, the tweezers, the huge concentration in his sleek, morose face as he brushed and scalpelled his way to perfection.

'What a tremendous thing you're doing,' he said, for the second time.

'Do you think,' I said, after serving Lucia another helping, cutting the chicken and vegetables into small pieces so she'd be able to scoop them into her spoon, 'that you could tell me about your relationship with my mother? I know most of it, but there are so many gaps. I'd be interested to hear your side of it.'

'Why?' he cried out, sudden shots of colour in his cheeks. 'Why would you want to know such things?'

'There's no one else I can really go to.'

'I think your mother was sick,' he said, 'literally, heart-sick for this girl.' He looked meaningfully at Lucia and stroked her forearm. 'Our relationship, whatever you want to call it, was really a friendship. She felt so alienated by your father.'

'But he's the one who was alienated. He's the one who agreed to stay in India, even though they were meant to travel around the world with his job.'

'And leave this girl here?'

He kept touching Lucia every time he referred to her, but she didn't seem to mind. She was transfixed by the deer heads on the club walls, their dead, glazed eyes.

'My mother could have done what I'm doing now. She could have left my father earlier.'

'And what would have happened to you?'

'What's happened to me anyway?'

It's an energetic week. We've been walking everywhere and Lucia looks better for it. Her face is tinged pink from the sun. Every morning she sits for an hour on the wall outside the room, warming her back before dressing for breakfast. The waiters at the club all know her by name and habit. In the morning they bring the box of cornflakes to the table as soon as they see us walking in. At seven in the evening, when I'm having my gin and tonic at the bar, they bring her a Coca-Cola and a plate of wafers without us having to ask. Uncle Sundar joins us most nights, and it is a relief to have someone to relay the day's adventures to.

We call Mallika regularly to check on the dogs. I put her on speaker so Lucy can hear her too. 'The dogs are fine,' she says, her voice phantom-like, disconnected. Lucia makes her say their names. 'Golly, Bagheera, Raja, Dimple. Yes, yes, all are fine.'

Valluvan phones one morning to tell me that he's going to stand for the Cheyyur district elections. His competitor is a man called K. Alexander. 'I need some funds,' he says. 'Otherwise that fellow and his goons will win.' I am tired of taking financial requests – Mallika, Valluvan, Teacher – all of them see me as some kind of never-ending ATM. And to what end? I am still alone in all this. I tell Valluvan I'll have to think about it. I had only just made a Rs 40,000 contribution towards the new village temple, and now he wants Rs 200,000 more. 'Have a good holiday,' he says. 'Good that you and your sister are able to enjoy some cool air. It is so hot here already.'

Everything in the town of Kodaikanal is as it has always been, except it has grown more dishevelled and pitiful, like an elderly relative who wanders about with stained shirt fronts. Lucia enjoys walking the flat path around the starfish-shaped lake, to charge downhill in the bazaar and at 7 Roads, but every time we arrive at the base of an incline, she flops down on the ground and shakes her head. I squat next to her and say, 'Come on, it's easy. You can do it.' And when nothing works, I say, 'Do you want a fresh lime soda?' For a while, it seems I can bribe her to do anything with the promise of a fresh lime soda.

People stare. Wherever we go someone is looking at us – gazing unabatedly, not with malice or curiosity, but some kind of stupidity. Families travelling with other families, honeymooning couples, busloads of day trippers from Kerala, mostly men. In them all I find something to despise. I see only smallness in their lives. Who am I to say? It could simply be that they don't know how to look. That, like the waiters at the club, they only need time to familiarise themselves. But I see only the imprint of failure. Those newly-wed women leaning into their husbands' chests – hennaed arms, bangles up to their elbows, incongruous in their jeans and T-shirts. Being steered around by men, who look like children really, overgrown children who have never been denied anything. They lead with their stomachs and hairy forearms, and the women follow to what surely must be a drowning. I want to believe otherwise, that in all the hordes there is beauty and potential, but mostly what I see is a beating down. The men and the women, and even the poor children, dragged around in their silly monkey caps and fluorescent sunglasses. What chance do any of them have?

'So you only see beauty in the singularity of self?' Uncle Sundar asks.

'I think most people don't look at the past. I think they're blind to their mothers and fathers, otherwise they'd choose differently, wouldn't they?'

I realise I'm collecting a tribe. The people I feel safest with are those who live alone in the world – Praveen, Auntie Kavitha, Uncle Sundar. Unmarried, unmoored. In America, the loneliness had haunted me. In India I long to see evocations of it because it seems from the second you are born there's always someone else's shadow casting over yours.

On our last day we take a taxi to the house. We turn off before PPCG and its looming arches and the Naidupuram market. I had been warned about what to expect, but you can never imagine the scale of ruin when it comes to the house of your childhood.

It has been forsaken – overrun with thickets of wild, cottony carrot bushes and shrubs of lantana. All the glass has been smashed out of the windowpanes and the tin roof sags like a hammock in the breeze.

There's a sign painted against the side of the house: *THIS LAND & BUILDING ARE ATTACHED BY THE RECOVERY OFFICER EPFO, MADURAI. TRESPASSERS SHALL BE PROSECUTED.*

The yellow board nailed to the trunk of a jacaranda still says *Mahalakshmi*, and it is uncanny to walk through her gates again, through all those derelict memories.

The taxi driver tells me that the family is in court. The old man is dead and all the children are battling for a larger share. 'Happens in all families when there's money,' he says almost cheerfully, as if relieved that he will never have to suffer this kind of ignominy.

He doesn't seem to be perturbed by our mission or by our flouting of the law. He stands at the gates watching, while Lucia and I cross the jungle of lawn and arrive at the portico, where the front door has been unhinged and dismantled.

The whole place is damp and bereft. The drawing room has been invaded by raspberry brambles pushing up through the floor and cascading through the windows. Cheap whisky bottles and cigarette stubs are scattered in corners. All the grey stone is eroded and the floors are filthy with excrement. Only parts of the walls show evidence of an earlier periwinkle blue with yellow trim.

There are two gaping holes in the walls of the sitting room on either side of the fireplace and the kitchen has been stripped bare. It's as if someone had redecorating plans and then just forgot the house existed.

There is my bay window overlooking Mount Perumal and Papi's office shed. The garden that Ma so painstakingly nurtured, completely overrun with devil's plague.

'I used to live here with Mummy and Papi,' I tell Lucia, who has parked herself on the dirty floor and is flipping the sleeve of her sweatshirt this way and that.

I try to imagine how our evenings in Mahalakshmi would have been with Lucia sitting on the rug in front of the fire, crouched over a jigsaw puzzle, her tongue stuck out from concentration, while her stubby fingers slowly pushed the pieces of the puzzle together.

'We had a dog, you know? His name was Salsicciotto. He was completely white and I loved him.'

At the mention of Salsicciotto Lucia perks up. 'That's Mummy's dog.'

'Yes, she took him with her when I went to college. Did she bring him with her sometimes when she came to see you?'

'That's Mummy's dog. He's gone to God.'

I ask the taxi driver to take a photograph of Lucia and me at the entrance of the house before we head down the hills to catch our train.

'Cheese,' he says, and Lucia answers, 'Paneer.'

The picture is blurry, and Lucia is standing on the step above me, making it so that she's the taller one. Two broken chimneys sprout out of the roof, and behind that, a ring of eucalyptus. We are both opening our mouths, exposing the pink tinge of our gums, and in that tremulous light, it's possible to believe we are sisters.

PART THREE

2 2

There's a tendency in failed marriages to look back and remember it all as suffering.

So much distance between us, but I can still feel the weight of Blake's thigh on mine. Prosciutto legs. That's what I used to call him. 'Get those prosciuittino off me,' I'd say, and he'd heave with greater force, squashing me until we were both laughing. I still lash out some nights, battling with his imaginary body.

We used to sleep like dead trees. Weight on weight. At first, there was a comfort to it, then a kind of dismay.

I shovel love for you, I will keep digging and digging. This is what Blake writes, what he remembers. The times we sat together in bed and binged on *The Sopranos*, the ransacking of each other's bodies, the glory.

In the beginning I could not stop touching him. The graze of stubble along his cheeks, the soft globes of his deltoids. He had small, pea-green eyes made to look sad and pulpy by the thicket of dark eyelashes that encased them. A neck of wire. Facing the mirror together, I sometimes thought, He is me, I am him – the longness in our faces, those high, heartbreaking foreheads.

No one ever said we weren't suited for each other. I had expected it from Papi, who could always be relied upon to scout out the souring in anything. But instead, he took

Blake to breakfast and said, 'I'm so happy to hear you're marrying Grazia. She was such an awkward, lonely child. Always in her room, listening to her Walkman. I always worried that she would never find someone because there is something so stubborn in her nature.' Blake and I had got engaged in Venice. I wandered the markets of Rialto while Papi offered Blake one of his Montecristos, to which Blake said, 'Thanks, Mr Marisola, but I don't smoke.' Later, in the room, Blake said, 'Your father was very kind. He kept asking me to call him Jack.'

When I rang to tell Ma, she said, 'He's a good boy. Slightly tepid, but a good boy.'

Over the years I watched him, as couples will watch each other, looking for signs of betrayal, and I saw that he was exactly as he was. Everything he presented of himself was true. Nothing in him would ever surprise me, and it was this lack of guile that began to gnaw at me.

We married at Blake's grandparents' farm in Penrose, North Carolina. Ida and Rush kept longhorn cattle and beef cattle, goats and sheep, pigs, horses and chickens. Their house loomed out of the fields like an exotic bird. Grandma Ida had apparently seen a picture of a Trinidadian house in a travel magazine and said that it was exactly the house she'd always dreamed of living in, so her husband built it for her – this grand, baby-blue Victorian anomaly with white Demerara shutters and fretwork. Everything in it was fitted out with pinewood and red cedar. There was no swimming pool but a large barrel-like thing that children and dogs jumped into in the summertime. I loved eating breakfasts in that kitchen with all those solid gleaming pans hanging from hooks above the stove. Grandma Ida whipping up fresh omelettes, Grandpa

Rush fussing over the coffee maker. Blake's parents Tom and Molly had moved there to help with the running of the farm, and Blake's sister, Liane, who was seven years older, lived in the house too, with her husband Gus and their boys. The Hendersons all shared the same oblong jaw, and it was reassuring to look into their faces in the morning light, those immaculate bones moving up and down like mechanical toys. I felt I'd married into some kind of stability.

Senior year in college I told Blake we needed to take a break. 'If we're really going to get married we should sow some oats.'

'But Grace,' he said, 'that's mad. I don't want anyone else.'

Two months later I heard a mousy blonde called Lorrie had attached herself to him in Chapel Hill. Misrak laughed when she told me. 'Now you're going to be all jealous when you're the one who started this.'

Every Wednesday Misrak and I would go out, and while she was generally encouraging of random men dry-humping her on the dance floor I preferred to create a box of air around me.

'Blake gets you,' she said. 'I don't know why you're pushing him away.'

I missed our weekends at the farm and I mistook this for longing. I had grown attached to Blake's family, and in that year of our apartness I understood that when you give up on a person you must relinquish their family too. Molly finally called, 'Why don't you stop all this nonsense, honey, and go get him. If I have to make one more gluten-free meal for that girl I will lose it, I swear.'

I had tried something with one of Misrak's friends – a beautiful Ethiopian boy called Dawit who was all bone and limb, whose stomach was a cave of muscle. As long as he didn't speak, I was content to look at his glistening body in bed, a rope of shells around his throat. With him I was someone else and it was this transformation I was interested in. When Dawit tried to tell me about his family back home, the words were so limited, so paltry, I had to tell him, 'Shush, darling, you don't need to talk.'

I'd come back to the apartment I shared with Misrak night after night, the place looking like some refugee camp. Ethiopians of every size sleeping on the couch and on the floor, all the groceries from the day before vanished, the kitchen in shambles. 'What happened?' I'd say, and Misrak, sitting in frayed lingerie, forking cheesecake from a Styrofoam box into her perfect mouth, would say, 'These people are driving me mad. I'm like some mother hen for them. How can I say no?'

Spring arrived and when the winter fat did not fall off me I believed I was homesick and bought $5 phone cards to hear my mother shout down the line. 'I can hear you just fine, Ma,' I'd say, but she'd shout anyway, telling me about how the air conditioner in the guest room needed replacing and how her neighbour, Mrs Dalal, had bought a flat-screen TV.

Blake did not call. He did not once break our pact. I saw him fleetingly through the windows of the students' centre. He was eating a burger with a stranger. Two decent-looking men wearing T-shirts and those stupid knee-length nylon basketball shorts. I ran past him, wondering what he was doing in Charlotte in the middle of the week, and who he was talking to. 'I felt pangs,' I told Misrak. 'Like he was someone else, like everything we've already lived didn't exist.'

Misrak blinked. 'It's all over in a second if you want it to be. You know that, right?'

Three months later we were married. I remember only Papi's face as he passed me over to Blake at the altar. 'Better take good care of her,' he said, menacingly. And Blake, crinkling those eyes, 'Of course I will, sir, of course.'

Later, in bed, 'What did your father mean by that? What kind of man does he take me for?'

In the summer of our third year of marriage I began yawning. I'd sleep eight hours and still gasp for breath when I woke. As soon as one yawn escaped I'd start thinking of the next, and the next – the delicious reprieve. 'Please don't think you're boring me,' I had to tell people. 'It's some kind of neurotic tic, I can't seem to stop.'

Months of this and Blake began assuming the worst – multiple sclerosis, a dissected aorta. All the shrinks I went to said it was anxiety. I told them about my dissatisfactory childhood, but they said no, it must be something more.

In bed I received Blake like a dowager, creaking my legs meekly apart and offering a few grunts of encouragement before even those fell silent. 'What's wrong?' he asked repeatedly. 'Don't you like me any more?'

Blake's father, Tom, fitted me out with a mouthpiece to slide between my teeth at night. 'You're clenching the hell out of your jaw when you sleep,' he said, skating a probe around in my mouth. I fell in love with the word 'bruxism', repeated it to everyone at work. 'I'm a jaw-clencher, a bruxist!'

*

There was a spring day in Charlotte, 2002, and I think it's possibly when I was happiest. The sky was wide and bright. The air tripping with the lightness of small birds.

Misrak and I are driving to the courthouse. She's wearing a white column dress bought on the cheap, a silver tiara set back in her curls, a netted veil. She's smoking, elbow propped out of the window, and we're laughing because it is all a moving picture story and we are the protagonists.

On the way there, Misrak screeches, 'Fuck, I forgot to get rings.'

'What rings?'

'Rings. Rings. We need fucking rings to get married.'

We detour to Wal-Mart and Misrak leads the way, marching giraffe-like on satin platform shoes, veil streaming behind her. 'Jewellery?' she barks at one of the name-tagged employees. 'Where can I get jewellery?'

We follow each other down the aisles. I am in a magenta Ethiopian dress that has been shunted around for different weddings. The fabric scratches against my knees, but I stride as if I'm the kind of woman who can withstand any kind of inconvenience.

At the jewellery counter Misrak says, 'Give me the cheapest ring you have. I need two of them.' The man at the counter smiles and says, 'You have a happy life now, you hear?' as we turn away from him.

At the courthouse, the boy Misrak will marry, Abebe, is hunched over a cigarette, wearing ivory silk pants and kameez. 'You look good,' Misrak says. 'I bet you didn't think to get rings, you bastard.'

Blake is there too, and it is a moment in our history when I'm still in love with the solidness of him. I stand next to him and he whispers, 'This will be us soon, but we'll do it differently, of course.'

Misrak's boss Patty arrives with her husband. They're carrying a fluffy white-fabric photo album and a bouquet of white roses.

'Please, no slips, okay?' Misrak says, when she sees them walking towards us. 'I told them it wasn't necessary, but Patty was hung up. She said if my family couldn't come, the least she could do is be here, can you believe?'

It is over in minutes. We sign our names as witnesses. We take photographs in the sun. It's an afternoon of giddy delight, as if we were standing on a high mountain, the oxygen in our lungs clipped and clean.

Later, at Applebee's, Abebe unbuttons the top of his kameez. 'Coronas for everyone,' he says, and the way he gesticulates, the great girth of him, makes me think that one day he'll make a woman burst with joy. Not Misrak, of course, but someone else.

'I feel bad,' Misrak says, looking at the card that Patty and her husband had placed in the album. 'They were so earnest. So full of good wishes, but it's also funny, isn't it?' We laugh so much the stitches in our sides seem to come undone. To an outsider we might have appeared like the subjects of a Bruce Weber photograph gone downscale – no Hamptons here, but look at this dewy skin, look at this golden light.

That night, as Misrak and I lie across from each other on our mattresses, the dirty grey shag beneath us, she says, 'They always tell us we need a man. All the old crones at home, they go on and on about how much we need a man. Even my lovely liberal father says it. He says it will make life acceptable. But what I need is America. And if a fake husband will get me a Green Card so I can stay, then fuck it, I'll take him.'

Five years later Misrak met Jake at a library meeting, a man of such checked-shirt regularity, it seemed unthinkable that they could love each other. But within weeks they fitted parts of themselves into each other's voids, voids they didn't know they had. There was a speedy divorce from Abebe, who laughed loudly when he heard the news. 'My wife is in love with an American man!' he chortled. 'And I am so happy.' There was another trip to the court-house – subdued, nervy. I yawned through the whole thing. 'Don't worry about me,' Misrak said, crushing me against her. 'I'm not going to change a bit.'

When I think of weddings now – all the waste and propaganda – I prefer to remember that fake spring union of Misrak and Abebe. We understood that the dangers of hours and hours of cohabitation would never touch these two, and as such, they were gleaming, like the afternoon itself. We knew as well that our own futures were bound to be different. About romance and companionship we knew little, but watching those two commit themselves felt honourable, the way marriage was intended to be, a transaction devoid of the complications of love.

23

There is an intimacy with women that is as domesticated and necessary as doorknob, pillowcase, wrist. I long to be fenced in that way. Sometimes I climb into bed with Lucia just to feel the heat off her back. I wait till she's asleep to slowly unhook the tangles in her hair. I press my nose into her neck and it brings me back to myself. Even Ma, who would rather rearrange rocks in the garden than stay enfolded in the sheets, understood my need to lie in the aftermath of her warmth while she fixed herself up for the day. I always lay on her side of the bed, never Papi's – covers up to my chin, watching as she rattled around with bottles of cream on the dresser. Polka-dot terry-cotton robe wrapped tight around her spare waist, socks up to her knees. This is when she was still thin, when I thought everything about her was as majestic and enticing as a holiday in a hotel.

I cannot know if men share this, if their anatomy allows it. In college, there had been a new friend, Elisabeth. 'Are you a dyke or something?' she asked when I did her hair in a French plait and pressed her shoulders afterwards. 'Of course not,' I said, fingers leaping away from her skin.

How to explain it, though? Always in bedrooms, always a distant sexual thrum. Even those tiny Madrasi friends, those pigtailed girls from Rosary Metric, whose faces I have forgotten, but whom I remember coming over to play – the shy tingle of pleasure of bringing down each other's panties and powdering each other's bottoms. The softness. The sheer peachiness of a girl's bum. And running out of the room afterwards to play hide and seek, faces hot with shame.

It is all touch, after all. With Queenie and Misrak it had been uncomplicated. We had been so obsessed with boys, trying to understand our bodies as weapons, not as playgrounds. But still, we would lie beside each other, the ease of tangled feet. And none of this had anything to do with the jiggle in my cunt while riding behind the neighbour boy Agostino Bernardi on his motorbike in Vicenza, or what I felt resting my knee against Blake's that first time. Certainly nothing to do with clambering on top of Vik in the dark of a dead-end street. All that had made me feel was that there was a ladder inside me – climbing, conquering, descending, dwindling. I tried explaining it to Blake once, how sometimes what you wanted was not a ladder but a lake. Something that spread all around you.

'I think it has to do with birthing,' he said. 'Only women are capable of doing it. Perhaps what you really want is a baby?'

Always, we came back to this.

We had moved from an apartment in Charlotte to a house and then a bigger house in the space of seven years. Blake's job paid for everything. He was frequently away on projects in counties across the state, working with farmers and their problems with soil contamination or fitting out waste-water management units in hotels and factories. On weekends, as if he hadn't tired of mud, he'd fuss with the pergola and the deck, coaxing wisteria, taming clematis.

When he was gone I walked through the rooms in the house trying to imagine what it would be like filled with the noise of children. I fought for air even though there was so much space.

I began working out. I'd always despised gymnasiums. All those people conscientiously sweating together on machines, gaping through wide, attractive windows. Silverbacks in tank tops pumping iron. Women in flocks of three clutching at water bottles. I was thirty-two, and what I was hoping for was an awakening in my body.

I quickly grew to love them – the new ridges in my thighs and shoulders, hard tongues of muscle that could stiffen and relax. My heart felt closer to me than it had in years. I listened to trashy music on earphones as I moved on the treadmill, legs pounding as though they had hearts of their own. I felt powerful. I began to watch people watch me. In the changing room I caught flashes of other women's naked stomachs, their dimpled thighs, the way they stepped leisurely into panties. The smells of deodorant and perfume were like infinity to me. I watched how dexterously frizz could be rolled out of hair with blow-dryers, so many pairs of arms furling and unfurling.

'It's shitty that we have to die,' I said to Blake one night.

We were lying in bed. I looked around at the things we had gathered, the most beautiful of which was the bed we were lying on, a four-poster behemoth. The coloured Murano-glass perfume bottles on the dressing table, the faux-Chola bronze Nataraja in the corner, the Marie Antoinette-style chaise longue, across which my gym clothes were draped – possessions that represented a collective purr of pleasure.

'I like watching your face when you grow pensive like this,' Blake said. The hair on the top of his head was beginning to grey and thin, which I knew bothered him even though he said nothing about it. Every morning, after showering, he'd sweep the bathroom for evidence, wrapping the wispy, treacherous flecks in toilet paper and disappearing them into the bin.

'It reminds me of how you used to be, back in Kodai,' he said. 'But we don't have to die. I mean, there are other ways to continue, you know.'

'Don't start, please.'

'You never ask what I might need or why. It's not right.'

'You speak of children as though you could ever really know them, as if you need them in order to live your life. Why can't you just live your life?'

'There's nothing missing from my life. That isn't what this is about.'

We lay beside each other without speaking. Blake turned over and switched off his lamp. When we argued he slept facing away from me, on his side, palms folded together as if in prayer. He slept easily, silently, with no debts to settle. I watched him as though he were some other person, someone who didn't belong to me, and I was hit by that familiar surge of tenderness whenever I began to contemplate a life without him. How sad it would be to lose this man who loved me so expansively.

Ma came to visit every April when the heat in Pondicherry began to crush through her skull. 'Just look at these blossoms,' she'd say, as we walked around the neighbourhood, its avenues of heaving magnolia and crape myrtle. But I always looked at her face instead, wondering how it had been allowed to grow into this – fruit-like, beyond ripeness. Her cheeks hung off her like kumquats. They juddered. They glowed.

The nights we didn't go out to dinner Blake threw slabs of meat on the grill.

'Sorry I'm not a better mother-in-law, I should be cooking for you.'

'You stay right there, Meera,' Blake would say. 'This is your holiday.' He carried plates of food to her, plied her with Prosecco and packets of Yo-Yos. She accepted these gifts happily like a child. 'I hope you realise what you've got,' she'd say from the island of her La-Z-Boy whenever he disappeared into the kitchen.

Sometimes, as we sat together watching television on those spring nights, I'd think about Papi, how if he were here, he'd be skulking around in the garden. I wanted to walk out and smoke a cigarette with him. I'd tell him I had looked through his diaries once, and seen naked sketches of Mother – her face always turned towards a window, her small, perfect breasts holding the light to ransom. It had been beautiful for me to think I'd come from this.

Ma wore baggy slacks with long shapeless tunics. She had learned to dress like a woman who always has something to hide. But there was no dissatisfaction about her. She was as limpid and happy as I'd ever seen her. In the mornings after Blake left for work, she and I would preen in deckchairs in the garden. Lemonade in a jug on the table between us, books folded on our stomachs.

'Can you really take all this time off? I can entertain myself, you know.'

She had grown interrogative, coaxing almost, and I wanted to ask, where have you been all these years? Who is this new person so concerned about my life? Everything about her now emanated a kind of openness. Even her hair – once long and rope-like, hanging uselessly down her back – had been etched into a spunky bob. She cared immensely for her nails, hair, skin – things she could still control. At the mall we leaned over counters, examining expensive products made in France, the sales reps daubing Ma's neck with regenerating creams and wonder gels. 'Guess how old I am?' she'd say. 'Ma'am, they should get you to endorse their product,' one of them said, and Ma loved it. Threw back her choppy little head and laughed. Even her laugh was changed, less guarded. Now she boomed. 'Yes, yes. Me the fashion model.'

The last time she visited she complained I was becoming a hoarder. 'Typically American,' she scolded. 'All this stuff you don't need.'

We spent a morning in the attic going through boxes. There were things I'd brought with me from India over the years – brass animals, bird feathers, report cards, a doll with a key in its back that had once been able to cry. Ma sat cross-legged on the floor, swatting away cobwebs, her elbows deep in my childhood. 'Look at this,' she said, opening a box of clothes. 'Oh, Gracey, remember these?'

Before I left home for college, Ma had taken me to the Anglo-Indian tailor in Kodai, Ms Bridget, whose workroom was part of a house she shared with her sisters. There were two mannequins in Valentinoesque lace outfits standing by the window and dated *Vogue* magazines stacked in a corner. For Kodai, it was impossibly glamorous. 'Sturdy girl,' Ms Bridget had said approvingly, as she took my measurements. She herself was a bird – thin-boned, blue-veined. 'These will be just lovely on you,' she promised.

Walking home, Ma pronounced, 'Never married. The famous Wilson sisters. So beautiful when they were young. All spinsters. One of them went off to be the mistress of a Tamil film star in Madras and had a bastard child and all, but these three have always lived together.'

And now here was this box of Bridget Wilson's clothes. All those pintucks and dropped waists. So many blouses and bubble skirts in shades of unflattering salmon. The purple jacket with padded shoulders I'd adored so much. Within months of living in America I had been forced to buy oversized jeans and T-shirts, but I kept these clothes out of loyalty, out of a misplaced sense of the glamour I expected college life to have.

'I suppose you'd better throw them away,' Ma said, sifting through the piles. 'You were so excited about them when they were ready. And I was excited for you.'

'I can't bear to look at them now,' I said. 'It reminds me of everything I've lost.'

'What have you ever lost? You know nothing about loss,' Ma said, struggling to stand, using one hand to lever herself up.

It began to rain. The sound of water slapping against the windows, softly first, then with a vengeance. Ma fussed with her fingers, examining her hands as if all the golden light that had just been in the room had slipped through them.

'What's the matter?' I asked. She shook her head. 'It's nothing. I'm tired.'

'Let's go, then,' I said, leading her towards the staircase. I watched her body negotiate the stairs, step by step, shoulders slumped as though she were cold. My fingers gripping either side of her neck.

Downstairs, the sitting room looked somnolent, hushed. Blake had left his coffee cup on the table near the television remote, and a note in the bowl of apples – *Home early tonight. Let's do Thai.*

Ma settled herself in the La-Z-Boy, legs spread, ungainly. 'Bring me something to eat please, kanna.'

I made chilli-cheese toasts and tea and brought it out on a tray. We sat together and watched the day grow dark. 'It's the most difficult thing to be a mother,' Ma said, chewing sloppily on the toast. 'You're right to resist if it isn't what you want.'

'I feel bad for Blake. This is one of those things that could divide us.'

'There are always things waiting to divide a marriage.'

'Do you ever miss Papi?'

'It's really not important.'

'How can you say that?'

'I mean exactly that. Whether I think of him or miss him or wish things had gone differently, we are where we are now, and it's better this way.' After a while she said 'Look at your garden. Your father would have loved it.'

I think about that now, how we always talked about Papi as though he were dead, even though Ma was the first to go. I think about Lucia and I living the way we do now. How we, too, are spinster sisters.

24

Blake arrives early one July morning. The neighbours are burning rubbish again, so the sky is the colour of lead. It has been three years since we last saw each other, but there is nothing surprising about the way he steps out of the taxi and says, 'Hey.' He looks thinner. The hair on his head meagre, clinging valiantly. Arms and legs whittled into sharp objects.

'Grace,' he says, those familiar lips askew. I go to him and put my face in his chest.

Kadar, my regular taxi guy, inspects the garden while Blake sorts through notes in his wallet. 'I brought you a curry-leaf plant,' Kadar says. 'You should put it here,' he points to a space in the garden bed.

He deposits the sapling in the mud and walks over to us. The dogs are at his ankles, licking and whimpering. Bagheera fat with new life. Raja, Golly and Dimple, pink-tongued, exuberant. He slaps them softly on their heads.

'What happened to all your other dogs?'

'They died. The villagers poisoned some of them and all the puppies got sick and died.'

Kadar's face closes momentarily. He makes a click-clicking noise with his tongue, which is meant to express the inexpressible. He moves on to another subject. 'Sir was full of tension for the journey, but I did what you said and drove slowly.'

After he leaves, Blake and I stand in front of the house, looking at each other. Mallika tries to take his suitcase and the duty-free bags inside, but Blake tells her in Tamil, 'No, no, I'll do it.' His accent is terrible, but her eyes widen when she hears him speak, and her mouth opens into a laugh. 'But how?' she asks, shaking her head. I tell her we are old friends from Kodaikanal. That he learned Tamil in school.

Blake stares at the house, the blue shutters. 'What a place this is. I'd imagined something more rustic. This is like a palace.'

Lucia wanders out to take a look. She's wearing a Bon Jovi T-shirt and a frilly tutu skirt. Her hair is loose around her neck the way she likes it these days. Her glasses are smeared with dirt.

Blake lifts a hand. 'Hey!'

She stares at him, pirouettes, retreats inside.

We've been different together after the poisoning and the distemper. The trip to Kodai helped, but I think both Lucia and I believed that when we returned, all our dogs would be magically restored. I do my duties of feeding, bathing, dressing, but I no longer reach for her hand at the dining table so she can give my fingers a squeeze. Our walks are desultory. After fifteen minutes, just as we approach the ashram arches, she presses her knees and says, 'Legs are broken down,' and demands we turn around.

Blake sleeps in the room downstairs. He wakes at six and goes running. I keep staring at his feet. We are always barefoot. In the house, on the beach. It's as if I've only just noticed that he has the most beautiful toes. Long, elegant, unmarred by hairs. When he sits in the cane chair reading, one leg crossed over the other, his toes open and spread like the swish of a shapely fan.

I consider what it might mean to fall in love with him again even though I've never believed in the return journey.

We sit out every evening after dinner. Lucia lies inside on the sofa watching *Tom and Jerry* on my iPad. We drink Cuba Libres or small sharp shots of Patrón. I try to explain what it means to live two lives, to inhabit two different spaces. 'It's genetic. My parents did it. I do it too. Except I think I'm being more open about it.'

'What will you do?'

He asks the question everyone eventually asks.

There are evenings here when you can't believe you're of this world. Everything is silent except for the sea's measured hush. Stars hang low. The moon is always rising. You think of the city far away – its harsh lights, its sodden ambitions. You feel excluded from everything that is alive.

He had written to announce his arrival. It hadn't been a request. *I miss India. I have meetings in Delhi about a waste-management project, which could be an exciting develop-ment, and afterwards, I'll go to Kodai, do a few lectures at the school and reconnect with some people. I land in Chennai on the 15th. Let me know if you could organise a cab for me, and if there's anything you need from here.*

'It makes you dizzy, doesn't it?' he said, when he first arrived. 'I had forgotten what it's about. The complete mania of it. It gets in your blood. Wakes you up. Kicks you in the balls.'

'It's why we stay here. Far away from all that.'

We drive to Pondicherry to buy supplies. Lucia sits in front with me, Blake in the back at the window, pointing things out uselessly. 'Look, a kingfisher!' he cries, before we get to the front gate. Salt flats, canals, women bent over digging around for things, leggy palmyras with parched hair. Look, he keeps saying. Schoolgirls in maroon with white ribbons. Bright yellow trucks piled high with green bananas wrapped in leaves that flap wildly in the wind like can-can skirts. Tiny village after tiny village manacled to the road, spilling out their people, goats, meagre vegetables.

At lunch, Blake looks tired and exhilarated. 'It's like being away for a very long time and realising that your mother and father, your sister, your childhood house, all of it still exists, alive, preserved. They've been waiting for you, wondering where you've been gone so long. It's so welcoming. You feel safe in the world again.'

'Did you notice there wasn't a single rubbish bin on that road for an hour? Those pretty little villages are going to be drowning in their own shit soon. You should think of setting up shop here.'

'I feel like I never appreciated it when we lived here. I was afraid for some reason. It felt insurmountable, a place like this. The problems. But I see things differently now.'

'Give yourself a few weeks.'

We make love that night. I crawl into bed with him. His body feels like a stranger's. He isn't surprised to see me. Drags me to him as though he's been waiting. I touch the muscles in his back, the soft flesh around his hips. We move slowly, enfolding, stroking. It is all wonder. He is above me, holding me tightly, our knees touching and rolling. I make noises I haven't made in a long time. Deep, unabashed.

Afterwards I stay there with him. A cool breeze from the sea blows in through the window grilles. A nightjar makes its chirr-chirr noise.

In the morning, I watch as he sleeps. I want to squirrel away parts of him. The bones in his cheeks, the eyes, the two small hollows at the base of his back. Those strong prosciutto thighs.

After breakfast we change into bathing suits. Blake sets up the umbrella. The dogs scamper around for a few minutes, dipping their paws into the waves before running back to the house to stretch their bellies out on cool floors. Lucia fixes herself into battalion position, bum deep in mud. Blake sits beside her. The waves come. I watch in astonishment. The ever-readiness of them. The way they come and come, rolling forever.

As a child I used to think the sea had a wall. The idea that it could be limitless was unfathomable. I dreamed of swimming powerfully all the way to that wall, touching the smooth tile of it, and swimming back. I was scared of sharks and other sea beasts, but I knew it was possible. When floods came, when the sea raged, I wanted to say, 'But if you could only keep going, you'll touch a wall.'

Blake leaves Lucia to join me in the shade. 'She's beautiful,' he says. We look at her together. This large child with inviolable arms and legs. She turns to look at us. All teeth. Her mouth spread wide with joy. The waves keep hitting her, pulling her out of her trench. 'Get back, Lucy,' I warn.

A huge wave unfastens her. She tumbles forward, and for a second she is lost. Blake is already in the water, reaching for her. He's taken hold of her wrist and is pulling her up out of a tornado of spume. She is snorting, giggling, wiping the sand from her eyes. 'Again,' she says, 'again.'

'It's not a game,' I yell. 'You're too far out. Blake, bring her in.'

He convinces her to sit with him closer to the shore. I look at them sitting side by side, fingers laced together.

Days pass by, lazy, unhurried. In the afternoons when everything is too warm we go into our rooms and lie under fans. The dogs find spots near the sprinklers in the garden where the ground is cool and wet. They lie curled like abalones, nose to paws.

I keep hearing Ma. It's as if she's down by the gate, locked outside, wandering around in a state of dementia, shouting. She's like that woman Blake and I once saw in Charlotte, who asked us if we were running out of people. Lost, confused, tapping at car windows, grimacing. I hear her all the time. 'Have you never lost anyone, then?' But it's Ma's voice. Soft, then urgent. She's always calling my name. I run out on the terrace, scalding the undersides of my feet, peering over the ledge, and of course, it's nothing – only the casuarinas, their windswept topiaries petrified into a kind of silence. The sea murmuring.

We drink tea with biscuits at four. The dogs wait patiently for their treats. When they hear the crackle of the Milk Bikis packet they start drooling. I pop creamy rectangles into their hungry mouths. 'Those are going to rot their teeth, don't you know?' Blake says. 'Don't you ever feel suffocated?' he asks.

'Sometimes I feel I can't breathe. It's all too much. Too hard. Then she'll do something inexplicable. She'll come over and squeeze my hand. She'll look at me and start laughing, really laughing, as though I were tickling her. Other times she's lost to me. She's in a place I can't know.

And it isn't sad so much, except I wonder what it's about. I can't explain it, but sometimes it feels to me that her knowledge is greater, grander than mine could ever be.'

'I don't mean by Lucia. I mean, don't you feel suffocated being here all the time? It's like a prison in a way. A beautiful prison.'

'Can you believe my mother did this? Bought this place. Kept this secret. Kept so many secrets?'

'You're stuck, Grace. You keep tracing everything back to them, but here you are. Is this what you really want to be doing? Is this the best you can do?'

'I feel I'm just beginning to understand things.'

'I think you've always known.'

We get stoned one evening and watch *The Sound of Music* in Blake's room. Lucia watches with us too.

'I haven't smoked since we were kids in Kodai,' Blake says. 'It's terrific.'

We are lying on his bed. Lucia in the far corner. Blake and I squashed up on the other half.

I sing all the songs. Loudly, with conviction. Raindrops on roses and the hills are alive. 'Isn't Julie Andrews' hair ridiculous?' I say. 'And honestly, the baroness is hot. Christopher Plummer is hot. Julie is just … it's not convincing, is it?'

Lucia is sitting upright with her legs spread in front of her. All the hankies and socks in a pile between them. She's swishing one sock around in her hand and she's singing her own song – louder and stronger than mine. She's moving forwards and backwards like a seesaw, droning.

'Do you believe in reincarnation?' Blake asks.

'I like the idea of it, but no, not really.'

'I think your sister is a prophet.'

I giggle. 'No more weed for you.'

'No, really. Look at her. There isn't a line on that face. Nothing needs to be explained if you can understand the body. See the way she moves. She's saying things all the time. Of course she understands everything. You don't have to explain anything to her. She understands.'

'Try that when we're out of Coca-Cola. She shouts like a freaking banshee for hours.'

'You've changed so much.'

'How do you mean?'

'You used to be a woman who needed stuff. You loved things. You had a shelf of toiletries. Now you're a woman who can travel with a toothbrush. It rarely works that way. Usually you start off with the toothbrush and get into accumulation. You're finding things out.'

There's a comfort in having known someone so long. All the shared bedrock of memories. We talk about the past as if it were a country we could return to any time we wanted. We dredge up moments. Sitting in his parents' house on Observatory Road in front of a fire. Molly asking Blake to lay down forks and plates for dinner, and Blake complaining that he's tired. Molly, looking at me, putting on her best Italian-American accent, 'My son, he has problems, eh? He was born tired.' All of us laughing. And later, after the table has been cleared, sitting against those uphol-stered chairs – Tom, Molly, Blake and I playing Scrabble. So, this is also family, I'd thought. We seem to have moved from house to house as easily as flies, and here we are, sitting in this house by the sea, chewing on olives, the flesh around their pitted hearts.

'What about Misrak?' Blake asks. 'Do you still keep up with her?'

'We're terrible communicators. We talk maybe once a year on the phone but it's always this hour-long conversation, rushing to say everything, and then we feel caught up and can move on with our lives. But I miss the every-dayness of having a friend nearby. Someone you can have coffee with, someone you can go out with.'

'And this man you're seeing?'

'That's finished now.'

'That's too bad.'

'I hadn't expected it to last.'

'The thing is,' Blake says, 'I've met someone too.'

He dismantles everything. He's telling me about her. She's an architect. English with American ancestry. Emma. Loves Bauhaus and the Brutalists. Keeps parrots. Grew up on a farm in Hereford. I'm listening to him and it's as if I'm travelling far from every place we've just visited. All those houses and fields, all those roads we just walked with our palms sticking together. Everything I had once wanted to move away from but now long to hold close. That girl I was getting to know again, she has vanished, leaving me only with this life, the one where I live alone with my sister, a pack of dogs and the wilderness.

'Stop talking,' I say. 'Please.'

But he keeps going, because he's earned the right to speak.

A sudden vision of the future. I am going to be one of those women who is alone. In her car, in restaurants, in the rooms of this house, waiting for a sign from the world. A telephone call. A letter. Nothing will come.

'We'll always know each other, Grace. We'll always be in each other's lives.'

'No we won't. You'll fall through. One day I won't remember your face.'

'That's crazy, come on.'

'What was the point of all this?' I say, my hands moving incoherently. 'Why come back? Why not send me a Dear Grace letter? I'm fucking used to those, you know.'

'I wanted to see you. I wanted to see the life you were living and know it, so that when we write and speak to each other I can imagine it.'

'Now you know. Good.'

'I missed you so much, I missed our life, but three years, I mean, you gave no sign you wanted to return. Life pushed me on.'

'I suppose she's dying to have children.'

'We've talked about it, yes.'

I looked at him and he was a stranger again. The days we'd just spent together were already beginning to crack and slip through the windows. That body I'd once known and had been relearning. Those toes. 'You should have said something earlier.'

'I tried. I did try. I'm sorry.'

Kadar comes to pick him up the next afternoon. He has brought a champaca tree.

'Where will you put it?' he asks.

There is none of the jubilation of the arrival. The dogs are out somewhere on the beach. Lucia is on the floor of the sitting room, flapping away with her socks. 'I'll put it in front of the house, so I can look at the flowers while I'm drinking tea.'

'No no,' Kadar says nervously, 'the sea air will kill it. Put it somewhere behind the house.'

Mallika and I stand at the steps and wave goodbye. Clutched in the centre of her palm are two 500-rupee notes, slipped to her by Blake as he was leaving. 'Nice boy,' she says, as the taxi disappears around the corner.

I go upstairs and wait for it, but the grief is lying coiled tight under my skin. It will roll out in waves. It will come from that faraway sea wall and hit me in the face when I've stopped expecting it.

I plant the champaca in front of the house. I want to see if it will survive. If it will bring forth flowers of salt.

25

Lucia wants to wear a *ghagra choli* for the new temple's inauguration. It is one of those bejewelled things she brought with her from the Sneha Centre – red velvet with gold sequins on the skirt, worn with great aplomb for Diwali and Christmas shows. Mallika has brought frangipani flowers from the trees. She makes a crown and places it gently on Lucy's head, saying, 'Now you're looking super.' Mallika herself is in a new sari – bright pink with gold checks – and a big red *pottu* in the middle of her head. Only I look like a faded nun in my beige salwar kameez.

Valluvan had said there would be an hour-long Carnatic concert followed by prayers, speeches and food. I'd hoped to time our entry towards the end of the concert, but of course, nothing is ever punctual, so they are still setting up the *shamiana* when we arrive. The musicians and the priest are sitting around listlessly drinking coffee from plastic cups. Six of Valluvan's men immediately guide us towards the row of chairs in front of the makeshift stage. We are chief guests of sorts, so there is no escaping the show. Men are fiddling with the wires of the speakers strung up on poles, which make menacing squeaking sounds. I think of Papi and stifle a laugh.

Mallika doesn't sit with us. She joins the throng of village women who are organising food behind the temple.

Only Lucia and I have nothing to do except hold cold glass bottles of Coca-Cola. I would have preferred a fresh coconut water, but these were brought over so ceremoniously, it was impossible to make a different request.

I had seen Valluvan a few times in the past month about the upcoming elections. 'You realise I don't work?' I told him. 'I have no regular income coming in. Whatever I have is invested in such a way that it has to sustain me for the rest of my life.' We agreed on half the amount he initially asked for. He was good-natured about it, although I don't think he believed me.

At one point there had been a plan to make his wife Nila stand for elections because of the 33 per cent reservation quota for women in the Panchayat system. It was a common practice. The wife gets in on the quota, the husband rules. But they had not thought of it early enough and all the paperwork had already been filed. So there were posters of Valluvan all over the place – smiling widely, giving the thumbs-up sign, and next to him – the leader of the party – an aged poet in dark goggles on a throne with a saffron shawl around his neck. Between them was the party's symbol, the rising sun, even though for some years now, the sun had been squashed by the current party in power.

Nila finds us. She is with her three daughters, and they have cut through the crowd like queens. 'Where's Lenin?' I ask. 'Playing all the time,' she says, making a face. The girls are told to sit with me. They have ribbons in their plaits and they wear glittery long skirts and tops. Coloured glass bangles make clinking noises all along their wrists. 'Hi Lucy-akka,' they say, patting her thigh again and again, till Lucy is forced to acknowledge them. She smiles and squeezes each of their fingers in turn and then returns to swishing the one sock I'd allowed her to bring. The girls have always been fascinated by Lucia. 'What's wrong with her?' they used to ask. Between Mallika and I, we tried explaining, but they didn't seem to understand, as they'd never seen anyone like her. Now they are protective of her, and when other village children come up to Lucy and stare, they call them rowdies and swat them away.

Midway through the speeches I kick off my sandals and bury my feet in the sand. The new temple is multicoloured and bright, its *gopuram* rising like tiers of cake into the trees. The sea lies a few hundred feet to the east. We cannot hear it because the speakers billow out in every direction, but it sends a sweet breeze down the long alley that connects us.

I have forgotten what it was like to be in love. To be in lust. To have my body filled in some way with desire. I was sixteen when I kissed the Bernardi brothers in Italy. Nonna Rosa, Ma and I would close all the windows and sit in the kitchen listening to Gino Bernardi playing Bach suites on his violoncello next door. It was the saddest, deepest music I'd heard in all my life. And even though Gino was a weedy, pretentious kid who wore bow ties and orthotic devices for his flat feet, which went smack smack smack as he walked up the stairs, I wondered what it would be like to kiss him. When we finally kissed – on Gino's bed, under a picture of his idol, Jacqueline du Pré, I had been disappointed. The kiss was startling, smelly, moist. It had none of the beauty of his music. I couldn't get past the halitosis, the awkward tongue. It was not the melting in the loins I'd hoped for, but I still listened to him play and kept up with the bedside kisses.

And then one day, Gino's older brother, Agostino, ambushed me at the gelateria. Agostino, who didn't speak much English, who led me with his rough hands to the smoky billiards hall in Arcugnano, where we drank beer with his friends and laughed, even though I had no idea what they were saying. Something was happening with Agostino, something mysterious and terrible, and when he took me behind the billiards hall afterwards to grab my neck like a brute and kiss me, there was no clash of teeth and tongue, just a warm smoothness, the start of a hurricane.

It was the summer of 1989 and I grew thin with worry despite Nonna heaping my plate with extra pasta. All the nervous energy ate into my bones. My parents had fallen into their usual state of heaviness. Nonno and Nonna slept like two ancient dogs, emerging only for meals. The June days, hot and mortifying, descended over Vicenza. Everything radiated guilt – the trees, the glass in the windows, the brooding clouds. Wherever Agostino was, I went. His broad shoulders and worn-out leather jacket, his stupid mouth, which had nothing genius to say, but did funny things to my insides. I have forgotten what those Bernardi brothers looked like, and I can't remember what the kisses felt like either. That bursting-out-of-your-skin feeling I had when I was sixteen has disappeared like a bird that once lived but has left no trace of itself.

Around us are fishermen, their wives and children, but also, small-town electrical engineers, plumbers and day labourers. There appears to be an informal segregation of the sexes. Except for Lucia and I, and a few grandmothers who have been parked in the audience, the chairs are mostly occupied by men. The women hold the periphery.

Children move seamlessly between. It is almost nine by the time we eat. Valluvan and Nila's girls watch Lucia while I get a plate of food from the tables set up outside. Halogen lights have been fixed to poles and coloured fairy lights hang from the trees. Tamil film songs thump mercilessly into the night. I feel lightheaded, dehydrated probably, but also, that wave of, What am I doing here? It is a feeling of displacement so strong, for a second, I must ask myself, Who am I? And what have I to do with these people?

I cannot imagine the security of being born in a place and knowing it to be mine. To think of ancestors whom I resemble, who knew this land, its language, its people. There must be such confidence in this existence, this knowledge that everything you have lived has been lived before by your parents and their parents. All my life I have stood outside, like my father, like my mother, standing behind glass, looking in. With Lucia, it's more pronounced – that feeling of not belonging. On days like this it overwhelms me.

'Akka, thanks for your contribution,' Nila says, at the food counter.

'Well, it's our temple,' I say. 'We are part of the village, so we are happy to contribute.'

It is not what I believe, but what I parrot anyway. I would have preferred to have used that money to educate children, or to hire someone to clear the giant mountain of rubbish that is accumulating as we speak from all the plastic cups and plates that will clog up the backwaters. But I had not been given a choice. Valluvan's men had come smiling with their request, and when I tried bargaining with them, they continued to smile but held their ground. In the end, I capitulated and gave them what they wanted.

'No, no, not the money you gave for the temple. I'm talking about my husband's election campaign. Unfortunately, we're still lacking some funds. We need a proper security team and an accountant. This is also for our village's benefit.'

I smile at Nila. The jewelled pin in her nose gleams. She is a handsome woman. I had seen her mostly at home, in a kaftan or a hurriedly tied sari. Today there is none of that sloppiness. She is in a crisp blue *kancheevaram*, face powdered, hair combed into an immaculate bun.

'It is out of my reach, Nila. You know I must look after my sister. And her old school has many poor girls whose families cannot support them, so I pay a lot. But I cannot be paying all the time, no? Maybe I should marry a nice rich man?' I say, laughing, hoping to steer the conversation.

'You are already married, isn't it? You should have children of your own,' Nila says, 'before it's too late.'

It is past midnight when Lucia, Mallika and I walk back home. The celebrations will continue for a few more hours. The path is dark and it has turned cold. I point the torchlight of my phone ahead, and Mallika beats a stick on the ground as we walk, in case there are snakes along the path. We are so rarely outside the house at night that it feels dangerous, this journey home. Only once, we had gone out to the beach on a full-moon night. The dogs and Lucia were both confused. I had packed a flask of tea and sandwiches. We had been sitting on the picnic mat for fifteen minutes when we heard sounds coming from the southern end of the beach. There was a light moving towards us and a man's voice, shouting. The dogs had barked, and the speed at which the light was moving unsettled me. I rushed Lucia back inside and, after bolting the doors, felt ashamed at my cowardice. It was probably just a crab hunter on his bicycle. He might have been calling out to someone he knew. But I hadn't wanted to encounter him.

Everything alters in the dark. It is one thing to be inside the house watching it, another to be standing outside. A motorbike putters towards us and slows down. I grip Lucia's hand tightly but she immediately shakes it away. The bike stops next to us. It is Mallika's half-sister's husband's cousin – the one who works as the head gardener at the ashram next door, who lost his young boy to fits. 'What are you doing walking alone like this?' he barks at Mallika. 'We were at the temple,' she says. 'Now we are going home.' The man's face is wide and angry, his eyes pop out like golf balls. 'Stupid bitch,' he says. 'That lady has a car so why didn't you drive there? Now is not the time to do all this. There are too many tensions. I'm just coming from Kadalur – there was a bunch of drunkards who wanted to come and make a noise here. All K. Alexander's men. This Valluvan thinks he's some kind of hero standing for elections, but he hasn't paid the right people.'

The man doesn't look at Lucia or me. All the force of his rage is concentrated on Mallika. 'Okay, okay, that's enough,' I tell him. 'We'll be fine.'

We walk away from him and turn into the gate. The house seems far away, but the dogs are running towards us, barking and shattering all the unease. Lucia starts to skip down the driveway, the heavy *ghagra choli* catching in the weeds, the frangipani crown long demolished. She's lifting her legs up and down, her sequinned skirt glinting in the torchlight. 'Wait,' I shout. 'Wait, Lucy!' But she refuses to hear. Up down, up down. She moves at the pace of a heartbeat. I watch the dogs circle her, running around and around in excitement. And it is girlhood, it is love, it is a word caught in my throat. Is that why they say my heart skipped a beat? Because before you can name it, you're breathing again.

26

What happens to old lovers? What must we do with them?

They line up in military fashion, in order of height and seniority. Blake, Dawit, Vik. To have lived this long and to have such paltry representation. Was there really no one else? No lone evening of love with a stranger? Are these the only faces I must recall when I'm swimming under-water, trying to bring it all back?

I've been living in seclusion ever since Blake left a month ago. The last conversation I had with Vik was at the start of the year in this café with its jungle of ferns. Here I am again, this time with Rohini. We face each other under a languid fan, stirring demerara sugar into our cappuccinos. I am gathering all the distances, all the grand vistas and low-lying ditches, wondering what happens to the days in between. What are they filled with? Life seems so waste-ful. I cannot account for much.

There are some memories that play repeatedly. The initial burn of desire with Vik. That first kiss. Leaning towards each other in the car, drinking of each other. I remember driving to the beach, listening to Nina Simone, laying my head down in his lap, watching the moon. I remember snatches of loving. But I don't remember the exact words. What did we say to each other? It's as if the rooms where these things happened still stand somewhere like an exhibition. They carry smells – salt, murk, rose petal – but the words are gone, even the actions are ghost actions. A caress. A crushing of limbs.

'Do old boyfriends always seem diminished to you?' Rohini asks.

'Not really. I'm the one who feels diminished. It's as if they've been released. As if I'd been the one holding them back in some way, stifling their potential. Blake is going to have a baby, you know. Finally, he's going to have a baby.'

'And Vik? Has he reached out?'

'A drunken text. One measly drunken text, saying, *Jaan, what have we done?* That's it.'

'You deserve better.'

Such a strange thing the body is. Sometimes you're living in the skin of it, you're inseparable. Then there are times you can't even hear one another. Everything is far. And there's dryness, such dryness. Is it about love, then? The body needing to be in a state of desire?

Rohini tucks a strand of hair behind her ear. I have thought of her disparagingly in the past, and I'm sorry for it now because I see she is not as cunning as I make her out to be. 'You'll find someone else,' she says.

'I wonder what the point is. But tell me, how do you survive marriage? Isn't there always the inevitability of decay?'

Rohini laughs. As always it is an unexpected sound. A gurgle. Those tiny pearl teeth flashing. That small pink tongue flickering, lizard-like. 'It comes down to a kind of duty, doesn't it? Everything is designed to wear us down, but we can't just abandon things when they become difficult.'

'But doesn't everything begin to drag?'

'It's about giving up or staying the course, that's how I look at it. You know, this morning I was thinking about this girl I knew in college. Beautiful thing with long beautiful hair. Brilliant as well, I mean she was a top-rank student. She hung herself from a ceiling fan in the college room. Everyone was so shocked. If someone like her was going to kill herself, what were we still doing alive? She always wore long skirts tucked into one corner of her waist so she looked like a flamenco dancer. I wrote a poem for her, and this morning on Facebook I saw that her boyfriend is now married and has a kid. His life has continued, and even though we're not really in touch, his presence is constantly validated. But for a moment I'd forgotten her name. I had to look for that old poem to remember her name. It's kind of unforgivable. Maybe living is about surviving, about being tenacious.'

'In this city?'

'Why not?'

'Look at these people. I feel most of them are here because they can't be anywhere else.'

'Maybe it's what you feel about your own situation.'

'Maybe.'

That night I get stoned and spend hours waving a mosquito bat in the air trying to kill monsters. I'm wearing a dress that normally makes me feel sexy, but something doesn't sit right. Either I've put on weight or the muscles in my stomach aren't as strong as they used to be, because my back droops and it requires too great an effort to straighten myself.

It is Samir, Rohini, Praveen, the neighbour girl Tanya, and I. The last time I'd seen Tanya the resident Pomeranians had shredded her daughter's toy pig on the floor, and she'd had to sweep the snivelling child up against her hip and storm out. She had been a heavy presence that evening. The disappearance of the father of her child had absorbed her every disappointment, and it seemed as if she couldn't get beyond this beseeching – *look what has happened to me*. She has advanced since then. The magic of Praveen's nocturnal visits, perhaps, or simply the understanding that life with that disappeared man would have been unbearable.

'You look well,' I tell her.

She is in an ikat jumpsuit, large silver anklets gleaming from under the cowl pants, breasts wide and settled, resembling the happy stupor of Loulou and Leela, brushed and fed, occupying two ends of the divan like bolster cushions.

'Life is good,' she says, stroking one elbow continuously.

Is it always so obvious when a woman decides to take a lover? Something changes, even though the body's dimensions remain the same. The way she holds herself, stakes her place.

'My mother is visiting so I'm getting some help with Mitali. I've rediscovered my sexual organs. Life is good.'

The bar room is an air-conditioned alcove with glass doors, old-fashioned rosewood furniture and tall, gleaming paper lamps. I kick my shoes off and enjoy the softness of the rug underfoot. There is an easy camaraderie to this alchemy tonight, and in the exuberance, Praveen suggests we make a master plan to take over administration of the city.

'I'll be in charge of public works,' he says. 'Grace – you take education. Samir, you're our chief minister. Ro, you take art and crafts. Tanya, what are you going to do? Want to take health?'

We pass the joint around and I propose that henceforth all children will be educated in matters of a practical nature. 'We'll take them camping. They must learn how to change car tyres, how to kill and cook the things they eat, everything, you know? Stuff that's actually useful.'

'Yeah, yeah,' Praveen says, 'that's it. And I propose that we microdose the water supply with LSD.'

'Hang on,' Tanya squawks. 'You got to pass that through my desk, buddy. I'm not sure that's a good thing for our citizens.'

'Are you kidding me? It's a known fact that LSD has curative powers. People with anxiety and depression. Dude, all those robotic people, they need a little injection.'

'As chief I'm going to step in,' Samir says. 'Recent studies have proved that while LSD in the short run triggers temporary psychosis, in the long term it increases optimism and openness. It's all about the serotonin receptors.'

'What bull!' Tanya shrieks.

'Why the fuck have I been given arts and crafts?' Rohini interjects.

It is joyful banter, one of those rare Madras nights when I feel entirely happy for existing. I can sit among these people with the knowledge that nothing I do is harming anyone else, that the only decision I need to make is when exactly I will need to get up and pee. There is no possibility of failure, and for these few hours, it is a kind of completeness.

'So, are the animals going to be drinking the same water?' Tanya is saying. 'I mean we're going to have a *Lord of the Flies* situation. Little camping children running around slitting pigs' throats and the poor piggies are going to be tripping out like crazy. It'll be anarchy. I can't allow it.'

'Fine. We microdose just once a week. Limited quantity, but steady. I'm telling you. It's what the people need. And the pigs.'

Rohini's cook has gone to her village for a wedding, so we decide to order food instead of making something ourselves. 'We're so freaking global now,' I say, scanning through food menus on my phone. 'Imagine doing this twenty years ago in this city. Forget about ordering food online, but sushi! Too much.'

'Why is the front of the body more shameful than the back?' Tanya says, suddenly. 'I know it's a weird question, but this morning I thought I saw someone in the opposite block of flats looking through to my bathroom window with a pair of binoculars, and the first thing I did was to show him my back. Why?'

The doorbell rings and all of us turn to look at it in dumb wonder. Have we progressed so much that food will appear just by thinking about it?

Rohini gets up to open the door and it is Vik. With him is a girl.

'We were passing by,' Vik says. 'You guys want to come? Golti's party, remember?'

They're standing at the doorway and Rohini is saying something to him that I can't hear. I march to the door. 'Hi,' I say. 'Oh, hey,' Vik says. The girl next to him is foreign, thin. She's in torn black jeans and a black tank top. Arms like letter openers – tapered, flat. The face is unimpressive. I've seen manhole covers more beautiful.

'Franny, this is Grace.'

'Hi,' she says, extending a sunburnt hand; her voice – car crunching over gravel. 'I'm Francesca.'

'So, no worries, we'll just head,' Vik says. The girl turns around and walks back towards the lift. 'Just hang on,' he says to her, 'I'll be with you in a second.'

He closes the front door gently behind him; Rohini disappears into the kitchen. 'I wanted to tell you myself. It's nothing serious, but I didn't want you to hear.'

'It's fine,' I say. I press the sides of my dress with both hands. 'I mean, you can do whatever you want.'

'Okay.' He inhales loudly and takes hold of my wrist with his hand. That leaf-like hand. 'Listen, are you okay?'

'I'm fine. You should probably go.' I turn away from him, back to the bar room.

They blink at me, four cows. 'All right, one of you can fucking say something,' I say.

Praveen is the first to speak. 'Miss G, it's not even worth talking about. I mean, that kid is clueless, right? He doesn't have the maturity you need. Like, I saw him a few weeks ago with this girl and I asked him, Where's she from, what's this about? and you know, he gives this sly smile and says how he met her in Hampi or whatever. So, okay, I go out with them one night, she's doing the usual Italian hippie thing, finding herself or whatever – lady can do some drugs, I can tell you – but she's messed up. That chick needs her chakras broken.'

'She's Italian, seriously?'

Tanya laughs. 'You know, when Mitali's dad resurfaced, every person I met started telling me about the Japanese art of broken things. I swear to God, everyone was going on about this *kintsugi* shit. They were like, you should think about it, Tanya, because the thing is more beautiful for having been broken or whatever. I could have strangled them all. I don't want a beautiful, broken, patched-together fucking thing. I want it whole. So I'm not going to say anything to you, except move it along.'

When the sushi arrives we sit at the table and eat from takeaway boxes. It's as if a season has passed. The dining room is warm and the dogs Loulou and Leela have followed us out but have chosen to lie by the threshold, where a conduit of cool air hits their fluffy faces. Later, after Praveen and Tanya have left, Rohini and I stand out on the balcony while Samir carries glasses to the kitchen.

'Sorry, I should have said something, warned you, but I thought it was just a thing,' she says.

'So it's not just a thing.'

'It's been a few weeks. Who knows what that boy thinks. I want to shake him.'

That night I lie on the fold-out couch and think of summers in Tranquebar, of things appearing to be what they are not. I see the house where Ma grew up – that squat, white, single-storey house on Queen Street, its low red-tiled roof and running veranda. The main room, where a portrait of Mahatma Gandhi hung alongside Jesus on the Cross, the three lime-green sofas facing the street like a firing squad, the arcades of wooden pillars, Grandpa's office, which was really his secret drinking room where his friends and him would drink rum from steel tumblers. The kitchens, the washing stones, the servants' quarters, the clothes lines and cowshed. All the servant girls around Grandma's feet peeling vegetables, grinding spices, pluck-ing chickens, drying rice, soaking lentils.

I remember Grandpa as he was in the photographs – shaped like a giant egg, pants hitched up to just underneath his impressive man boobs, walking regally down the street with his black umbrella, shooing off stray dogs, haggling with fishmongers and fruit-sellers. I see him sitting in his armchair quoting his hero, the father of the nation, 'I will let the winds from all corners blow freely through my house, but I refuse to be blown off my feet.'

Ma telling me on one of her spring visits to Charlotte, casually, 'He was a terrible husband. Jealous, petty. He used to beat Grandma if she smiled too sweetly at other men.' How hearing her talk made it sound like it was a story from someone else's life.

And how it happened when they began dying – the family breaking into small groups, the hushed courtyard. My mother's brothers selling the house and dividing the profits between them.

A year later, a tsunami would storm across the rocks and knock down half the houses in that town. It was like a recurring dream from childhood – a house by the sea that is lifted like a tree by its roots into the sky. I mourned for that house, went to stand again and again on the spot where my mother was born and where my grandparents had made a life, and I can still hear my grandfather rocking determinedly in his chair, challenging the winds, proclaiming how no one was ever going to blow him off his feet.

27

It's August and I feel a tiredness in my body. I want to lie down and forget about the city. I want something different. I drive slowly to the house. A cluster of brown birds scuttle off the path. The dogs run up the driveway to greet me, barking and howling. Bagheera's puppies are due soon. There is something majestic about her, even though she has grown so heavy and slow. After this round of birthing, we'll have to find a way to fix her.

The house looks silent, all the blue shutters closed. The dogs' dishes are scattered on the porch, empty of water. I sound the horn. 'Mallika!' I shout.

The garden hose is coiled in a heap on the lawn. 'Mallika!' I shout again.

I leave the groceries in the car and walk around the house to see if she's watering the trees along the stone path. I look through the French doors. Everything is hushed. The patio furniture has been pushed inside, the cushions heaped one on top of the other. 'Lucy,' I yell.

I walk around the house again, past the car, towards Mallika's little house. Everything is eerily neat. No vessels outside, no hanging clothes. The sand has been raked and there's no sign of a recent wood fire. There's a padlock on the door.

I run now, heart erratic, body warm and light. I stare at the wall of the bathroom downstairs. The shower area is open to the sky and it's where I always imagined an intruder could enter. All they'd need to do is jump the wall, and if the door to the bedroom wasn't locked, as it frequently wasn't, walk through. I lift my arms up against the wall and try jumping. It's not so easy to climb a wall without a ladder or someone's hands to push you over. I make hopeless movements and slump in the grass.

Raja, Dimple and Golly are around me, barking, excited. 'What's happened?' I say. 'Where is everyone?'

My mouth is dry and there's a bad smell coming from it. I want to lie on the ground and stay here. I think of who I can call and, suddenly, I'm overcome with tears. I feel there should be someone I can call. Someone who's doing this with me.

I get up and move towards the car, reach for the phone in my handbag and dial Mallika's number. Nothing. I get in and start the engine. The dogs begin to howl in confusion. I go back up the driveway, through the gate to Valluvan's house. I've never driven there before because I was always embarrassed to show them my car, but I don't know where I must go and what has happened.

There's no place to park so I stop the car a little ahead of the house, blocking the small tarmacked road. The door of Valluvan's house is open, as always. I stand at the threshold, lean my body in. 'Valluvan,' I say. 'Are you here?'

Lenin, the boy, appears. He is taller and there is a new mannishness to his limbs. 'Hi akka,' he says. 'Did you bring me chocolate?'

'No,' I say. 'Is your father here, or mother?'

His face closes. 'Amma,' he shouts, and runs out of the front door.

I hover there, not sure if I should go inside and wait, or keep watch here. Lenin is stroking the flanks of the car doors admiringly. He opens out the side mirror and smooths down his hair, juts his chin out and makes faces at his reflection.

'Nila,' I shout. 'Nila, are you here?'

Nila sees me at the door. Her hands are full of clothes. 'Where have you been?' she says, accusingly.

'What's happened?' I say. 'I don't understand what's happened.'

She drops the bundle of clothes on the floor and starts beating her forehead softly. Tears stream out as she begins to convulse. A noise starts coming from within her – a harsh, painful sound. No words that I can understand except for 'they are coming for us'.

'Who?' I say. 'What's happened? Where's Mallika? Where's Lucy?'

'How can you ask this?' she keeps saying.

I pick up the clothes and heap them on the two jute stools by the almirah.

'You,' she says, her body shaking slowly now, as if she were dizzy. 'You can leave whenever you want to, but what about me, what about my children?'

'Nila,' I say, shaking her. 'Tell me what it is. I don't understand anything.'

At seven I walk down the stone path to the beach with a torch. The dark comes so quickly here, turning the edge of day into something altered and treacherous.

'Golly, Golly!' I shout. I try whistling, but the noise coming from me is feeble, like the sound of wind slipping through the small crack of a window. She had disappeared after I left for Valluvan's house. Raja and Dimple follow alongside me, sometimes tearing ahead at an imaginary shape in the distance. I cry, a steady weep, and somehow this is comforting as I shine the torchlight across sand. The beach is deserted. I scan left and right. A bright orange moon is beginning to emerge from the sea.

Kavitha had taken three hours to drive from the city. 'Slow down,' she'd said, when I phoned her, frantic after speaking with Nila. 'You're like a horse going off the rails.'

Nila had given me the house key. 'Two days,' she said. 'I've been waiting two days for you to come and get the key. What you do is not right.' If she had been silent about her denunciations in the past, she was making the force of them clear now by repetition.

When Kavitha arrived we walked into the house together. Lucy's room had been emptied out. All her clothes and shoes, her retinue of friends – hankies, socks, and the newly added oven mitt – the tar shampoo for her dandruff, the silver anklets we had bought from the Kashmiri shop in Kodai, all had been taken away. How little the sum of her possessions, I thought. Only the soft toys remained in their usual corner, and I was ashamed, looking at the sad state of them.

I went to lie on my bed while Kavitha set about making a stew for dinner. I kept thinking of what Nila had said – *What you do is not right*. I had wanted to explain that I had tried to do something right.

'You came here and suddenly he starts thinking he's a great man. That he can make changes in our village with someone like you to support him. But you didn't support him, did you? So much money you're sitting on, holding on to it like some queen's cunt, but you're just a common whore, stingy bitch.'

'What are you saying?' I said, shocked, breathless.

Nila had laughed, imitating my disbelief. 'Oh, sorry, you didn't learn these Tamil words? You don't understand? No one taught you? Everyone is so nice to you all the time. Bowing and scratching at your fucking feet. As if you're some kind of saint because of your sister.'

'You think that's easy?' I shouted. 'You don't think what I do is hard?'

She laughed meanly. 'What do you know about hard? My husband lies in a hospital now. He might die. Then what will happen to me? How will I live?' She was adamant, shrieking, 'Everyone talks about accepting this, accepting that. Everything must be accepted. It's God's will. It's someone's will. As if we are nothing – mud – shit – I do not accept. You listen to me: I do not accept.'

'Where are the girls?' I asked.

Lenin had stalked back into the room. He looked worried. 'Amma,' he kept saying, but she turned to him wildly. 'Shut up! How many times I told you, now is not the time to talk. My daughters! Yes, what will happen to those girls now? They are at my mother's. They're not safe here.'

'I must find Lucy. You call me if you need anything.'

'Yes, yes,' she sneered. 'You are always so available.'

When I go downstairs, Praveen is standing with Kavitha by the kitchen island fixing martinis, plopping olives into long-stemmed glasses. 'Come here, darling,' he says, wrapping his arms around me, squeezing my ribs.

I feel like how I used to when Papi and Ma fought. It was always a kind of battering. After long arguments, after everything had been said and nothing could be taken back, one or the other would make a small touch, an advance. Usually Ma. And it always surprised me how that managed to restore things. But isn't everything broken? I wanted to ask. Haven't you shattered everything that you've taken so long to build? All the days of calm. Aren't you exhausted by each other?

The sun appears cauldron-like, and by nine in the morning the whole sky is milk-white with heat. The sea murmurs beneath and I can hear the sounds of a few catamarans puttering across the water. I look at the tops of the casuarina trees from bed. They are motionless, not a hint of breeze. There is clattering in the kitchen below. Kavitha, always an early riser, would have returned from a walk. She would have known to take the dogs with her. I wonder if Golly is back. I know I should shower, descend, begin, but my legs feel like axes – leaden, directionless.

I thought I heard Lucia shuffling down the corridor last night. She had been so excited about Bagheera's new babies. It had become a ritual – talking about the new pups, how many they'd be, what colour, what names. It was almost a way of getting back together.

I reach for my iPod, push the earphones into my ears. Jacqueline du Pré. Elgar's cello concerto. I know there will be emails from my lawyer Mr Sriram waiting. Praveen will want an extensive breakfast discussion about how to proceed. But I feel like a person dying or dead. I want to be alone.

A hand at my shoulder. 'Grace, wake up.'

Dried spit on my chin. 'What time is it?'

'Eleven. You should get up.'

Kavitha is pulling on the ropes of the blinds, allowing lashes of light to hit the floors.

'Sorry, I must have gone back to sleep. It was a rough night. Is Golly back?'

'Yes. She was on the patio this morning. I fed the dogs some rice and curd.'

'I feel wrecked.'

'I think you'll have to go and visit Valluvan at some point. Praveen will go with you. I'll talk to Sriram about what our options are legally.'

'Have you been able to speak to Teacher?'

'She's not taking my calls.'

'And Mallika. What's her story?'

'Nothing yet.'

There are two guards at the gates of the Sneha Centre. Men who wear uniforms, who are hired out by security companies on a part-time basis to lend a sense of propriety to establishments.

'Entry not allowed,' one of them says, in English.

Praveen is cajoling at first. 'Listen,' he says, 'we just want to make sure that her sister is okay, that she's here. We just need to go in and speak to Mrs Gayatri.'

'Madam is out of station,' the guard says. 'Nobody is allowed inside. If you try, we will call the police.'

Kavitha pushes Praveen aside and leans over the gates. 'Gayatri!' she shouts. 'Stop this nonsense, this is serious. At least, let us know she's here.'

The guards try to wrest her off the gates and Praveen is on them, punching wildly. People emerge from houses along the street. Some run into the fray, shouting with authority even though they cannot know what the matter is. Others stand and watch, shielding their eyes from the sun. Kavitha is on the phone talking to someone who knows the Inspector General. I start screaming, Lucy Lucy Lucy.

The teachers at the Sneha Centre file out, creating a barricade behind the guards. There are five of them — women who have committed their lives to looking after these children. Nothing like this can have happened here before, because their eyes gleam with drama. Two of them have been with Mrs Gayatri since the beginning. They have known Kavitha since before they were married, and now they have children who are almost ready to be married themselves, but still, they look at her as though she were a stranger and tell her they don't know where Lucy is.

'You mean you've lost her?' one of them says.

'If you have nothing to hide, then let us in,' Kavitha says. 'What is this behaviour? I don't understand.'

Finally Teacher barrels through the line. 'That's enough. What is your business here?'

'I want to know if you have Lucy,' I say. 'I just need to know she's okay.'

'So you can beat her, is it? So you can abandon her for days? You know that lady you keep to look after her disappears as soon as you're gone? She feeds her once and then goes and sees some fellow she has in the village. Poor child. Bathroom, everything, she has to do by herself, and she cannot manage. You know that. You think that lady feeds your precious dogs? You think she does anything the minute you go? You should have seen the state I found her in.'

'What are you saying?' I say. 'Mallika always speaks well of you. Why are you talking like this?'

'These children — can they say anything? Can they say that someone is abusing them, or taking advantage of them? How can you leave your house open there with your sister? And what? To go off and have fun in the city?'

'What proof do you have?' Kavitha says. 'This is just talk, come on.'

'Do you deny it?' Teacher says, looking at me.

'What?'

'Do you deny that you hit your sister? Did you not beat her, poor thing, when your dogs were poisoned and she was grieving? Did you?'

I tear up with all the shouting. Everyone looks at me, including Kavitha and Praveen. But I cannot speak. I cannot be in this place any more.

'That's what I thought,' Teacher says, turning away from us. 'Don't let them in.'

Days pass. All is subdued and hushed. The house feels different, larger somehow. I cannot remember how it used to feel when I lived here alone, before Lucia came to stay, but it did not feel like this.

Praveen and I drive to the government hospital in Cheyyur where Valluvan was taken after he was attacked. It had not been about land, as I had initially suspected. The perpetrators were from a neighbouring village. Valluvan had been speaking to their people, trying to get votes for the elections. We don't know whether there had been a failed dialogue where they asked him to back off and he disagreed, or whether they thought it would just be easier to maim the man, but we knew that there had been three of them and they had used fish hooks.

There are rows of chairs cemented into the floor of the hospital waiting area and all of them are full. One woman is talking dramatically, slapping her chest, knots in her hair, sari in disarray. It's some kind of plea for help. People sit around reading newspapers, playing games on their mobile phones, calmly ignoring her. The receptionist is wearing a burgundy sari and looks bored until Praveen goes up to her. He's a man used to getting things done.

We sit in a side corridor under a row of tube lights, examining the ceramic-tile floors with lines of dirt separating them. Two nurses are gossiping beside a man on a stretcher. A young boy with a mop and bucket walks past us barefoot.

Praveen is restless. He jogs his left leg up and down. I put a hand on his knee to settle him.

After an hour the receptionist comes over to us. 'Okay,' she says. 'Now you can go.'

Valluvan is in a room with another patient who is corpulent, turned over on one side, the great back of him shrouded in a green hospital blanket. Beside him Valluvan looks like a tiny relic. There's a stool beside his bed with a mobile phone and a photograph of Amma, the hugging saint.

He's covered in bandages — legs, arms, head. One eye is covered with a patch. There are stains of yellow through the bandages and whatever little we can see of his face is blue and bloated. The receptionist hovers behind us. 'I told you he's unconscious, but you wanted to see, so here. But you must go soon. Actually, this is not allowed.'

I walk up to Valluvan and peer into his face. I want to say something about how worried I am for him, for us, but I just pat the air around his arm lightly, too scared of touching him.

'Bloody thugs,' Praveen says, as we leave the hospital. 'This state is run by thugs and we are surrounded by thugs.'

'I just want to get out of here.'

'Three of them. I mean, they fucking sliced this guy and he's still alive.'

'It was just one extra day that I stayed,' I say. 'Just one extra day.'

We drive towards the city. The traffic moves with purpose. Outside, the flash of paddy fields through the window in quick succession. We pass under a canopy of wide-limbed trees, and the effect of the dappled light on the road is so beautiful, so incongruous, it feels like we've momentarily been transported somewhere else, to a country where gangs of men cannot set upon a man without fear of retribution. I feel a sense of confidence returning. Valluvan will live. Things will be put back to what they were. I do not need the freedom I imagine I need.

28

I occupy Papi's flat like a bird. I make multiple nests in different rooms. I need a space to sleep, a place to read, a nook by the window. I hear the heavy labour of his breathing wherever I am – guttural sounds. 'Grazia,' he'll call, but only when he needs me. He's lived with such staunch ideas about the limitations of responsibility. Now that his body is showing signs of diminishment, he wants to be sure to uphold those ideas.

'Get out of here,' he says in the mornings, after I've taken him breakfast and antibiotics. 'Get some air. You look like an animal in a cage.'

The streets of Venice are intolerable. I walk past glass-fronted shops, all in the business of selling mirages. Trinkets and masks. Rows and rows of pointless coloured glasses. There are a few treasures. A printer, close to Papi's apartment. His name is Gianni. He looks like he has travelled here from a different century. He spends his days with gargantuan, laborious, hand-printing machines. He was the last to learn the art from the Armenian Mekhitarists on the island of San Lazzaro. He still speaks of Venice as if it were the centre of the world. I glide through his shop touching the array of visiting cards and thank-you notes – the paper, creamy and thick, far too luxurious for the disposable times we live in. '*Guarda*,' he says, showing me the *ex libris* he made for Joseph Brodsky. It is an image of a cat reading a book. Gianni caresses the cat's coat.

There is a woman who makes shoes. Soft, kidskin boots in bright colours. I think of childhood stories – 'Puss in Boots', 'The Elves and the Shoemaker' – all those beauties could have come from this shop. They glow in windows – ankle boots, eighteenth-century-style slip-ons with short, sturdy heels, glamorous lace-ups trimmed with fur that sits at the widest part of the shank. I'd had no use for shoes in Paramankeni – just rubber slippers for the beach to protect against thorns, and a few pretty things for the city. The shoemaker sits in a chair, bent over her work, thread in her hands. I would like to go in and watch her, learn something of how she works. It feels ridiculous to have lived so long and learned nothing of a craft.

Venice is a kind of banishment. I take vaporettos to the islands. In Burano I point my phone at coloured buildings. They seem unreal – reds, blues, greens, yellows. A book I read mentions that the palazzos in Venice were once painted like this too. So much colour.

In Peggy Guggenheim's museum I wonder what I would have done if I'd been incredibly rich and eccentric. Would I have surrounded myself with staggering beauty? Would I have had sex unrepentantly with other women's husbands? And the dogs. I certainly would have had all those dogs.

The accident of birth. Papi and I have been talking. 'I don't think much of my parents now they are gone,' he says. 'But you feel it very much, cara, and you must move forward in your life.'

He doesn't understand my conundrum, doesn't see why I insist upon being stuck in my life. Even the fact that I am here taking care of him does not strike him as being ironic.

He will recover, but it is his first setback, and he's at an age where this signals a decline.

More and more he will need to rely on other people. 'It need not be you,' he says. 'That's what I'm trying to tell you. I have money. I'll get a nurse. And if I outlive my money, then I'm the problem of the state. Not you.'

'But what will have been the point? Why breed? Why have the structure of family? Why live together for years and years, bearing each other's inconsistencies, only to abandon them?'

Papi's fingers itch from inactivity. He's been forced to give up smoking but he still asks for his papers. He makes stacks of beautifully rolled cigarettes. 'Take them and distribute them on the streets,' he says, laughing.

I gather up the rollies and put them into Nonno Danilo's silver cigarette case. This too is an act of connection. The smooth age of it in my palm.

There's an afternoon when I eat lunch in Campo San Polo. It's one of the widest, sunniest campos in Venice, so it's always filled with children and dogs in the afternoons, and in winter they put in an ice-skating rink and around it there are stands selling sweets and glossy pink *zucchero filato*.

A family at the restaurant – American I think, drinking tall beers, smiling at their pizzas. Three boys, golden-haired, one of them with Down's. He is shorter than his brothers, squatter, and his mother has cut the crusts off his pizza. They are smiling, looking at the pigeons, enjoying the post-card of their family vacation. The parents are suntanned, the father perhaps a little too pink. He leans towards the boy, squeezes his hand. It undoes something in me. I have been keeping the story of Lucia to myself. Papi will not hear too much of it, so I must ration out bits and pieces until he signals that it is enough.

I walk up to the family. 'Excuse me, I'm so sorry for interrupting.'

The woman is in a striped long-sleeved T-shirt, her face an explosion of freckles. 'My sister is like this,' I say, and I look to the boy. 'She lives in India. I'm sorry for coming over. It's just I miss her, and I think she would like it very much here.'

The woman nods. 'This is Daniel,' she says. The other two sons don't get an introduction. Daniel smiles. He has widely spaced teeth and his eyes could be Lucia's eyes.

'Hello Daniel,' I say, and reach for his hand. He flips my hand over and chivalrously plants a kiss on it. 'How do you do?' he says, with flourish.

The parents gleam. It's obviously a thing he does, but the effect on people is always different.

I start crying. Silly crying, deluge crying. 'Sorry, sorry,' I say. They look at me, perplexed. I have momentarily broken the sanctity of their vacation. I hurry back to my table, pick up the bill that has been brought with the food, walk into the bar and pay at the counter. 'All okay?' the waiter asks. 'Yes, yes,' I stammer, 'I'm not feeling so good.'

Papi and I have philosophical arguments about happiness and suffering. He believes that both exist in equal measures of one another, refuses to be brought into any conversation that involves the word 'decency'. 'Morality is a false qualifier,' he tells me, 'it cannot have universal applications.' His cough has become less severe and the doctor has suggested taking short walks on days that aren't damp. He grants himself a cigarette a day. 'You would not have me living with no pleasures at all, Grazia?'

We stop at the café around the corner for *aperitivos* in the evening or coffee in the morning. Bangladeshi men shove roses in Papi's face and look at me in a manner that is both leering and sweet. 'She's my daughter,' Papi spits. 'Idiots, get away from here.'

He looks shrunken, his hands especially. He seemed so voluminous to me as a child, but now I see he has always been delicate in some ways. The eyelashes, the ears, the bony arch of his elbows. We walk arm in arm and I wonder what people looking at us might think. Whether we are from a far-off place? Whether we share the same blood? I catch sight of my reflection, at the lines around my mouth, which seem to have deepened over the last few months. I look exactly as I feel – a woman who is slipping out of the prime of her life.

'What will you do?' Papi asks.

That question again.

There are parts of the city I am getting to know. I understand the importance of narrow passages. I catch glimpses of secret gardens. One afternoon, in my old neighbourhood of San Giacomo dell'Orio, I notice Roberto, the mathematician from Ca' Foscari, heading for the bridge that goes towards the train station. 'Roberto,' I yell. 'Man with the keys!'

I feel a strange sense of relief that he recognises me. It is important somehow to be known by someone other than my father here. It makes me feel less alone. 'Come,' he says, 'let's sit somewhere.'

Later in the afternoon, we lie in a room that smells of cigarettes and basil. I lie under the blanket, while Roberto lies naked beside me. There's a smoothness about him that's unnerving. Barely any hair on his chest or arms. He's like an anorexic seal making sounds of pleasure as he slides towards me. We hold each other and I wonder when I can leave. Already the act has become something forgettable and sad.

Roberto insists on walking me to Papi's flat. 'So you will stay some time?' he asks.

'One more week.'

'Let's eat dinner soon,' he says. 'I know a wonderful fish place in the ghetto.'

I wave before turning to open the front door. I know we will not see each other again.

Kavitha is lifting the new puppies one by one towards the eye of her laptop. There are five of them – fat, fluffy things. Mostly black with tinges of white, except for one, who is completely white. 'I've called him Giorgio Armani,' she says. 'He's the coolest one.'

She's been staying at the house, looking after the dogs. Valluvan has just been released from the hospital. He has recovered, although he drags one foot around and there's a palimpsest of scars on his arms, back, legs. 'Tell her my wife was distraught. Tell her she must come back to the village, she must find a way to bring her sister back too.' This is the message he sends.

Kavitha has locked up her Madras home and brought the couple who used to look after it to stay in Mallika's house. They are middle-aged people unused to living so close to the sea. They complain there's nothing to do – no teashop, no market, no cinema. But she trusts them, so she gives them money to water the garden and wash the dishes, to lie in the heat of their room watching television the rest of the time.

Mallika has vanished. Nobody seems to know anything about it. At the Cheyyur police station where Kavitha went with Praveen to file a missing person's report, the constable had asked what their relationship to Mallika was. 'Any husband, children, parents?' he asked. 'There was a flair about him,' Kavitha tells me, 'the way he said, "A woman who has come from nowhere and disappeared into nowhere." He told us to forget about it, as if we'd been robbed on a bus, the likelihood of recovery so minuscule.'

Of Lucia I hear little. Kavitha has not managed to see her yet, but we know she is with Teacher at the Sneha Centre. There has been an exchange between lawyers. 'They're going on about you hitting her,' she says, 'and this thing of you leaving her for days, they are making a big deal out of that. But I think we can find a way to come to a settlement.'

I listen to her like I'm listening to a story that isn't mine. It feels distant – that place, that wilderness, Lucia. I stand in Papi's kitchen, the windows open to the sound of people walking below, pigeon wings.

'Don't worry,' Auntie Kavitha says. 'We'll sort it all out.'

Papi has gone to buy fish from the Rialto market. He's turning the key in the door and walking through, setting the bags down. 'Bye then, bye,' I say, quickly, slamming down the lid of the computer.

'You behave like a child of divorced parents,' Papi says, laughing. 'When Father comes in, get off the phone with Mother.'

'I am the child of divorced parents,' I say. 'I just know you have issues with her, so I don't want to get entangled in all that.'

'She was a good friend to your mother. Too good, perhaps.'

He never asks about the situation, isn't curious about the outcome of all these lives I've spoken about. There's a friend of his he wants me to meet. She's coming over for dinner. Her name is Marcella. He tells me nothing more except she can be a little grand.

Papi sets to work in the kitchen. He's a good cook, able to put together meals that are simple, but over which you can linger. Nothing like my hearty, one-pot dishes that made you want to immediately lie down. 'You make nothing well,' he complained when he'd been in bed with pneumonia. 'How is it possible that you learned nothing in the kitchen?'

Marcella arrives early and is dressed in that slapdash aristocratic way that Italian women of a certain generation have – elegant, but nothing too thought over. Slacks, a silk shirt, beads from an interesting country, impeccable shoes. Face clear of make-up except for a smear of coral lipstick. She has maintained herself well: there's a slight thickening around the waist and hips, but she keeps a straight back and when she looks at you, it is with a kind of hunger. I feel the mysterious need to be liked by her.

'Why did you leave America?' she asks. She listens sympathetically. 'Matrimony is such a bore, but oh, North Carolina,' she scowls. 'No, no. A person like you should really be in New York.'

When I tell her how I've come to hate cities, she smiles at me as though I were a child telling a lie.

I watch them sitting side by side across the table from me. Jack and Marcella. There's a warm octopus salad with fennel and potatoes, anchovies with parsley, a caprese salad, and gnocchi in cavolo nero sauce. For dessert Papi brings out a chocolate salami – beautifully dark and nutty. He looks pleased about the way Marcella eats. Her arms are long and white. One of them stretches across the bench she shares with Papi. 'You always feed me too much,' she coos. A mock complaint.

Afterwards, she stands by the window in a feline pose, blowing smoke circles away from us. She is a woman contained, nothing like the hysterical Italian female proto-type Papi was so fond of conjuring.

'This city was made for night,' Marcella says. 'We should go for a walk.'

We crowd over Papi, making sure he's warm enough to step out. He has the face of a victim – stoic in his accept-ance. Hat, scarf, coat. Marcella leads us over bridges and along small canals where boats are moored and bobbing in moonlight. There's always music coming from somewhere in the streets of Venice. We are in San Marco now, a place Papi and I hardly ever pass through because of the tour-ists. It is peaceful at this hour, even though every table is filled. Two competing quartets play on opposite ends of the square. People leaning back in their chairs have a look of deep satiation.

'Isn't it strange that it's never too much?' Marcella says. 'It's always a surprise.' We walk past the statue of the Lion of Venice, around the corner towards the Bridge of Sighs. Gondolieri are singing the usual songs, and the lights of San Giorgio gleam across the Grand Canal. Now we are back into secret passages. 'This place has the most divine hats,' Marcella says, turning to look at me. I'm trying to take note of the shop – a name, or a landmark, but it's hopeless. I'm lost. All the streets have started looking the same. Night closes in with a gradual September chill, our feet move noiselessly over cobblestones, and all of Venice feels like the inside of a cathedral, sacred and unreal. Here is a perfect scene – a cluster of trees, restaurant tables with red-and-white checked tablecloths, dogs curled at table legs waiting to go home. A man on a saxophone is playing 'Come Fly With Me'. Papi grabs Marcella by the waist and she emits a small cry, a pretence of not wanting to. But then they move away from me, slowly, in circles and with great care, as though a river were sleeping beneath them, as though they had lungs of glass.

29

These hours between countries are a kind of limbo. Timelessness and stupor, a place where everything stops and moves. I look through the aeroplane window and my nostrils imagine seaweed, decay. I see the fish shape of Venice below, and it is all clarity now. I understand her streets and bridges. There and there. I see now, that's how it all connects. This winter, when Papi sends me a photograph of the snow in Cannaregio, the avenue of bare trees, Marcella standing at the entrance of the Biennale in a red beret looking like one of Modigliani's women, I will be back at the beach, Lucia might be with me, our best days ahead of us — sun, dolphins, a legion of dogs.

I had sent an email to Vik before leaving, knowing I'd have a day of erasure, of travel, before expecting any kind of reply. *I think of Madras as a barren place*, I'd written. I wrote loftily of the man he might become, as if the great encounter of our love might transform him into something more than he could have been by himself. *I hope to still know you*, I might have written. Or a version of that. A future where we could come together and acknowledge one another, because to have given so much only to let it fall to the wayside seemed wasteful, a derelict approach to love.

There are other words in my handbag. Ma's letter. I had received it at Mr Sriram's office in Teynampet a few weeks after her death. I had taken a taxi there from my hotel. It was a warren of a place. A haphazard office in a ground-floor corner of a haphazard building. There was a reception area that smelled of old newspapers and stale *agarbathi* smoke. Slow-turning fans hung from the ceiling, and a few scattered administrators – women who seemed to have been unlucky at everything in life – sat at large pachydermal desks in front of typewriters. One of them led me to Mr Sriram's office, a coffin-shaped room with a file cabinet slung against one wall and a row of wispy plants by the window.

Mr Sriram did not sit at a desk. There was no room for one. He padded softly across the perimeter of the room like a dancer testing the length of the stage. 'Bring tea,' he said, to the secretary. 'And two chairs.'

We sat facing each other. Me staring into Mr Sriram's small, ruined face. Him holding Mother's letter, and perhaps feeling some of the messenger's burden. 'You have all our support,' he said.

I touched the cup and saucer lovingly. There was something poignant about the design of a small orange flower etched into the corner of a cheap china saucer. The gift of tea.

To see her handwriting on the envelope – the letters narrow and blue and upright. The same hand that had written to me when I was in America. Those first years before email. The thrill of reaching in my letter box, seeing those stamps, knowing that inside was a voice of a living person. *Dear Grace.* She always wrote the way she spoke, but this letter was different. She had taken time over it. She might have written several drafts but this is what I'm left with:

Nothing I say will make you understand this, so I can only plead forgiveness and ask you to read this through. If this comes at a point in your life when you are happy with your own family, in a place far away, then I hope you will make the time to know your sister, even in the slightest possible way. A visit, once a year. Some connection, whatever you can manage, because you are together in the world, bound by your father and I. I can hear you saying, It's impossible. I know, kanna. We never imagine the kind of decisions we have to make. There is no guide for such things except the body, the heart. And these are changeable things as you know. I was afraid. That is the truth. Your father was lost. When we heard the news, there was so little anyone could give us. Where should we go? What must we do? We were young, not that it's any excuse, but we were alone in the world together, and we could not decide. My instinct was to bring the baby home and care for it. I wanted to change our lives but your father thought it would flatten us. I heard him speaking to his brother on the phone. The baby is a Mongoloid, he said. He kept using that word even though I told him that's not what it's called. The baby isn't right, he said, it's got one extra chromosome, like Cousin Emilio. They'd had a cousin with Down syndrome when they were growing up. He'd stayed with the family and it had been diffi-cult. It embarrassed your father to think of having to raise a child like that. What about other children we might have? he said. How can we put them through this? We went to look for places that might help, and you should have seen them, Grace ... horror chambers. Children and grown-ups with nappies on because there weren't enough staff to toilet train them, children in straitjackets and, sometimes, chains. I told him to leave, to go back to Italy, that I would manage alone. Although I knew I would not manage alone. I thought I'd go back to Tranquebar, however difficult it would be, but I might have done it. Then I met Mrs Gayatri. She was teaching at the Clarke's School for the Blind at the time, but she wanted to start a centre for girls with disabilities. We drove out one day to see the plot of land she had bought. She needed money to build her centre. She said if we could help her with that, she would take Lucia, and it would be a way for us to continue our lives. I thought I wouldn't survive, that I would lie awake at night and everything would be broken. What I felt was a kind of relief. The kind of work Mrs Gayatri does requires a selflessness, and perhaps your father was right in recognising that neither of us would be capable of it. You are wondering why we stayed together, why we had you so many years later. And the answer is I do not know. I'm writing this in Pondicherry, looking out of my window, where I cannot see the sea but I can smell it. It was a kind of love we had. Not the best, not glorious, but there was deep peace in those days with your father. I know you will not remember it this way. But those outbursts were so few. When I think of our life, it was a cocoon, and we had you, our happiness. I wanted to tell you, many times. I tried. But it is difficult to rewrite the story of your life, especially when you have been telling it one way for so long. I wonder how you are now, if you feel my presence, if you believe in any of that. You should know that whatever you decide, no one will judge you, because in this you are not culpable. Live your life. Your father and I have made provisions so that Lucia can live her life, regardless of what you decide.

The letter had made me sick. Everything about it was cloying, desperate. I'd read it in the taxi to the Connemara. Auntie Kavitha had asked me to stay at her house but I had wanted the anonymity of a hotel. I didn't want her scratching around, inserting her ideas, because she'd been complicit too. It was only later, when Mr Sriram took me to Paramankeni to see the house – the rutted village road, the brick wall and the heavy wooden gate, a kingfisher flying in front of us, the blaze of its blue wings winking all the way down the driveway – that I understood Ma had made plans for an alternative future. That I might find my place in it.

We land in Madras to the usual scrum and rush. A darting-up of bodies to drag luggage from cabin bins. I want to stay in this place of resolve where everything is clear. 'Are you okay?' the flight attendant says, coming up to me after the plane has emptied. 'Do you need help?'

At immigration, people constantly jump queues trying to figure out which line is the fastest. A shift of gears. Outside – there it is. The heave.

Where's Kadar? 'Madam,' he shouts. He takes the bags off me, and I let him. 'Have you eaten?' he asks. Cheerful man. He's always asking about the state of my stomach. We stop at one of the roadside restaurants for idlis and filter coffee. 'Come and eat with me,' I say, but he shakes his head, 'I've finished.' He waits in the taxi, pushes the headrest back and plays the radio softly.

By now this road should be familiar to me, but I keep forgetting which village comes after which. There are always new scars of apartment buildings clawing into the sky. The sun is at my face, restrained, but as we move through the widened highway, past Mahabalipuram and continuing on towards Pondicherry, it ascends with great vigour, the sea beneath it a pitiful blue rag.

'Roll down the windows,' I say once we get to the turnoff, relishing the warm air rushing in. The canal gleams to our right, dunes and jagged palmyra, and beyond, stretching to the water, paddy fields, a shimmy of white egrets. A woman with her goats is crossing, stick raised in the air, voice shrill and menacing. 'Slow, slow,' I say, as we watch them pass. They move in a mass, one or two of them breaking free in a trot, the sound of their panicked goaty noises reverberating through the flock.

Is it fear? Something like it. It shoots up my body from my toes, and my eyes fill with tears, the way Lucia's used to. They fill and stop. This homecoming, all this uncertainty. The small houses in the village with their open doors, the *kolam* patterns in the mud outside them, bushes of jasmine, boys playing cricket, piles of brick and hay.

The boys stop their game and gather in a huddle as we pass. They are bare-chested, in shorts. They wave and holler. Further down the road, water is gushing uselessly out of a pipe, and there are new trenches on either side, freshly dug, but it's as if they've been abandoned, people having forgotten what they needed them for in the first place.

'Happy to come home?' Kadar asks. And I say, 'Yes, of course.'

There are new speed bumps in the road, tiny clumps of tar in groups of three. Kadar flies over the first set, and again I say, 'Slow, slow.' There are always things crossing a village road. Dogs, chickens, children. How to explain to Kadar that I want to take all these creatures home with me. Even the mean-spirited, superstitious adults. I want to belong to them, instead of this estrangement.

We stop at the gate and I open the car door. 'I'll get it,' I say. I'm wearing the wrong clothes, aeroplane clothes. Jeans and sports shoes and a hoodie. The air so sweet and warm. I heave the gate to one side, the blue paint peeling in places. The long grasses down the centre of the drive-way are unruly and parched. Kadar honks the horn twice. A signal to the dogs. As I climb back in and move towards the house, they start running towards us. Raja, Bagheera, Golly, Dimple and, flagging behind them, the new pups – racing madly, howling, tongues like pink sails trailing out of their heads. And so there is this, I am filled with it, a sweetness.

'It's not about thanking,' Kavitha says, but I insist it is. 'What would they have done without you? Papi or Ma. They were like children, completely clueless, and what would I have done without you?'

We are sitting on the veranda, watching the moon rise. The hush of sea. It's the most peaceful sound in the world. Womb noise. I'm still in a place of two places. Venice, Madras. In a day or two, all that will be forgotten and it will just be this – the heat, the dogs. But for now it's still in my body, that strange afternoon with Roberto in his professor's quarters, the midnight walk with Papi and Marcella.

'Papi is happy, you know? I haven't seen him happier. He says coming back to Italy was the best thing for him. He found a kind of peace again. He told me it was about finding a level of hypocrisy you could deal with.'

'And Lucia? What did he say about her?'

'He is unmoveable. He listens but offers no advice. He has not changed his mind about anything, and in a way, I suppose, it's a kind of relief. Imagine, if you were going to begin to feel guilt.'

The dogs are lying on the patio around us, bellies full, bodies stretched out like mats. 'The dogmatics,' I say, laughing. 'Look at them. The good life.'

Kavitha's face is lean and tanned. The lines around her eyes look more pronounced, but there is something fresher about her. 'The sea air has done you good,' I say. 'You look rejuvenated.'

'I feel close to her here,' she says.

'To Ma?'

'She was the most stubborn person I knew. We met at a yoga centre in Madras. Did you know that? She decided I would be her friend. She had that command with people. I don't know how she lost that. It's as though she got thwarted a few times and she just gave up. But being here in this place, I understand that she never truly gave up. She was just tired. It was your mother's idea to move to Kodai. Your father was so unhappy. He was talking of taking a job in Africa, of going back to Egypt where he had worked before. Your mother was terrified it would mean cutting all ties with Lucy. We stayed up one night talking about it and she kept saying, "It will be like being in exile. I can't allow him to do that to us."'

'She got her way.'

'She frequently did.'

After dinner we go upstairs and lie on the bed together. A small bat flies around in a frenzy until it finds its way out through the terrace doors. Kavitha lies on her side, facing me. She wears a robe tied loosely at the waist. A pedestal fan in the corner of the room moves its head slowly from side to side. I bring the sheets up to my chin. 'It's easy to grow tired,' I say. 'It's easy to give up.'

I wake intermittently, drink sips of water, tread over to the bathroom in the dark.

'You're flopping around like a sole fillet,' Kavitha complains. 'What time is it anyway?'

'Sorry. It must be the jet lag. I'm completely awake. I'll go read in the other room.'

I leave her and walk down the corridor to Lucia's bedroom. There is a smell of her. I can't say what it is — something powdery and musty. The room has been closed for a while. I open the side window. The stuffed toys arranged in a pyramid glare at me in the dark. I should burn those things.

I put the bedside lamp on, looking for something to read. There are a few children's books that I used to read to Lucia, but she soon tired of those. I lift the pillow so I can lean against the bed comfortably. Underneath the pillow there's a crumpled napkin, military green, made of rayon or something synthetic. Lucia must have stolen it from a restaurant. I think of her howling for it at the Sneha Centre, and Teacher looking at her without being able to help. 'Which one, kanna? Aren't they all here?' A night, a day, and maybe then she would have stopped with her noise. I squash the napkin in a ball and crush it in my palm. When Kavitha brings me tea in the morning, she finds me splayed out on my stomach with the lamp on, the napkin in my fist.

A few days later we drive to a village fifteen minutes away. There's a new roadside restaurant at the top of our street called Saravana Villas. A man in a ramshackle Mickey Mouse costume waves to cars speeding down the highway, trying to flag them down and direct them to the restaurant.

'Poor little shit,' Kavitha says. 'What a job.' She slows down as we pass by, and thrusts ten bucks into his paw. A group of men dressed in white are leaning against a white jeep drinking coffee from plastic cups. Even their sandals are white. Local politicians of some sort. They all have healthy moustaches and paunches. 'Do you think the reason they're so committed to white is because it's so obvious they're corrupt assholes?' Kavitha says.

'Stop staring at us,' I want to shout. 'Turn away and mind your own business.' I don't know what it is about seeing groups of men together, but it unsettles me. The way they hold their bodies, the ownership of space. Nothing they offer by way of their togetherness engenders a sense of safety. It is all gnarl and hair and ball sac and matted heel. The world needs softness. Not this.

There is dereliction all around. A gated community called Luxor lies in semi-finished abandon. Incongruous, trying to recall some kind of pharaonic glory here in Tamil Nadu. The builders must have run out of funds or neglected to pay off the right people. Already neem bushes are growing horizontally and wildly into the half-built foundations. The Sphinx-like statue in yellow stone, positioned as the centrepiece of the property, is covered in bird shit and has nothing of the grandeur of its Egyptian ancestor.

It's only nine in the morning but my shirt is already damp. We pass the Marakkanam Lake to our right, which is flat and white in the heat. 'There,' I say. 'That's the road we need to take.'

It is always a surprise, leaving the main road for the interior. How rapidly the scale alters. An Indian village will cling to the side of any highway. In most cases the village was there first, but when the highway arrives, dissecting it, the village remains in this amputated fashion, growing any which way, adjusting itself within the new parameters. There is no discernible centre except for a large banyan tree, under which meetings with village elders supposedly happen. Kavitha parks near a temple because the road has become too narrow and muddy. We step out and walk behind a group of children – boys and girls who are fixing to play some kind of game.

'Where's the dog doctor?' Kavitha asks. 'Do you know?'

The smell is something awful. Burnt hair, burnt flesh. As we approach the crowd, the noise escalates. A man in a golf shirt, jeans and trainers stands in the middle of the crowd. He has white hair and glasses, and he is speaking in a patient, measured tone to the men around him. The majority are village men, barefoot, in shirts and lungis. They are thumping their chests extravagantly. Kavitha unsheathes her massive SLR camera and starts photographing the scene.

Burnt corpses of dogs lie in heaps. There are hundreds of them. The earth has been turned over in ridges, and volunteers continue to dig with shovels. When they find another one, the digging stops. Someone goes into the crater and pulls out a charred rigid thing. 'Okay,' or 'Got it,' they shout, and the digging begins again.

The man from the Blue Cross, Kavitha's friend, with whom I've spoken a few times on the telephone, gives us masks and gloves to wear. 'It's cyclical,' he says. 'The dogs multiply because of all the rubbish, there are packs of them, and so of course there are accidents. People are scared to walk around, some children get bitten, people complain and so the *panchayat* just decides to do a mass culling.'

Was it easy for these men to corner the dogs one by one and inject them with cyanide? Did they wait to set them alight or did they burn them immediately? I have to walk to a corner and vomit to feel steady again. One of the village women is crying. 'They killed my Tikku. He was like my son. What right did they have to kill him?'

She's dragged away by family members and there is more shouting. I can't understand everything that's going on, but there is a sense of fear. Everyone knows the police are on the way so there's a scattering, but a few tenacious ones remain. The man from the Blue Cross is on his mobile giving directions to a journalist.

Kavitha lights a cigarette. 'Can you believe this shit? It's inhumane, not to mention stupid. Don't they think that after injecting cyanide into four hundred animals, burning some of them and burying them right by the lake that it won't affect their water supply, their soil?'

'Please,' the Blue Cross man says, walking up to us quickly. 'Do you mind not smoking here? Things are tense as it is.'

Kavitha squashes the cigarette under her sandal. 'Just to be clear, I don't give a shit about their sensibilities.'

She strides back to a group of volunteers who are bagging corpses. They are college students from the city. Many of them have never been in a place like this. Even they look at her with confusion and admiration. She's wearing a man's shirt as usual, with jeans and sandals. Every few weeks she gets her head shaved so the salt-and-pepper bristle is maintained. Her face is achingly symmetrical, nose sharp, lips full, but there is a hardness about it that you can tell has accumulated over the years.

'I'm sick of this,' I say. 'There's no need for us to be here.'

A few hours later we make our way back to the car. The door handles are impossible to touch. I fold the cuff of my shirt under the bottom of my palm and lift up the handle. Three of the volunteers climb into the back seat. We drive with the windows down and the air conditioner blowing hard. We let them off at the Koovathur bus stop. They are all chummy, shouting, 'Bye auntie, thanks auntie,' at us. On the way home I cover Kavitha's hand with mine on the gearstick. I hold it as if it were my sixth finger and I were reclaiming it.

'Papi was right,' I say. 'We're living with savages.'

30

The house is secretive at this hour. Kavitha is still asleep, and the dogs are lying in cool patches of mud in the garden. We've had rains, so everything looks powerful and unstoppable. I put the kettle on and stand beside the counter with one leg tucked into the other, tree pose, waiting for the water to boil. Everything seems so closely bound in the mornings. I sit on the veranda with my cup of tea and biscuits. The lawn gleams, choked with weeds. A bird in a tree is making a sound I've never heard before.

I could not give any of this up. There is a kind of silence in these early mornings broken only by faraway truck horns and flies slamming themselves against window glass, guiding you into the day.

Teacher had told me to come alone.

I'm wearing one of Ma's saris – the white Bangladeshi cotton with the red border. I hardly ever used to wear them, but Kavitha has been teaching me how to drape them so that my limbs aren't inhibited. Strange how a piece of cloth can transform you, fool you into thinking you're stronger than you are.

The compound wall is in such a damaged state, but it would cost a fortune to fix it up again. In a place like this, where decay is inevitable, it feels simpler to submit. I have wanted to belong to this world. I think this as I drive out.

It's sentimental, but how else are we to look at things? To move through life at a distance, without having participated, it seems wasteful somehow.

I drive past groves of trees. The flame trees we planted to cover the ugly orange house. Champaca, hibiscus, laburnum – all sprouting from the mud of our dead dogs. I feel peaceful driving into the city, even though I haven't seen Lucia in five months. We had spoken on the phone a few times. Teacher held the phone to Lucy's ear and I shouted, 'Hello, Lucy, how are you? I miss you.' And Lucy, after saying the first hello in her way, the h caught in the throat like a well, the long extended ooooo, would fall silent. 'Huloooo.'

'Golly misses you.'

'That's Lucy's dog,' she'd say.

Eventually, Teacher would get on the phone. 'Okay, bye for now.'

'Will you bring her back?' Valluvan had asked when I went to see him.

He was an old man now but his face held no malice. He would not talk about what happened except to say that he had survived because of the grace of God. A rare man. Strident in his house and village, humble before the universe.

Nila did not meet my eye. She had revealed too much already. She was a loyal wife, a strict mother, no one could say a word against her. When Valluvan was in the hospital she had been in charge. She looked at her husband as if he were a saint. She brought him a shawl, she brought tea. When he said, 'Leave us,' she left. We both knew she was standing by the kitchen wall, listening. She would have to get used to standing on the sidelines again.

'What shall I do?' I asked.

He explained there were only two ways of living. The life we desire and the life we are born to. Sometimes these lives can be the same. Sometimes we must make them the same.

'Are you scared?' he asked.

'I'm always scared.'

I went home in the late afternoon knowing that the real days were ahead of us. Our dogs were strong. They did not leave us at nights and they no longer knew hunger, so they were less exposed to danger. There were tomatoes in the garden and chillis. All around the trees grew close and high, protecting us. Lucia would know all this again.

Teacher brings me a pair of scissors. Her eyes are limit-less pools of authority. 'Pastor will be joining you,' she says. There must be a hundred people gathered. I recognise most of the girls, but there are a few new faces. They are dressed in long sequinned skirts and velvet blouses. I know not to expect to see Lucia there, but I look anyway. Someone has switched the fans off for the lamp-lighting ceremony, so there are armpits soft and wet all around. People from the neighbourhood have come. Shopkeepers, housewives, a judge who has been given a plastic chair to sit in. Everyone else stands. The staff are passing out plastic packets of water. Pastor and I are given tumblers of Fanta.

'God bless you, child,' Pastor says. We cut the ribbon together and are asked to move closer to smile for the camera. 'Please,' I say, 'after you.' We leave our footwear outside the building. It smells of fresh paint inside. I'm sad again. There is something hopeless about the window grilles.

After everyone gathers inside and sits down on jute mats, the girls are pushed into the centre of the room to sing 'Vande Mataram'. I can hear the scraping of spoons against vessels from outside the building, where caterers are making large vessels of biryani. Teacher makes a speech where she thanks me for my generous contribution for completing the new wing. She speaks for a long time because she has prevailed. If others will not praise her, she will praise herself. Everyone praises her, though, even her husband, who had once seemed ferocious but now walks respectfully two paces behind her.

Later, in her office in the old building, after everyone has left, she cries. She tells me one of the girls had been having breathing problems. Valli. Did I remember her? Not really. She kept putting her fingers down her throat and nobody could understand what was wrong with her. She couldn't say what was bothering her. They took her to a government hospital and kept her there overnight. Teacher called the parents to inform them. They were separated, she told me. Brahmin couple, she added. The husband lived downstairs and the wife lived upstairs. They couldn't afford two separate houses. 'They said they couldn't pay for the hospital so we brought her back here, but she was still uncomfortable. She kept putting her fingers down her throat. I feel so bad that we can't know what they're thinking. After two days she expired.'

I think of that word, 'expired'. What does it mean? She ran out of steam? She stopped? She gave up? 'I'm so sorry,' I say.

'How can we know what's going on in their heads?' Teacher goes on. 'I feel so bad.'

'You do what you can.'

'You and I must always work together,' she says, using the end of her sari to dab the corner of her eye.

I am unable to console her, unable to fill this gap with empathy. I want her to be quiet and take me to Lucia. I have waited long enough. I have done as she asked.

'When I met you at your mother's funeral I was happy because I thought Lucy has lost a mother, but will find a sister. I could see that you were weak. But still, I thought, Lucy will be saved. Are you ready now?'

I had sold all Ma's jewels. There were boxes of the stuff in a bank safe. Treasures collected over decades. When I think of her earlier in her life, it's as though she were a different woman. In the photographs she reclines on sofas, leans against balconies, wears filigreed gold chokers and emerald peacock earrings, hair swept into dark towering beehives. For a while, she wore only white with long strands of pearls. Her eyes rimmed with kohl, watery, disdainful. Papi is in some of these photographs too. All the wide space of his forehead exposed. The same dark-trim suit.

I kept a slim ruby necklace with uncut diamonds and Nonna Rosa's ring, but the rest I sold. 'Won't you regret it?' Rohini asked. 'You don't need the money, do you?'

It is a moment of death to understand you will not continue. Nothing in my life will pass on. I will not have daughters. I will not make Fisher-Price villages with them on bedroom floors or scoop them into the cave of my stomach when they are ill. I imagine these ghost children Blake and I could have had. Flaxen-haired girls with oblong jaws. They would not be weak. They would not be strong. They would not give birth to beautiful lonely creatures of their own.

There is a line that divides us. Rohini cannot under-stand what it means to travel lightly. She wants imprints, a kind of eternity. 'You need it too,' she says. 'You're fooling yourself if you think you're not after the same thing.'

I want to tell her that a woman who moves from her parents' house to her husband's house is never uncertain. She has not walked through rooms searching for light switches. Someone is always showing her the way.

It is January in the city. We sit on Rohini and Samir's balcony, surrounded by towers of concrete. Impossible to think that a sea breathes beyond, that animals and birds make their nests amongst these multitudes. One day all this will collapse. The sea will rise and swallow entire suburbs. Almost as unimaginable to think that this was once all paddy fields. The nights were completely black and all you could hear were nightjars and koels, the long insistent bark of a dog tied to a post.

'You played it right,' Praveen says. 'You've come out of this stronger.'

He is methodical, always pushing for extremes within the constraints of his obligations. He tends to the edges like a gardener. This is where friendships are nourished. This is where sex lives. Beyond is the whole territory of travel, where a man can be subsumed, where he can re-invent himself. Then he must return to the centre. The centre is where he sleeps, where his mother lives, the house, the dog. The car that takes him to the office every morning. A joint in his pocket for when the day presses in too hard. He wears floral shirts to prove his ruggedness. He notices a woman's handbag and shoes.

'It's better this way,' he says. 'You'll have your space and your sister will have her peers. There'll be a bit of back and forth, so you should just hire a driver. It's a good balance. We'll see more of you.'

'I had this maths professor in Charlotte. Dr Shah. He used to invite all the Indian students to his house for a meal once a semester. There were only ever five or six of us, and we'd sit around his kitchen table eating pakoras and roti, dal, *sabji*.

'He had young children, but he seemed so old then. One summer his wife had taken the kids back to India. The food wasn't as good. I said to him, "Dr Shah, you must be glad to have the house to yourself." He was a sweet man, really. He said, "You know, once you have kids you'll understand. There's never any peace. When they're there, when they're not there."

'Men are always telling me what I don't understand because I don't have kids. I think he may have been right, though. The house isn't the same without her. It's as though I'm either too big for it or too small. It makes no sense to be living out there with the sea and those trees. All those pretty china plates in the crockery cupboard, for what?'

'It's like some fight against obscurity,' Samir says. 'The whole thing. Everything we do. We try to fill it with purpose. We try to find tasks. For some people it's their kids, for others, their jobs, their art, whatever. Why worry?'

It's impossible not to think of time passing. Even in the city. We are all of the age where we turn our hands over repeatedly, examine our faces in mirrors, watch the past recede. We sit on the balcony listening to Lou Reed. We have not said anything of survival. For most people the point is to live.

That night I write to Lucia, which, in a way, is writing to myself:

255

I want to take you to Venice to meet Papi and Marcella. Now that I've had the idea, everything is clear. It's not about living away from the world but living in it. It's a longer journey than you're used to making, but I'll give you the window seat, Lucy, and you can sit with your knee tucked into your arm, and yes, we'll bring your friends. You have to climb many steps to Papi's house, though. It's at the corner of a street where there are cafés and pigeons. We'll take the vaporettos to the islands, darling, and I'll show you everything. We can't take the dogs with us, but Kavitha will look after them. Kavitha is going to stay with us for some time. Everything will be different. You'll like Venice, I think. There are so many ice-cream shops and whenever you're tired of walking we can sit on a bench, or get into a gondola. They glide like swans. You look up, Lucy, and you see buildings, old as forests. At night when you close your eyes you hear the soft sounds on the water, and it'll be like being home, listening to the sea.

I follow Teacher to the new wing. The two buildings are separated by a concrete courtyard. There's a poster hanging lopsidedly along the front wall, made especially for the inauguration ceremony. The words *Sneha Centre* are written in bold English, there is more writing below in Tamil. A portrait of Teacher in a Victorian-style frame dominates the poster. It's an old photograph. She looks more determined in it than she does in real life.

'I don't know why they want to waste money on such things.' Teacher flushes as we walk by. 'But the staff like to do all this. It's a way of honouring me, they say.'

I think of Lucy in her new room. Napkins, socks and an oven mitt arranged like a fan around her. If there's a window, she'll be sitting by it, so she can catch the sun. She hums softly. She isn't waiting.

I think of the train journey we made to Kodai. The terror of those small railway towns we stopped in, the valiant lives that might be out there. Lucia insisting on the top berth, her feet gingerly placed on the rungs on the wall. Me giving her bum a little shove up. For hours afterwards, she hung her face off the berth looking down at me, switching the lights in the cabin on and off. I kept apologising to the other passengers, an older married couple – the man recently retired from teaching, his wife fat-cheeked and cheery. 'It's okay,' they reassured. How she settled into the sheets eventually and slept. The light flutter of snores. I remember the tin can of a bathroom. The stench of it. Hauling Lucy into it in the morning and holding her while she squatted over the hole in the floor of the train. 'Weeeee,' she said. 'Lucy is doing wee wee.' The slow bustle of the Kodai Road station. Coolies in blood-red shirts hauling their ancient faces around. Lucia and I treading over the railway tracks with our luggage, taking deep breaths of that sweet balsamic air of the foothills. The haggle with taxi drivers. 'I want to go in that car, Grace.' The two of us in a white Ambassador, one at each back-seat window. 'Look, Lucy, look at the monkeys.'

'Do you think she feels happiness like you and I do?' I ask Teacher. We are at the entrance of the new block. The room where the singing and speeches just happened this morning is cluttered with paper plates and cups. Two tree-like women are bent over, sweeping everything into a corner.

'It's like how I was saying,' Teacher says. 'We can't know what's in their heads. But we can understand when they are comfortable, when they are happy, when they are upset. We can't even know what we think ourselves, so how can we know about others?'

I wanted to tell her that I had seen Lucy excavate a hole in the seashore and fasten herself there like a canon, letting out sounds of rapture as the waves bashed her about. And how, when we walked into enemy territory of pariah dogs and she bent her knees and put her mouth to the sky, howling with Bagheera, it was a song of triumph. There could be no doubt about the force of the emotion. But it was regular life that concerned me – the washing of elbows, the getting in and out of nighties and pyjamas, the chewing of food. Did she ever feel oppressed by it all? Did she ever think of settling herself in a bed, never to move again?

I knew not to expect anything momentous.

Teacher opens the door. 'Look who's here!' she says.

She is as I imagined. Sitting on the single bed, positioned in the ray of light. Shoulders slightly sloped, legs splayed. Her eyes widen when she sees me. She shows me her jagged teeth.

'Hey Lucy,' I say. I sit on the bed and take her hand. 'Give me a kiss, will you?'

'Hi Grace,' she says. She lets me kiss her cheek. She looks at me, not with suspicion or any kind of demand. Her look merely says, here you are.

'Here I am.'

I open my handbag and take the military-green napkin out of it. 'See what I found?'

She snatches it from me and practises feeling it in her fingers. Flip flip. Oh, it's been so long, hasn't it? Flip flip.

She looks paler, somewhat chubbier in the stomach. 'Are you ready to come home, Lucy?'

Her bag is already packed in the corner of the room. She becomes something else when she travels. I don't know how I know this for sure, but when she's on the move all her idiosyncrasies are suspended. The rooms of her life collapse and open into something larger. 'Are we going on a choo-choo train?'

'We're going in the car to see Raja and Golly and Dimple and Bagheera and all the new puppies.'

'What about Hunter and Thompson and Flopsy?'

'They've all gone to God, remember?'

Is she my child, then? My daughter, my sister. There is something pure about her fingers, the misshapen right index finger with the nubby nail, the deep brown lines in her palms. I take her hands and squeeze them between mine.

'You'll be coming here too, kanna, don't worry. We'll be seeing you soon,' Teacher says, stepping out of the way as I take hold of Lucy's suitcase.

We walk down the stairs. All the girls have lined up by the gates to say goodbye. Sugandhi, the albino, stands above them all, almost six feet tall. She's waving her long arms from side to side. They are nobody's treasures, these girls. It's hard to look at them all together.

'Will you be calling us for Lucy's birthday party, akka?' It's Priya, Lucy's old friend, who waddles up to us and puts her hands on her hips. 'Will you?'

'Of course she will,' Teacher says. 'Why don't we take a photo?'

Teacher's husband faces us, his back to the street. What have they done to you? I want to ask each one of them. Why have they abandoned you, your families, your blood?

They are still in their velvet blouses and sequinned skirts. The material sticks to their skins. We welcome the heat, the closeness. We stand together, our decaying bodies. I want to believe in old-fashioned ideas of goodness and evil. There is such a thing as giving shelter. In the days to come there will be children engineered to resemble our ideas of children. They will be born in Petri dishes and every chromosome, every strand of genetic evidence will be tampered into perfection. And still, we will fall short.

Lucy and I walk to the car, carefully avoiding the stagnant puddles of water. She seems pensive, her limp brown hair touching her shoulders. There are two cows chewing on rotten banana leaves next to a rubbish bin. We steer away from them. It happens in a flash. I open the boot to put the suitcase in and Lucia makes a run for it, sprinting away from me and the Sneha Centre. She stops at the crossroads, bending her knees as though she were going to jump from the pavement into the oncoming traffic. She is smiling wildly. It is only a joke. A game from childhood where she used to run away. She's moving back and forth on her legs, one hand hitching up her pants. 'Come back, Lucy,' I yell. I know what to do this time, I want to shout. I won't let you down. Motorbikes and cars flash by her like schools of fish. I think of us underwater, the dolphins in the blue, our dogs on the beach. Everything that's going to save us. 'That's enough,' I say, making towards her.

Soon we are home and the dogs are scratching at the doors, trying to get in. Kavitha is in the kitchen, making noodles for dinner, the air thick with the smell of burning wood fires. 'Let's go put our feet in the sand,' I say to Lucy. The dogs rush out of the gate before us, scrabbling about to catch crabs. It is a comfort to sit there watching the coconut trees in the distance sway over the village. We count the fishing boats parked up on the ridge. Flocks of white birds that look grey in the twilight make patterns above our heads.

Kavitha walks out when it's dark. 'I know you must be hungry now,' she says. We walk up the path together, trying not to get thorns in our feet, holding each other up as the breeze blows by. We pause at the edge of the lawn and look at the house with its blue doors flung open. Soft lights gleam from every room. We don't say it aloud, but we look at each other and know we can keep doing this. We can keep being who we are.

ACKNOWLEDGEMENTS

Thanks to Angela Dorazio for the gift of Canonica where the idea for this novel began. To Jasmine Dellal, Vikrom Mathur, Editta Dal Lago, and Patrick and Fiona Clements for providing salubrious roofs under which parts of it could be written. To Art Omi: Writers for a timely residency equipped with ping-pong table. To Jin Auh and Tracy Bohan at the Wylie Agency. To Faiza Sultan Khan and Alexandra Pringle at Bloomsbury. Thanks as well to Manu Joseph and Carlo Pizzati for reading early drafts. To Mandira Moddie for all her support, canine and otherwise. And to Eira and Vinod, goes without saying.

A NOTE ON THE AUTHOR

Tishani Doshi was born in Chennai. She is an award-winning poet, journalist, essayist and novelist. Doshi has published seven books of fiction and poetry, most recently *Girls Are Coming Out of the Woods* in 2018. She is the recipient of an Eric Gregory Award for Poetry, winner of the All-India Poetry Competition, and her first book, *Countries of the Body*, won the Forward Prize for Best First Collection in 2006. Her debut novel, *The Pleasure Seekers*, was shortlisted for the Hindu Literary Prize and long listed for the Orange Prize and the International IMPAC Dublin Literary Award. Doshi is also a professional dancer with the Chandralekha Troupe. She lives in Tamil Nadu, India, with her husband and three dogs.

tishanidoshi.com

A NOTE ON THE TYPE

The text of this book is set in Perpetua. This typeface is an adaptation of a style of letter that had been popularised for monumental work in stone by Eric Gill. Large-scale drawings by Gill were given to Charles Malin, a Parisian punch-cutter, and his hand-cut punches were the basis for the font issued by Monotype. First used in a private translation called 'The Passion of Perpetua and Felicity', the italic was originally called Felicity.